"I thought I might get a head start on identifying this guy if you recognized him, but I've also asked Lieutenant Fowley to pick up the yacht captain to see if he can identify him."

"If the dead guy was on staff, the captain would be the one to ask." She glanced back at the photo. "Does Simon know what killed him yet?"

"Early autopsy reports suggest it was a flare gun."

"A flare gun? Can one of those actually kill a person?"

"When shot into the abdomen, at close range, yes, and that seems to be the case here."

Addie shivered and rose to her feet.

"Not so fast." He collected the photo and placed it back in the folder. "Identifying him was only a hunch since I had you here, but the real reason I thought that you might be able to help us out is this." He pulled out a small evidence bag from the folder and handed it to Addie. "Is there any chance you can identify this?"

Addie turned the red-labeled plastic bag over in her hand. "It appears to be the torn corner of a book. Why, what does it mean?"

"Is there any way you can tell what book that came from?"

She studied the slip of paper inside the small package. "No, there's no ink markings, no title, nothing on here except an edge of what appears to be the bottom right corner of a book page. Maybe the title page, otherwise there would be some print given the angle of the tear. What does this have to do with the dead guy?"

"It's the only thing we found on his body . . ."

Books by Lauren Elliott

Beyond the Page Bookstore Mysteries

MURDER BY THE BOOK
PROLOGUE TO MURDER
MURDER IN THE FIRST EDITION
PROOF OF MURDER
A PAGE MARKED FOR MURDER
UNDER THE COVER OF MURDER
TO THE TOME OF MURDER
A MARGIN FOR MURDER
DEDICATION TO MURDER

Crystals & CuriosiTEAS Mysteries

STEEPED IN SECRETS
MURDER IN A CUP

Published by Kensington Publishing Corp.

UNDER
THE COVER
OF
MURDER

Lauren
Elliott

KENSINGTON
PUBLISHING CORP.

www.kensingtonbooks.com

KENSINGTON BOOKS are published by

Kensington Publishing Corp.
119 West 40th Street
New York, NY 10018

First Kensington Books Mass Market Paperback Printing: April 2021

ISBN-13: 978-1-4967-2713-8
ISBN-10: 1-4967-2713-4

ISBN-13: 978-1-4967-2714-5 (ebook)
ISBN-10: 1-4967-2714-2 (ebook)

10 9 8 7 6 5 4 3

Printed in the United States of America

Chapter 1

Addie pulled her red-and-white Mini Cooper into a parking space in front of Beyond the Page, her book and curio shop. She leapt out and raced around to the passenger side, grabbed the two dress bags on the back seat, took a quick glance at the size tags, and snatched up the top one. She jerked and glanced back over her left shoulder at a frantic tapping sound against glass. Martha Stringer, her white head bobbing back and forth, frantically waved at her to come into the bakery.

Addie swiveled on her high heel and rolled over on her ankle. Her arms flailed, and panic surged through her. She made a grab for the side of her car to steady herself when she and her precious cargo made a beeline for the gutter. Her dress-bearing arm shot high in the air, wrenching her shoulder and sending a hot pain shooting up her neck. Addie grimaced but managed to keep the bag high and safely out of the reaches of roadway dust and grime. She inhaled deeply, stretched out her throbbing ankle, took a few more deep breaths or ten . . . hobbled up onto the curb and limped toward the bakery.

As she approached the door, her chest tightened, and she paused. The cake displayed in Martha's window was the one her best friend, Serena Chandler, and her mother, Janis, had ordered for Serena's wedding today. Right down to the antique cake topper of an early twentieth-century couple—one Addie had untreasured in her great-aunt's attic. Who the topper belonged to was a mystery because as far as Addie knew, Anita Greyborne, her bene-factor, had never married. Oh well, a mystery to solve an-other day. Today was all about Serena. This was her day, but it broke Addie's heart to know the cake Serena had dreamed about was now preserved and placed in a win-dow as a display. Addie shored herself up and stepped in-side the front area of the bakery where she was greeted by a heavily perspiring Martha.

"Are you heading over to the yacht soon?" The short plump woman's faded-blue eyes pierced Addie's.

"Yes, why?"

Martha produced a large tray of petite pastries from the counter behind her. "Here, take these for me. Being as Saturday is my busiest day of the week, I won't be there until later, and I promised Janis that at least one thing they ordered for *her* daughter's wedding would be served."

"Yeah, it's really too bad that Zach's stepmother, Veron-ica, went ahead and changed everything on the menu. I feel so bad for Serena. By the way, the cake you made looks beautiful. It's exactly like the one in the pictures Serena picked out."

"Just too bad it's only window dressing now. Not hoity-toity enough for Lady Veronica Ludlow, I guess." Martha harrumphed. "But at least the display has brought in three more wedding cake orders for the next few months, and I heard this morning that Bernadette Garland's daughter was planning her wedding for next spring and there might be an order there, too."

"It's just sad that Serena won't be the benefactor of your beautiful five-tiered creation."

"Yeah, but it has helped boost my newest wedding cake line."

Addie bit her tongue to stem the words she wanted to scream, retelling all that had taken place over the final preparations for this day. Even though she and Martha had resolved many of their past differences, Addie still wasn't certain that her onetime nemesis was completely trustworthy. She dared not vent her frustrations only to have them used against her in some way. So, she settled for a nod of the head. "Yes, it's too bad everything turned out the way it did, but I think Serena is coping with the changes well, don't you?"

Martha snorted.

"What? Do you know something I don't?"

"I saw the poor girl go in your shop as soon as Paige put the sidewalk sign out this morning, and she didn't look too chipper to me."

"Is she still there?"

"Haven't seen her come out."

"Oh dear, I'd better go see what's happened today."

"Don't forget these." Martha thrust the silver tray in Addie's hand. "See you this evening."

"Yes, thanks." Addie balanced the large tray in one hand, trying not to crush Paige's dress that she'd hung over her other arm, as she maneuvered the door open and headed next door to her bookshop.

She stopped long enough to admire the fairy lights around her window. The flower-covered mini-trellis, vintage bridal books, and classic romance novels painted a perfect wedding theme if she did say so herself. The smile brought on by the window display continued as she stepped inside and took in the heady scent of old leather and books, an aroma she could never seem to get enough of.

"Ta-da," she exclaimed, holding the dress high over her head.

"Is that my dress?" squealed Paige Stringer, her assistant manager. She clapped her hands together, and her china-blue eyes lit up her face as her gaze took in the image of the marine-blue bridesmaid dress through the plastic garment bag.

"Yes, it is," Addie said, and stepped toward her. "I think you'll agree when you put it on that my cousin Kalea did a great job on all our dresses."

"Did she manage to get rid of that weird pucker under my armpit that we noticed during my last fitting?" Paige's voice reflected the concern in her eyes as she fidgeted with the plastic covering.

"She said she did, but she wanted me to let you know that she'll be at the yacht early enough to make any last-minute alterations if she has to." Addie limped over to the Victorian counter she used as a cash and coffee bar, set the platter down, and laid out the dress beside it.

"What's wrong with you? Why are you limping?"

"Oh, silly me forgot to change out of my heels after my fitting this morning, and I rolled on my ankle. It's fine, though. It doesn't look too badly swollen."

"There's ice in the freezer compartment of the fridge in the back."

"It's fine." Addie pressed the dress flat on the countertop. "You know, for a woman who never showed a talent for anything other than landing a rich man, I think my cousin's shop, Hudson's Creations on Main, is a real hit around town. She does have a knack for sewing and design."

"It makes sense though because she's such a fashion diva herself, so I guess it turned out perfect for her when she bought that dress shop from my sister. She finally found her calling. Heaven knows working as a bookseller wasn't it."

Paige's comment brought a chorus of belly laughter from them both, and then Addie's elbow jarred the tray of goodies sitting beside her on the counter, causing it to teeter precariously on the edge.

Paige sprang toward it with the dexterity of a cat and snatched it before it tumbled off onto the floor. "Phew," she gasped, as she eyed it while setting it safely back in place. "This looks too fancy for our midmorning snacks, so I'm guessing it's for the wedding?"

"Yes," Addie managed to burble as she choked back her last laugh brought on by the sight of Paige's ninja-style rescue.

"Then you should know that I think there might have been a change of plans."

"What are you talking about?" Addie croaked.

"I think the wedding's off."

"Did Serena and Zach have a fight?"

"Nope."

"Then what?"

"You'd better ask her." Paige jerked her head toward the backroom. "While you're dealing with the latest crisis, put some ice on that ankle. I don't want to have to carry you up the aisle." Paige scoffed as Addie started limping toward the back room.

"Yeah, yeah, yeah . . ." Addie waved over her shoulder. She stopped at the door, sucked in a deep breath, pasted a smile on her face, and with all the grace of a chimpanzee, hobbled into the storage room.

For all her false bravado it only took one look at her friend's tear-streaked face for Addie to crumple. "Oh hon, what happened now?" She collapsed beside Serena on a wooden book crate and wrapped her arms around Serena's trembling shoulders.

"What hasn't happened?" Serena sobbed and sniffled. "You were at the rehearsal and dinner last night. Did it look like the wedding party and family event *I* planned?"

Addie shook her head.

"That's right because Her Highness, *Lady Ludlow*, had over a hundred friends *she* invited who weren't on *my* wedding list for today, let alone for a small family dinner last night. All because *she* didn't want them to miss out on the celebrations and was mad at me for not inviting them to the actual ceremony today!"

"If it's any consolation, you looked beautiful, and everyone appeared to be enjoying themselves."

"That's not the point!" Serena barked, and rose to her feet.

Addie shrank back when Serena began pacing and wagging her finger in Addie's face.

"I planned a nice quiet dinner in that private dining room at Smugglers' Den after the rehearsal for the wedding. Then two weeks ago she informed us that she had canceled the reservation because she had something else in mind." The shrillness in Serena's voice rose to a fevered pitch as she mimicked her soon-to-be step-mother-in-law, "*Don't worry, it will be lovely. Trust me, I know what Zach really wants.*" Serena leaned into Addie's face. "How can she know what my soon-to-be husband really wants? As his stepmother, she barely knows or tolerates him." She straightened and resumed her pacing with force. "No, this woman has gone too far. I should have known it would get worse, not better, when she put a kibosh on the reception venue *we* booked last summer."

"Yeah, that was too bad. The community hall was perfect," Addie said wistfully. "It holds so much history."

"Right." Serena spun toward Addie. "She walked in and took one look around, turned up her surgically created perfect nose, and said, 'It's too old.'"

"Of course it's old. It's a two-hundred-year-old stone building."

"Can you believe she wasn't impressed with what the restoration committee had done? Not even the period furnishings, polished planked floors, the beams, and the wood-paneled coffered ceiling could sway her. Nope, she said, 'No son of mine will have a wedding reception in such a shabby outdated facility.' Then she turned and walked right out." Serena huffed and crossed her arms. "She even objected to using your house and grounds as an alternative. Nothing's good enough for the high-and-mighty Veronica Ludlow, it seems. I know that crushed you."

Afraid to look up at her friend and not certain the tirade was over, Addie nodded and wrung her damp hands in her lap.

"Yeah, but she rules the roost, and everyone kowtows to her. I'm surprised she did listen when I adamantly objected to her plan to have our wedding at their estate in Connecticut so my friends would not be left out completely. Apparently, it is her mission to bring a representation of the estate to us so *her* friends don't have to deal with any less than *they* are all accustomed to. Who on earth has a supersize yacht the size of a cruise ship?"

Very rich people. Addie pursed her lips when she recalled what Serena had said when she first started dating Zach—that he and his family came from the poorer side of the Ludlow family. Though, she'd like to see how the rich side lived if that monstrosity of a yacht was considered poor. "What did Zach say about last night?"

"Nothing. He just squeezed my hand and told me everything would be okay. Yeah, it'll be okay when I call off this stupid wedding." Serena dropped back onto the crate and sobbed into her hands.

"Serena, you have to talk to Zach before you make any rash decisions about calling off the wedding. Maybe he can talk some sense into her, or his mother and father can?"

"He's tried," she choked out between sobs. "His mother is none too happy about it, but what can she do? The poor woman has been relegated to smiling and keeping her mouth shut as the *new Mrs. Ludlow* runs the entire event and his father . . . well, all he says is 'everything will work out in the end.' Like father like son, I'm afraid." She wailed through renewed tears.

Addie drew in a quiet breath and waited for her friend to give some indication that the familiar rant of the last few months had burnt itself out. When no sound except sniveling and sniffles followed, she knew they had crossed another hurdle and reached over and pressed her friend's hand into hers. "Do you love Zach?"

Serena nodded.

"Does he love you?"

Another head nod.

"What's the most important conclusion of today?"

"To be married," Serena choked out.

"Exactly, and even though most of your dreams of your perfect wedding were stolen from you, the outcome is one dream Veronica can't steal." She swept a chestnut-red ringlet from Serena's face, tipped her friend's chin with her finger, and forced Serena to look her in the eyes. "Now, you know as well as I do that when you get stressed or upset, your freckles pop out every which way."

Serena's hazel-brown eyes filled with panic.

"You don't want to ruin the perfect picture of your big day with a blotchy face, do you?"

Serena emphatically shook her head.

"Good, my suggestion is to go next door to your tea shop. Make a big pot of chamomile tea, drink it all down, relax, and then go to the yacht for your hair and makeup appointment as scheduled, and no more talk of calling off the wedding."

"Will you come with me just in case Dragon Lady strikes again?"

"I'll be there for my appointment at two."

"Promise?"

"I promise. You're looking at the number one dragon-slayer, and I wouldn't miss this day for anything, not even a fiery dragon lady." Addie gave Serena's hand a reassuring squeeze. "Think you can go and relax for a while for me before I get there with my sword and shield?"

Serena nodded and stumbled out the back door into the lane.

Addie closed the door once Serena was safely inside her shop and hadn't dropped to the ground to curl up in a fetal position. Addie banged her head repeatedly on the metal door and heaved out a heavy breath. "Give me strength to make it through this day."

"Addie?"

"Yes," she said, glancing at Paige, who stood in the doorway.

"I hate to interrupt, but . . ." She looked toward the storefront and smiled and turned back to Addie. "Marc's here, and he wants to speak to you."

"He's here and didn't barge into the back like he usually does?" She chuckled.

"I told him you were talking Serena off the ledge again, and he said he'd wait, but he's doing that pacing thing, so I thought maybe it was urgent."

"Okay, well she's gone now, so you might as well send the next Chandler with pre-wedding jitters back."

"He's dressed in his uniform . . . so I think it might be official," Paige said, waving him to the back room.

"Great. What have I done now?" Addie sank back down on the book crate. "Chief Chandler, what a surprise to see you this morning. Shouldn't the brother of the bride be at the tuxedo fitting right about now with the other groomsmen?"

Marc loomed in the doorway and toyed with his police cap in hand. His honey-brown eyes darkened and he averted his gaze, studying the toes of his boots. "Addie, I'm afraid I'm going to have to ask you to come down to the station with me."

Chapter 2

"Can you at least give me a clue as to what this is all about?" Addie followed Marc through the bookstore to the front door.

"It's a police matter," he said over his shoulder.

"Okay, you've already said that much. Can you give me a hint what police matter you're talking about?"

"You'll find out soon enough."

"What? That's it? That's all you're going to say?"

He nodded but remained mute as he opened the front door, waited for her to scramble through, and closed it behind her. The fury and adrenaline coursing through her veins had diminished the throbbing in her ankle, and she no longer hobbled as she made her way to the curbside where he stood, holding the police cruiser door open for her.

Paige's pale face was clearly imprinted with questions

and concern as she stared out the bay window. Addie could only shrug her reply as she dipped her head and took a seat in the front passenger's side. Marc got in, and his continued deafening silence screamed in her ears.

"Marc, what is all of this about?"

"I told you that we'd discuss it at the station."

"Could you just give me a"—she pressed her thumb and pointer finger close together—"teeny-weeny hint now?"

He shot her a side glance under a creased brow.

"At least tell me if I've committed a crime I wasn't aware of or broken one of this town's archaic bylaws?"

His gaze fixed straight ahead as he turned the key in the ignition and pulled out into traffic.

"I admit that I did jaywalk the other day in front of the library but really . . . is this how Greyborne Harbor's finest treats jaywalkers?" She glanced over at him and didn't miss the telltale tic of his jaw, proving she'd struck a nerve. "That's it! You're actually arresting me for jay-walking? This is your sister's wedding day, in case you forgot, and she fully expects me to be there in"—she glanced at the clock on the dash—"in three hours!" Addie crossed her arms and glared out the side window as he did a U-turn down the block and back toward Main Street and the police station.

Marc pulled into his parking spot around the back of the historic sandstone building. He got out and opened her door, and despite her pleading, she still couldn't get a word out of him. He gestured for her to go ahead of him on the exterior back staircase and opened the door, steering her through the back room, around the reception desk, and into his office. After removing his cap and hanging it on the coatrack by the door, he sauntered over to his desk, took his seat, settled into position, and then motioned to the chairs in front of the desk for her to sit. She did, begrudgingly, while cursing him under her breath.

"This better be good." She pinned him with a look as he folded his hands and laced his fingers together in front of him on the desk. "The only thing that either of us should be focused on today is your sister's wedding."

"I wish that were the case, but something has come up."

"You said it was police business, is that right?"

He nodded.

"So, what is it?"

His eyes narrowed.

"It is the jaywalking thing, isn't it? I knew it." She sat back in her chair. "You've put up those surveillance cameras like they have in the big cities, and you've hauled me in here for a safety lecture?"

Without a word, he slid the top drawer of his desk open, removed a beige file folder, and placed it in front of him.

"You have a file folder of my misdemeanors?"

He shook his head.

"Then what is going on and why all the secrecy?"

"Addie"—his Adam's apple wobbled as he swallowed—"I need your help with something . . . and I don't know quite how to ask you."

"How about 'Addie, I need your help'? Did those words not come to mind ten minutes ago when you escorted me out of the bookstore?"

"Yes, but . . ."

"But what?"

"Since I'm always telling you to keep your"—his

voice dropped to a whisper—"snoopy nose"—he cleared his throat—"out of police business, I wasn't sure you'd accept my request."

Addie sat back and folded her arms across her chest. He was right, of course. Why should she help him now after all the times he'd lectured her on keeping out of his investigations and sticking to what she, apparently, did best: sell books? She crossed her arms. If he wanted her help, he was going to have to work for it.

She masked all emotions from her face and fixed her gaze on his equally unyielding one. She waited. The clock on the wall behind his desk ticked off the seconds, and just when she thought she was going to burst at the seams with questions, he finally made the first move and averted his eyes. She did a mental fist pump. Once again, she had outwitted and outlasted the great police chief Marc Chandler. She hadn't lost her touch with him, and she relished in the moment until he opened the folder and placed a photo of an obviously deceased man in front of her. Her celebratory mood shifted to one of instant remorse.

"Who's this poor fellow?" Addie gazed at the grisly image and hoped she'd be able to erase it from her memory.

"That's what I need your help with."

"I'm not sure I can help you with this." She pushed the photo toward him and out of her line of sight. "I've never seen him before."

"Are you sure?"

"Pretty sure. Why, am I supposed to know him?"

"I thought since you've spent more time than me on the yacht this week with all the cocktail parties and bridal teas Veronica Ludlow has put on that you'd noticed him on staff."

She shook her head.

"Do you recall seeing him at the rehearsal dinner last night? Maybe he was a guest?"

She glanced back at the photo and then averted her eyes. "No, I don't think so, but there were over a hundred people there last night. I could have, but nothing about him stands out to me."

"Take a closer look." He pushed the photo back toward her.

She pressed her eyes closed and counted. *One* . . . *two* . . . *three*. After quelling the churning in her gut enough to take another peek, she opened her eyes. "Is this from the crime scene?"

"Yes, he was discovered on the beach about six this morning by a man out walking his dog."

"This looks like it's not far from where the yacht is docked at the cruise ship pier."

"Yeah, it isn't far from there." He tapped his finger on the image. "Does this look like the uniform that the serving staff on the yacht wear?"

Addie squinted at the photo. "I'm not sure. It's definitely similar, but there's something just off with it. If I could see the actual jacket, that would help." She sat back in the chair. "It's so hard to tell from a photograph."

"Unfortunately, the clothing is in Doc Emerson's lab over at the hospital. Simon's examining it now for trace evidence. I thought I might get a head start on identifying this guy if you recognized him, but I've also asked Lieutenant Fowley to pick up the yacht captain to see if he can identify him."

"Yeah, if the dead guy was on staff, the captain would be the one to ask." She glanced back at the photo. "Does Simon know what killed him yet?"

"Early autopsy reports suggest it was a flare gun."

"A flare gun? Can one of those actually kill a person?"

"When shot into the abdomen, at close range, yes, and that seems to be the case here."

Addie shivered and rose to her feet.

"Not so fast." He collected the photo and placed it back in the folder.

Addie plopped back into her chair.

"Identifying him was only a hunch since I had you here, but the real reason I thought that you might be able to help us out is this." He pulled out a small evidence bag from the folder and handed it to Addie. "Is there any chance you can identify this?"

Addie turned the red-labeled plastic bag over in her hand. "It appears to be the torn corner of a book. Why, what does it mean?"

"Is there any way you can tell what book that came from?"

She studied the slip of paper inside the small package. "No, there's no ink markings, no title, nothing on here except an edge of what appears to be the bottom right corner of a book page. Maybe the title page, otherwise there would be some print given the angle of the tear. What does this have to do with the dead guy?"

"It's the only thing we found on his body."

"So, you're saying, just this"—she wiggled the bag in the air—"is all the guy had on him? Not even any ID?"

He shook his head.

"What about his cell phone? Can you get into it?"

"No phone on or around him."

"That alone is unusual today, isn't it? Who walks around with a torn scrap of paper in their pocket and not a cell phone?"

"Exactly."

"Perhaps if I could touch it to feel the paper. I might have a better idea, at least, as to what century the book was published. Not sure that would help but it might be something to work with."

"I'm afraid not yet. We haven't finished processing the fingerprints we managed to pull off it. After we get results, then maybe, but no promises." He took the bag from her hand and tucked it back into the folder.

She glanced at the wall clock. "Well, if that's all, I'd better get moving. I still have to pack an overnight bag, and I promised Serena I'd be there for my two o'clock appointment."

"I take it that you and Simon are staying on board after the reception."

"Yes, aren't you and Ryley? I mean I just assumed everyone in the wedding party had accepted the Ludlows' invitation to a stateroom after the party."

"We were planning on staying." He glanced at the folder. "But now, I think as soon as Serena and Zach leave at ten to drive to Boston to catch the red-eye flight to London, we'll both be coming back here to work." He escorted her to the door, which flew open in his hand. A red-faced Lieutenant Jerry Fowley bumped into him.

"Sorry, Chief, but Captain Gary Nevins is here."

"Thanks, Lieutenant, bring him in."

Jerry waved toward the waiting room, and a moment later a tall man with sun-bronzed skin and salt-and-pepper hair blocked Addie from leaving. She smiled a greeting at the captain whom she'd had the pleasure of meeting over the past week through the various onboard festivities.

However, as his sultry gaze locked on hers, a warming flush surged through her. She understood in that moment why the normally meek Ida Biggs, a book club member, and the usually prickly Martha had both schemed to get closer to him during this past week's festivities. A competition, which had ultimately caused a bit of friction to develop between the two old friends, because Addie had to admit herself, he was a fine specimen of a middle-aged gentleman.

Although, his good looks shouldn't have surprised her. Veronica only held court and surrounded herself with *beautiful people*, staff included. Addie gave the captain another once-over and blinked at a realization. The dead man couldn't have been on staff. Even though he probably had been attractive enough with his squared jaw and wavy, light-brown hair, he was not a standout Adonis like the other staff Veronica had on board. He wasn't exactly what could be called one of *them*. She would be very surprised if the captain could identify him.

"Miss Greyborne," the captain said, returning her smile, "nice to see you again."

"Yes, nice to see you, too." She glanced at Marc, hoping he hadn't notice the flush on her cheeks as he stepped aside to allow the man entry.

"Jerry," Marc said. "Could you get me the latest update from Dr. Simon Emerson on the autopsy and find out if he's found anything useful on the clothing?"

"Yes, sir." Jerry skittered into the back room that led to his office on the lower level as Marc motioned for Captain Nevins to take a seat.

Addie hung back by the office door. After all, Marc

hadn't actually asked her leave, and she took this and Jerry's absence from the desk area as a sign that Marc wanted her to hear what the captain had to say about the dead man. She smiled at the young officer on desk duty and casually leaned toward the open door. From her vantage point she could see the captain studying the photograph Marc had placed in front of him.

He shook his head and sat back. "Sorry, Chief, he's definitely not on staff, and I don't recall ever seeing this fellow before."

"Are you certain? Take another look. Could he have been a guest last night at the dinner?"

"He might have been, but there were so many people coming and going." The captain shrugged. "I didn't notice him in particular."

"Okay." Marc raked his hand down his face. "I guess that's all. Sorry to drag you in today, but we'd really like to find out who this guy is—"

The captain stood up and pushed his chair back. "Well, if anything comes to mind, I'll call you." He glanced back at the photo. "But I really don't think I can be of any assistance in this."

Addie jolted around at the sound of a throat clearing behind her. She came face-to-face with Jerry and his famous stink eye whenever he caught her eavesdropping.

"I was just leaving," she muttered, and scurried across the waiting room toward the main door. She glanced back at the sound of soft chuckles coming from the desk and flashed a wry grin back at Jerry, who was tsk-tsking her and shaking his head.

Chapter 3

The excited screeches of a flock of seagulls circling overhead brought Addie to a halt at the foot of the wide pier. She drew in a deep breath and filled her lungs with the invigorating briny sea air. The Stargazer lily bouquets attached to each of the wooden dock pilings added their own aroma to the afternoon and helped settle the day's chaos in her mind for a moment. She took the time to notice the ivy-vine garlands adorned with red roses and pink wisteria blooms—a symbol of love and happiness—that decorated the rope handrails between pillars along both sides of the dock. The sights and fragrance created the perfect awe-moment for guests as they arrived for her friend's wedding, and she slowly drew in another rejuvenating breath.

Even though it wasn't the wedding venue of Serena's dreams, at least it was still in Greyborne Harbor and not miles away in Connecticut, which seemed to be the alternative in Veronica's mind. Serena did tell Addie later that she felt somewhat of a sense of relief when the harbor master gave permission for the Ludlows to moor their yacht here for the weeklong celebration even under the condition that the yacht was to be gone by this coming Tuesday afternoon. He'd stressed the fact to both Zach's father, Oliver, and Veronica that this pier was constructed by the town council to accommodate the small cruise ship that graced Greyborne Harbor every second Tuesday during the spring, summer, and fall months, and it had first priority on mooring rights. At least it meant that, in spite of all the drama Veronica caused over the location, Serena could still have a hometown wedding as planned.

Addie scanned the six-level superyacht emblazoned with the name *The Lady V* across the bow. Serena told her it was originally called the *Melly-May,* a name Oliver Ludlow's first wife—and Zach's mother—Melinda, had christened it with. However, Oliver's new wife, Veronica, insisted on renaming it something more in keeping with her past title as the wife of a now-deceased British lord.

Addie gripped the leather handle of her overnight case, adjusted the garment bag over her arm that contained her bridesmaid dress, and began the long trek toward the ramp to what was the second but otherwise known as the lower deck. At the gangway entry, she was greeted by an easel and sign announcing the Chandler-Ludlow wedding and a man simply known as Gerard, who served as the yacht's butler. He looked like an actor from a British Regency movie and was just one of the twenty-four regular staff on board.

She followed behind the dignified gray-haired gentleman dressed in a black jacket complete with nautical-

patterned brass buttons at the cuff. The entranceway
opened to a mahogany-paneled room with a double-wide
internal stairwell that allowed access to the above decks.
Addie recalled that when Veronica had taken the wedding
party on a tour earlier in the week, she had mentioned
there was also an elevator located close to the staff staircase in the stern or rear of the boat. Although guests were
permitted to use it, the elevator mainly served as a food
and housekeeping cart lift.

As Addie followed Gerard toward the staircase, she
grinned as she passed the garage entrance. She had already discovered, due to her snoopy nose as some people
liked to say, what a garage was for on a yacht. It wasn't
for storing land vehicles. Instead it housed the family's
many water toys, including a ski boat and various Jet Skis
along with a retractable water sports platform. *Never too
old to learn something new, I guess.*

To Addie's right off the gangway entranceway was a
door that led into the passageway to the crew cabins and
the kitchen/galley. Veronica had stressed in no uncertain
terms that the entire area was off-limits to guests. Below
them was one more level, but it wasn't counted as being
one of the six decks. It was simply referred to as below
deck and couldn't be accessed from the central staircase.
It housed the mechanical room, the engineers' and head
housekeeper's cabins, and the housekeeping supply room,
and could only be reached from either an outside stairwell or by the elevator and staff staircase.

Just as on her previous visits the past week, Addie was
taken aback by the lavishness of the finishings and the
decor surrounding her as she ascended the oriental-
carpeted, double-wide mahogany staircase to what was
called deck three, or the main deck, as Veronica had re-

ferred to it. According to Zach, before Veronica had re-
decorated, there had been a more casual beach theme to
the interior design. However, since her *Ladyship* had become mistress, the yacht had been redone to what Addie
saw today—an ostentatious display of wealth that would
even have left the shipping magnate Aristotle Onassis
breathless.

A small well-appointed guest salon with floor-to-ceiling
windows, decorated in a mix of art deco and contempo-
rary styles, was located at the top of the staircase. The sleek
leather chairs, sofas, and ornate tables were obviously
meant to inspire awe in visitors as they ascended to the
heart of the ship. The lounge, like most of the other rooms
on board, had glass doors that allowed guests easy access
to the outside deck areas. A feature that was definitely
worth it for people like her in order to escape the stifling
opulence of the interior and catch a literal breath of fresh
air.

Deck four above them was where four of the sixteen
guest rooms were located, in addition to the extravagant
owner's suite, a formal Edwardian-styled lounge with
double-wide doors that opened into an equally lavish dining room, a small office, and a library. Addie had been
itching to explore the library since her first day. She knew
the ceremony would make that impossible today, and
mentally crossed her fingers that tomorrow there would
be time before they disembarked.

There was a second dining room on deck five above
that, one much more casual in its presentation and decorated more in line with the beach theme Zach had mentioned his mother designed. That was the area that he and
Serena had chosen for their wedding ceremony and reception, much to Veronica's horror, as she wanted it on

the Edwardian level, which she'd apparently modeled after her estate in England. On the very top of the yacht was deck six, which contained the bridge, an outdoor swimming pool, a pool bar, and a massive sundeck.

From what Addie could remember of her initial tour of the ship, aside from the lounge area she currently stood in with its piano bar, deck three also housed the other smaller twelve guest cabins, a games room, a fitness room, a massage room complete with sauna, and a beauty salon, where they were headed now.

Gerard indicated with a gesture of his hand that they had arrived at her destination and stepped aside, allowing Addie to enter the beauty salon. "I'll take your bags to your stateroom, but you'll need this." He dropped a brass key into her hand, bowed at the waist, and disappeared down the passageway.

"You're late." Serena glowered at Addie by way of her refection in the wall mirror in front of her salon chair.

"By a whole ten minutes," Addie replied with a chuckle as she dropped the key into her handbag.

"Well, at least you're not cooling your heels in a jail cell, *this time*," Serena scoffed.

Paige piped in from her chair beside Serena's, "Speaking of heels, how's your ankle feeling?"

"Not bad. It's still a wee bit swollen, but I think I'll be able to get my high heels back on in time for the ceremony. They may not last all evening, but at least I'll be able to wear them for the big event." She elbowed Serena's shoulder good-naturedly as she passed her to take the last of the chairs on the other side of Elli Hollingsworth, Serena's assistant and Paige's best friend.

"What ankle, and why are we worried about it?"

"Oh, it's nothing." Addie waved off her look of panic.

"I just had a little run-in with a curb this morning. That's all. Nothing for you to concern yourself with." Addie winced as her stylist ruthlessly brushed her hair.

"I did," said Serena, staring into the mirror, giving her a side-glance, "have a bit of a panic attack when Paige told me you'd been taken away in a police car again."

Elli's chocolate-brown eyes reflecting in the mirror widened.

"Yeah, what was that all about?" asked Paige. "Your text later only said, 'Everything's okay, and close up whenever you can. I'll meet you at the boat.'"

Addie gazed mutely at the three via the mirror reflections. *Should I or shouldn't I relay the tale of the body on the beach?* She didn't want to cast the shadow of a murder over her friend's big day, but news would get out soon enough, so she had to say something. Since it had nothing to do with the yacht or the wedding, as far as she knew, she wouldn't have to supply details and could brush it off . . . well, as much as someone can brush off a murder.

"Oh, Marc only wanted to know if I recognized the photo of a man whose body they found on the beach this morning." She waved her hand in nonchalance and looked up at her stylist. "Jenny, is it?" She glanced at her gold name tag.

The young woman, sporting a black asymmetric haircut, nodded.

"Good," said Addie. "I was thinking that since my dress is a one-shoulder strap to my right then perhaps a low side ponytail held with a clasp that I found. It will match the crystal floral-ribbon headbands the other girls are wearing. Do you think on my left side would be the best style?"

Jenny glanced at Serena in the mirror. Bridal approval

given, Jenny nodded. "Would you like the ends curled or spiraled?"

"You and Serena can decide. I just think with the one shoulder strap it would look better balanced, don't you?"

Serena's stylist, Tiffany, murmured her agreement, and it was settled. The others would have an assortment of updos, and Addie would sport a side-spiraled ponytail.

"Getting back to the body Marc asked you to help identify. Was he murdered or was it natural causes?" Serena's gaze in the mirror pinned Addie with a loud and clear message: *If you say murder, don't you dare start your sleuthing thing today.*

"The autopsy results aren't in yet." Addie hoped she was coming off as convincing as Serena needed her to be. "He just wanted to know if I had seen the man before, that's all."

"Is it someone you're supposed to know?"

Addie shook her head.

"Then why ask you, or is he bringing *all* the residents of Greyborne Harbor in one at a time to see if they can identify him?"

Paige and Elli burst into laughter. "That would take like a year to solve this case, wouldn't it?" Paige chuckled.

"Exactly my point." Serena glared into the mirror. "So why *you* this morning?"

"Well . . . you were busy and I was . . . well, around and he . . . just thought maybe the guy had been in my bookstore or I'd seen him around town square. You know, just trying to get a lead on this, I guess, so he could wrap it up before your ceremony. Which, my friend, is the only thing you should be thinking about right now."

"Okay, if you say so, but if you disappear on me this evening and run off to do any of your sleuthing because of this, I'll, I'll—"

"Don't worry. I don't know the guy. Never seen him before, and besides, *nothing* will distract me from making sure you have the best day *ever*!"

Chapter 4

Addie eyed her finished hairdo in the mirror and locked her eyes on Serena's reflection. "Soooo, Bridezilla, does this *one* meet your approval?"

"Bridezilla!" Serena sputtered. "What? Me?"

The three bridesmaids snickered and nodded in unison. "Yeah, just a wee bit," Addie said, chuckling softly. "You have these poor girls doing and redoing our styles so often that I'm sure they're all thinking of new careers by now." Addie glanced in the mirror at Jenny behind her and gave her a wink.

"I can't help it, but I want everything to be perfect. Dragon Lady stole everything else from me. At least let me have this."

"Now, now, my friend, remember the freckles." Addie flashed a teasing grin. "I'm just saying and I believe you have to admit that after four different attempts to please you with various versions of a side ponytail *failed* . . . even though you didn't agree at first . . . you have to confess now that Jenny was right when she suggested a messy-curly side bun for me instead."

Serena glanced in the mirror. Her scrutinizing gaze studied Addie's makeup and hair, then Elli's, and then Paige's, and she nodded.

The four stylists behind them heaved a collective sigh of relief.

"Okay," Addie said pushing herself up out of the chair. "Hair and makeup done. Let's get round three of preparations complete and then go get you married."

"Isn't the mother of the bride going to have a little pampering herself?" asked Tiffany as she helped Serena to her feet.

"No, um, she, well . . . has her own hairdresser that she's used for years. So . . ."

"I see." Tiffany smiled knowingly. "Then I guess we're done here, and if I do say so myself, Serena, you look absolutely stunning."

Serena took one more glance in the mirror at her half-up, half-down hairstyle. Addie knew the finished result wasn't even close to what Serena had envisioned. For the last two hours, they all had been on pins and needles, waiting for the explosion that was sure to follow the tug-of-war between Serena and her stylist. For one, Tiffany hadn't placed the two crystal-and-pearl floral comb headpieces across the crown of Serena's head as she'd wanted. Instead, the hairdresser used the combs as fingers and swept masses of wavy red hair up at the sides and used the ornate combs across the back of her friend's head to secure the curled locks on top. Long, soft coils of hair hung freely down her neck. *Like a fairy princess*. The smile on her friend's face told Addie that Serena approved of the end result.

"Thank you," Serena whispered, fighting tears that threatened her reddening eyes. "It's perfect. I'm glad now that I abandoned the idea of having a braided coil on either side of my head like my mother had on her wedding day."

"Yeah," Elli said, "but that wasn't until Paige pointed out that you'd look like Princess Leia."

"I know," snickered Serena, "and then I decided taking on the Dragon Lady this week has been bad enough. I really didn't want a go-around with Darth Vader, too."

Addie's face crinkled in laughter, and she let out a sound somewhere between a snort and a laugh. Paige and Elli fared no better when they doubled over bursting with knee-slapping hoots.

The foursome, still giggling from Serena's quip, noisily made their way down the passageway to the central staircase. "Addie, I hope you don't mind that I asked Gerard to take our bags and dresses up to your stateroom."

"Of course not," Addie said as they ascended to the deck above. "I think using my cabin as a dressing room is a perfect alternative since you and Zach aren't staying on board tonight and you don't have one of your own."

"Are you sure? We could use my mom and dad's cabin instead, I guess." Serena shot her a side glance. "But it is so much smaller than yours and Simon's."

"It's fine, really."

Paige grabbed Addie's sleeve. "Wait a minute, did I hear right? We're going up to *your* cabin, not Serena's parents'? I just assumed they'd be the ones up here in a glamorous stateroom."

Addie glanced helplessly at Paige as she removed her

freshly manicured claws from her arm. "Be careful. You don't want to smear your nail polish."

Paige frowned, glanced at her hand, shook her head, and then looked back at Addie. "I just want to know how you scored one of the fancy staterooms on this deck while Catherine Lewis and I have to share a small cabin on the deck below."

"What can I say? Veronica has a thing for titles, and once she heard that Simon was a doctor, well, that was it. She insisted we take the stateroom across the corridor from Zach's stepbrother Preston Buckley and his wife, Annabel."

"Well, at least Kalea and her boyfriend, Jared Munro, will be on my deck, too."

"No, they won't." Addie winced. "Apparently Jared is a business associate of the Ludlows', and they're in the stateroom next to mine."

"Pffttt," Paige sputtered.

"I'm sure your cabin will be just lovely," Ellie said, glancing at Paige. "How could it not be? Just look at the rest of the yacht." She waved her hand around the Edwardian lounge area as they stepped onto deck four.

"Besides," Serena chimed in, "Addie being up here works out perfectly since the groomsmen are using Preston's suite as their dressing room, and I overheard Veronica say it's fitting that the wedding party stay together for the big entrance to the ceremony on the above deck."

"That's a first," chirped Elli.

"What do you mean?"

"I think that's the first time you've agreed with Veronica on *anything*."

Serena mumbled something completely incoherent

and continued to make her way past the lounge and dining room and down the mahogany-paneled passageway. When they came to the double-wide glass doors of the library, Addie's pace faltered.

"Later, my friend." Serena shot her an impatient glance. "We have a wedding to get to, in case you forgot."

"I haven't forgotten." Addie stared longingly into the ornate room. "I only hope I have time later to go in and explore."

Serena grabbed Addie's hand and tugged her forward.

"Wait a minute," Addie balked. "I actually thought I saw an early edition of Leo Tolstoy's *Anna Karenina* on the table by the door."

"You can stick your snoopy nose in there after we get me married, after I'm finally free of Veronica Ludlow, and after I am off exploring the tea shops of England for the next two weeks."

Addie wistfully scanned the bookshelves that she could see from the passageway and reluctantly followed her friend into the stateroom wing of the yacht.

"Which one is it?" Serena glanced over her shoulder at Addie.

"I have no idea. I guess that would help, wouldn't it?" She chuckled as she fished around in her handbag to retrieve the brass key Gerard had given her. "It's 4-C. It looks like it's up here on the right," Addie said, noting the brass plate room numbers 4-D on her left and 4-E on her right. She stopped in front of the polished mahogany door of 4-C, fit the key into the lock, and flung the door open, letting out an involuntary gasp as she hesitantly entered.

Serena released a low whistle as she stepped inside the massive stateroom behind Addie.

"Wow!" Paige exclaimed as she entered.

A bug-eyed Elli followed her in. "Is this for real?" Elli's eyes sparkled in the sun-drenched room. "You have your own walk-out balcony *and* two queen-size beds!"

From the doorway, Addie eyed the wall of floor-to-ceiling windows with sliding glass doors opening out onto a small private balcony. The room was finished in a dark teak and screamed pure luxury. The double built-in wardrobe had an inset beveled-glass mirror on each of the two doors, and past it—from what she could see—was a lavishly finished en suite bathroom. If she wasn't mistaken, the bathroom floors were covered with Tau Ceramica, designed by an exclusive Spanish tile company.

"Catherine and I have two single beds in our cabin, and you have all this!" Paige waved her hand.

"It is bigger than I thought it would be," marveled Addie, unable to believe her eyes. "When Veronica switched us from a room with only one bed. I had no idea it would be . . . this!"

"What do you mean she switched you?" asked Serena.

"Umm, earlier this week she told me she had put Simon and me in one of the king-size bed staterooms. I informed her that we preferred . . . umm"—she cleared her throat—"separate sleeping arrangements and that one of the twin cabins, like Paige has, would be just fine. She said, 'Nonsense, a doctor of Simon Emerson's stature deserves far better,' and she said she'd switch Jared and"—her fingers hooked air quotes—"'his little friend' into the king room."

"His stature?" squeaked Serena. "What does she know about Simon other than him being a doctor?"

"Apparently"—Addie opened the wardrobe doors—"his reputation from New York preceded their introduction this week. I mean I know he's good at what he does, but who knew that at one time he was considered one of New York City's top trauma surgeons?" She shrugged. "Anyway, we have an hour, so we'd best start getting ready."

Addie removed the garment bag containing Serena's cream-colored, full-length chiffon sheath dress from the hanger and held it out to her. "Why don't you go into the bathroom and put the slip on, and then I'll help you get into the dress later? We don't want any mishaps with makeup all over the front of it, do we?"

Serena took the dress bag from her hand and headed toward the en suite.

"Is it just me," Elli said, watching Serena, "or does she suddenly seem a bit out of sorts?"

"I think she's fine. Probably just a case of last-minute nerves." Addie handed out the other two bridesmaid dresses to Elli and Paige. "Here, we'll get ready, and then I'll check on the bride and help her get into her dress."

Addie slithered into her georgette mid-length dress and let it drop around her. A knock on her door stopped her fingers from fiddling with the material. "Who's there?"

"It's just me." A silvery voice accompanied a half-up, half-down-styled, coffered auburn hairdo as her cousin stepped through the door. "Your dress designer and alterations expert, Kalea Hudson."

"Hi, cuz, you're just in time. So, what do you think?" Addie smoothed down the tulip hemmed, dark-marine-blue bridesmaid dress, twirled in front of the mirror, and admired how the faux-wrap front had a very slimming effect on her not twenty-five-year-old-anymore waist size.

Kalea's hazel-green eyes scanned each of the women before her and nodded approvingly.

The overall style and material of each dress was the same, but they all had a different neckline to set them apart. Addie's was a one-shoulder creation, Elli's had spaghetti straps, and Paige, the least endowed of the three, pulled off her strapless dress perfectly.

"I can't believe it!" Kalea laced her red-nailed manicured fingers together and clasped her hands to her chest. "They all turned out perfect if I do say so myself." She beamed broadly. "How does the bride's dress fit?"

"I was just about to go in and give her a hand," Addie said, heading toward the bathroom door. "We'll find out in a second." She raised her hand and knocked. No answer. She knocked again. Still no answer. Addie's gut tightened as she turned the handle and peered in behind the door. There sat Serena, wearing only her full-length slip, shivering. "Are you okay?" Addie asked as she stepped in and closed the door.

Serena stared blankly at the dress hanging from a hook on the back of the door.

"Serena, is everything okay?"

Serena turned her blurry eyes to her. Her bottom lip quivered. "It's real, isn't it? I'm about to get married. That means *forever*. I mean, sure we've been happy living together, but once we're married, what if we end up hating each other in ten years, what if—"

"Stop it." Addie scurried to her side. "You and Zach love each other more than any two people I've ever known."

"I know, but what if this is all a mistake?"

"Can you imagine your life without Zach?"

Serena shook her head.

"Then remember, you don't marry someone you can live with. You marry someone you can't live without."

Serena's eyes widened, and she stared at Addie.

"You're right. I don't think I could live without him, and I don't ever want to try to."

"That's my girl. Now, let's get this gorgeous dress on you and—"

The door opened and a faded, graying red head appeared around the door. "It's just Mom. Can I come in?"

"Yes, please. I need you, Mommy." Serena sniffled and held her arms wide open.

Janis Chandler darted toward her and tightly embraced her. "Got a little case of cold feet?" she said, looking down at her daughter.

Serena sniffed and nodded.

"It's okay . . . it's normal." Her mother held her close to her chest.

Addie took that as her cue to leave and slid out the door. "Hi, Mr. Chandler. Your little girl's nearly ready and should be out in a few minutes."

"Thanks, Addie, but please call me Wade. I feel like we're family, and I want to thank you, all of you." He glanced at Paige, Elli, and Kalea. "You've been my baby's rock these past few months. I know things have happened that have upset her, and I don't think we've been the kind of support she needed."

Addie glanced at Paige and Elli standing beside the tall, graying-haired gentleman, who at the moment appeared so small and humbled in his dark-gray linen suit that she wanted to hug him. "Serena is strong because of the base you and Janis gave her to fall back on. It's you who's made her the marvelous woman we all know and love today."

To the murmurs of agreement around the room, Addie took Wade's hands in hers and squeezed them. "You have a lot to be proud of." She smiled up at him. When his

dark-brown eyes met hers, a shiver raced through her. It
was as though she was looking into Marc's eyes. The resemblance he had to his son always caught Addie off
guard. She shook it off and turned toward the bathroom
door as it opened. Then like everyone else in the room,
she gasped. Addie glanced over at Wade, who was obviously fighting the tears blurring his eyes.

"Oh baby," he choked, "you are the vision of the perfect bride. You're absolutely beautiful."

Addie thought that Wade couldn't have said it better.
Her best friend was a vision of innocence and beauty
draped in her flowing sheath dress. It was the perfect
boho-style wedding dress for a very unconventional bride
who had fought tradition along with all Veronica's pomp
and ceremony. The top flowy chiffon, covered in tiny
eyelet flowers, was softly ruffled at the bodice and had
two front slits that flowed to the floor over a matching
sheath slip-dress. It was pure Serena in its simplicity and
style and perfect for the outdoor wedding on the promenade deck.

Addie glanced from Janis, dressed in a light-green
mid-length suit that highlighted her faded-red hair, to the
proud father and had to fight back her own tears. Elli was
the only one thinking and produced her cell phone from
her small black evening bag and snapped photos of the
group.

The door flew open and there in the doorway loomed
Veronica. It was clear by her imposing stance and her
floor-length silver evening gown that her vision of an in-
formal family wedding greatly clashed with Serena and
Zach's. Her coffee-brown eyes flashed a cool greeting toward Wade and Janis. Then she glanced dismissively at
Addie, Paige, and Elli, skimmed her eyes over Kalea's

stunning fitted, floral summer dress, and paused. A slight smile tugged at the corners of her pursed ruby-red lips, and then she focused her attention on Serena.

"I only came in to let you the groomsmen have headed upstairs now, so whenever you're ready . . . hmm." Her eyes scanned Serena from head to toe. "I really do wish you'd taken my advice and seen my dress designer in New York." Her neat brows arched subtly, her dark, coiffured feather-bob didn't sway, and her Botox-injected face didn't move, but the disapproval in her eyes of Serena's choice in wedding dresses was clearly evident as she spun on her spiked heel and disappeared from the room.

"Well, I never!" Kalea gasped, and thrust the door closed behind her.

"Relax, Kalea," Serena said, smiling. To her credit, not one freckle popped out, which was completely out of character and a huge contrast to the hot mess her friend had been the past few months.

"I love my dress. It's exactly what I wanted and knowing Dragon Lady doesn't approve . . . well . . . it makes me love it even more. Now, Daddy"—Serena held out her arm—"are you ready to walk me down the aisle?"

Chapter 5

Addie smoothed the whisper-soft fabric of her skirt and steadied herself in front of the closed lounge door leading out onto the open promenade deck. Paige reached around her and pulled a corner of the door curtain back and then glanced at Addie, her eyes reflecting sheer horror.

"What's wrong? Didn't anyone show up?"

"How many invitations did you say Serena and Zach sent out?"

"About thirty. Why?"

"Take a look and tell me if I'm seeing things."

Addie drew back a corner of the curtain and promptly dropped it. "Don't say a word," she whispered, keeping her gaze focused straight ahead. "Just line up behind me and act as naturally as you can."

Paige nodded and took her place beside Elli. When the

string quartet outside the door finished playing the pre-arranged melody cue, Addie reached out and gave a small rap on the door. In choreographed unison, the French doors swung open, flanked either side by a male staff member dressed in the yacht's black jacket and brass-buttoned uniform.

Addie fought to refocus the panic overtaking her. There was no telling how Serena would react when she marched down the aisle and realized that, yet again, Veronica had ignored her and Zach's wishes for a small, intimate ceremony. She conducted a quick mental count of the chairs and stopped when she reached over sixty. She didn't recognize half the guests and questioned if even Zach would as they were no doubt high-society friends of the Ludlows'.

When the quartet began to play the introductory wedding march, Addie took a hesitant step out onto the warm, early-evening sunlit promenade. Giddiness of what was about to occur overtook the momentary panic she'd succumbed to. She only hoped her friend's freckles would stay in check upon seeing the number of guests, and that when she reached the makeshift altar on the bow, it wouldn't appear as if she had chicken pox.

Addie glided up the white carpeted aisle bordered on either side with rose petals. Her feigned smile became heartfelt with every step she took toward the window-styled arch draped in flowing sheer fabric and flanked on either side by a square pillar topped with massive crystal vases overflowing with an assortment of roses and wisteria blossoms. If her friend could keep this view of the harbor dotted with boats and a few of the many smaller islands off the mainland, she might overcome Veronica's dictatorial spectacle.

Addie's smile broadened when her gaze met Simon's. The picturesque sea behind him highlighted the blue of his Armani jacket. It didn't hurt that his ebony hair framed sea-blue eyes. He took her breath away. He was the most handsome man in the room. She glanced at Marc, who stood beside him, and had to admit that he, too, didn't look half bad. Both these men cleaned up pretty well in their light beige slacks and summer-weight, medium-blue linen jackets, which paired well with the bridesmaids' marine-blue dresses. Even Preston, who was Bond-esque in his everyday clothing, pulled off the more casual look that Serena and Zach had insisted on.

To Veronica's earlier vocalized angst, Zach wore a full light-beige lined Armani suit that matched the grooms-men's trousers. Addie glanced at Oliver Ludlow in the first row. Zach's father had obviously lost the battle of suit color with Veronica and wore the more formal navy version she had unsuccessfully attempted to dictate to the entire male entourage.

Addie took her place along with Paige and Elli and scanned the rows of guests, recognizing only about five people in every fifteen. When Serena, her arm looped through her father's, began her march toward them, Addie mentally crossed her fingers that her friend wouldn't notice the expanded crowd size. She glanced back at Serena as her father presented her on his arm to Zach and then stepped back to stand beside Janis directly in front of Addie. She didn't have to worry about her friend being put off in the moment by the increased guest list as she only had eyes for the man she was about to say *I do* to. Addie doubted that her friend would be able to see past the tears that filled her eyes right now anyway.

By the time the couple exchanged their personal wedding vows and was pronounced husband and wife, Addie couldn't contain her own tears. It took a nudge from Simon for her to realize it was time to form a procession behind the happy couple down the aisle and into the lounge where the reception would be held.

"You look incredible today by the way," he whispered with a wink as they made their way to the lounge entrance.

"Thanks, you look pretty good yourself," she murmured, giving him a light hip check.

When they reached the double-wide French doors, her breath caught in her chest and her fingers clamped down on Simon's jacket sleeve.

"What's wrong?" His hand covered hers.

"Do you see who's here?"

"I see how many people are here, and I tell you, Zach was none too pleased. I thought he was going to have it right out with his parents before the ceremony."

"No, I mean did you happen to see the uninvited guest standing over past the string quartet?" she asked, stepping into the reception area.

"No, but I find it hard to believe that anyone would be here that wasn't invited. I thought Zach was going to rip Veronica's head off when we lined up to go outside. If it hadn't been for his father dragging her away, we might have had a murder on our hands."

"We still might when Serena sees who showed up."

"Why? Who's here that shouldn't be? Well, aside from about fifty extra guests?"

"Lacey Davenport! Marc's high school sweetheart, remember her and the trouble she caused me the last time she blew into town?"

"She's here today? But I thought you said she wasn't invited after all the commotion she caused the last time, not to mention the little matter of her stealing money from Serena's safe and then disappearing again."

"I know. I helped Serena and her mother compose the guest list, and she certainly wasn't on it."

She glanced toward the door as people filed in. Her hand tightened on Simon's arm again. "See?" She jerked her head toward Lacey, a tall, leggy blonde. Her stylish blue gingham-patterned sleeveless dress, belted at the waist, billowed out in a full skirt. Addie had to admit the woman looked amazing, but she also knew the true personality all that glamour was attempting to camouflage. Unlike others, not being a fashion diva herself, she wasn't distracted by the flash because she knew the kind of person the stunning outfit was disguising.

"I see her, but if she wasn't invited, how did she hear about it? Last we heard she was living in New York City."

"I think the better question is . . . why is she here?" Addie glanced at Serena, who was smiling dumbfounded at an elegant couple Addie didn't recognize. Serena glanced past the pasty-faced plump woman, and her eyes screamed *help me* when they met Addie's.

"Oh dear, I'd better go save the bride. She looks like she's drowning in unwanted attention." She dropped Simon's arm, scooted over to Serena's side, and glanced apologetically from the short balding man to the woman. "I'm sorry to interrupt, but Serena is needed over by the hors d'oeuvre table for a moment." Addie smiled and tugged her friend away.

"Thank you," whispered Serena. "I have no idea who those people are, and I really don't care." Serena studied the crowded lounge. "I don't know who half these people are." Her bottom lip quivered.

"Don't worry about them. You know full well Veronica would end up getting her way in the end, so all you can do is focus on your friends who are here, the people you and Zach did invite. Smile and nod at everyone else, and once in a while take a look at the table in the corner piled high with gifts and be grateful Veronica has such rich friends."

"Addie, that's horrible. You make it sound like that's all that is important about this fiasco."

"What are you going to do about her ignoring your wishes? It's too late, so make the most of it and enjoy. You leave in a couple of hours anyway, and then you won't have to think about her until—"

"Until she wants to have another family event. I guess when I married Zach, I married his entire family, too, didn't I?"

"I somehow don't think she's all that family-oriented. I heard that Preston, her own son, was shipped off to boarding school when he was very young. All you can do going forward is to take it one holiday at a time and re-member that up until the wedding planning started, Zach didn't have much to do with his family. He's made Grey-borne Harbor his home, so I think he'll support you when you tell the Dragon Lady you'll be spending holidays here with your family." She glanced over at Zach, who appeared far more relaxed speaking with his employer, Dr. Lim, from the local naturopathic clinic, than he had earlier talking to a couple of high-society types from his hometown in Connecticut.

"Thanks, I needed that." Serena smiled.

"That's what best friends do, plus . . . they make sure their friends eat." She popped a small canapé from Martha's tray into Serena's sparrow-like mouth.

Serena swallowed and nodded her gratitude, then her eyes flew wide open. "What the . . ." Her gaze drilled a hole in a certain blue gingham dress.

"Please," Addie said. "Tell me you didn't invite her out of lamenting a lost friendship or feeling some obligation at the last minute?"

Serena never took her eyes off the willowy woman toying with her champagne glass. "Not a chance after what she pulled the last time she floated through town and then left with *my* money. Nope, our friendship sailed out of here with her that day. I can't believe her audacity by showing up today, and just look at her, chatting away merrily with Kalea and Jared like they were old friends."

Addie put a plate of appetizers together. "Here, you take this and go find Zach. I think I saw him and Dr. Lim heading to the table over there where your parents are talking to your aunt and uncle. I'm sure he needs to eat something as badly as you do. I'll go talk to Lacey and see why she's here."

"You know it's to cause trouble. Just look at her. First, she was cooing and cawing all over Jared, now she's set her gaze on Marc. Just watch her claws come out when he puts his arm around Ryley."

"You eat. I'll go see if I can defuse an imminent situation while I try to find out what brings her to a place where she knew she wouldn't be welcome."

Addie shuffled toward the bar. Her ankle had done fairly well all day, but with the standing, it was throbbing again. She slipped out of her heels and kicked them under the piano by the bar. When she came face-to-face with Lacey, Addie regretted her decision as the lanky woman towered over her.

Lacey stared down her perky little nose at Addie and feigned a smile. "Addie, what a pleasure to see you again."

Chapter 6

"I'm sure it is." Addie nodded, squeezing the napkin in her hand into a tiny ball. "However, I don't recall seeing your name on the guest list, Lacey." Addie crossed her arms and waited for the excuse of the day.

The air around them all but sparked with the electricity born from their dislike for each other.

"Oh," squealed Kalea, "you know each other? What a small world. Addie, I was complimenting Lacey on her beautiful dress and well"—Kalea's hand swept down her own floral skirt—"she loved mine and asked who the designer was. When I told her it was me, why, we've become the best of friends." She giggled nervously as her eyes flitted from one unwavering woman to the other. Kalea pointed to one of Lacey's pockets. "See, her dress has hidden pockets just like the ones I put in my creations. I wish I had thought of adding those to the dress I designed for Ryley, too, though, now I know they're all the rage of the New York designers."

"Ryley's dress is beautiful as it is. Besides, it's form-fitting and perfect for her shapely body. Pockets wouldn't have worked in it." Addie's annoyance with her cousin's constant babbling bubbled to the surface. "Well, Lacey, you still haven't answered my question. Why are you here today? Did you forget you owed Serena a few thousand dollars and come to pay her back as a wedding gift?"

"Oh, that little misunderstanding. Is that what this is all about?" Lacey knocked back her champagne, finishing it off, and motioned to the bartender to refill it. "I left Serena a note explaining I was only taking the money I earned by doing all the hard work of relaunching her little tea shop." She waved her hand dismissively. "I'm certain that if you talk to her, she'll explain."

"I have talked to her *many* times, and no, she doesn't see it that way."

"Semantics, my dear Addie." Lacey gulped down another mouthful of her drink. "I'm fairly certain I was meant to be invited, but I recently moved into a new apartment. My invitation must have been lost in the mail."

Addie spread her feet apart and leaned toward Lacey, her blood and her words boiling in her throat. She opened her mouth to give Lacey what for, but the woman grinned and said, "I see you finally came to your senses about Marc not being your type."

Addie stared at her and snapped her mouth closed. Serena was right. The audacity of this woman was unbelievable. She glanced at Lacey's half-full champagne glass, noted her teetering in her high heels, and knew any words she had with her now would be lost, given her current state.

"And you know," Lacey glanced at Simon, her gaze lingering for a moment, "I definitely approve of the doctor." Then she fixed her baby blues on Addie and smirked. "He really is a catch and one I myself wouldn't have minded reeling in, if it wasn't for the fact that Marc and I have so much history." She circled an imaginary ring around her left ring finger. "Being engaged to a person does that, you know."

"Marc asked Addie to marry him, too," Kalea piped in, "but she got cold feet because she couldn't get over David."

"Is that right?" Lacey eyed Addie from head to toe. "Well, well, well, Miss Greyborne, you really have made your way around town, haven't you?"

Addie bristled momentarily, forgetting where she was, and took a step toward Lacey, her fingers curled into a fist at her side.

Jared glanced at his phone, which had distracted him since Addie joined the little group, and shoved it in his jacket pocket. "This has been lovely," he said, reaching his outstretched hand between Addie and Lacey, as he took her hand in his. "It was a pleasure to meet you Lacey. I'm sure we'll be seeing you around New York the next time Kalea and I are there on business."

Addie relaxed her fingers and gulped in a breath, trying to quell the bile rising in the back of her throat and the blood boiling in her veins—a common reaction for her whenever she had to deal with this she devil. Addie tried to shake it off, remembering this was Serena's wedding, and she had vowed to let nothing spoil the day for her best friend. Lambasting Lacey, no matter how well de-served, probably wouldn't be her best move right now. That could wait until later and Addie reluctantly took a step back.

Jared kissed Kalea on the cheek. "See you in a few days, darling."

"Are you leaving now?" Lacey's lip shot out in a little-girl pout. "But we've all just gotten to get to know each other."

"Yes, it's too bad," he said. "This has been enjoyable, but I'm afraid I have to fly to Switzerland tonight. There's a problem with one of the ski resorts a client is building, and if we lose this summer weather, it will put the project back a year." He glanced at Addie. "Please make sure your cousin behaves herself tonight and doesn't do too much celebrating." He dropped a brass key into Kalea's hand. "I guess I won't need this now." He kissed her. "I gotta run, or I'll miss my flight. I'll call you later tonight from the airport." He turned and strode off toward the central staircase.

Lacey's gaze followed the tall, dark-haired lithe man across the room, and she sighed. "You got yourself a good one there, my new friend." She laughed and clanked her glass against Kalea's.

"I have a great idea." Kalea dangled the key in her fingers. "Since Jared won't be here, why don't you stay in my stateroom with me tonight? It would be a great time to get to know each other, and you can tell me all about your New York City dress designer friends . . . and maybe give me some pointers on how to break into that market."

Lacey took the key and slipped it into her pocket. "Sounds like a plan," she said with a wide grin. "Now, getting back to you, my old friend." She swiveled toward Addie. "Do you really think I was going to miss my best friend's wedding?"

"Best friend?" Addie was taken aback by her cousin's offer and Lacey's question. "You don't steal from best friends."

"Oh, get over it, really. I've known Serena since she was in diapers and nothing was going to keep me away from her big day. Bartender, another." She motioned with a swirl of her glass. "Now, tell me"—she leaned across the bar—"who is that raven-haired beauty in the red, sleeveless, choker-styled minidress with my man, Marc?"

Addie coughed on the *my man* words.

Kalea glanced over her shoulder and then at Lacey. "That's his girlfriend, Detective Ryley Brookes. Don't you know her?"

"Nope, but I'm about to." Lacey smoothed her hands over her skirt, adjusted the narrow blue rhinestone-studded belt, squared her shoulders, and strolled toward the couple who were chatting with Mayor Bryant, his wife, Zoe, and a few other guests by the open promenade doors.

"Now there goes a woman on a mission who knows exactly what she wants and isn't afraid to go after it." Kalea chuckled softly as Lacey draped her hand on Marc's left shoulder and whispered in his ear.

"Even if that mission is total destruction." Addie leaned against the bar and waited for the drama to unfold.

"I like her. I can't believe you never told me you were friends with such a cool chick." Kalea gave her a teasing wink. "Everyone else in town is so stuffy and appropriate, but Lacey"—she eyed the lanky blonde across the room—"feels like my soul sister and having her as my roommate tonight is going to be fun."

Addie choked on her drink and wiped her chin with a bar napkin. Her gaze never strayed from following Lacey's antics. She sensed the inevitable fireworks when Ryley, standing on Marc's right, calmly turned, removed a glass from the passing server's tray, twirled with the grace of a dancer between Lacey and Marc, and delivered a hip check that sent Lacey shuffling to the side.

Lacey swung around, her long hair whipping in defiance, and stood her ground. The leggy detective merely smiled and extended a limp hand toward Lacey by way of introduction. There was no mistaking the back-off warning that flashed in Ryley's dark eyes as they fixed unyieldingly on Lacey's baby blues, which shone with disbelief at the detective's setdown.

Addie took a sip of her drink and smiled. It appeared as though Lacey had met her match in the detective. From experience with both women, Addie didn't foresee a catfight but battles of wit outplay until Lacey got bored and moved onto some other poor unsuspecting victim. She glanced sideways at her cousin and could see why Kalea referred to Lacey as her kindred spirit. They were two peas in pod.

The band that had set up in the adjoining dining room began playing and the crowd from the lounge area heeded Serena and Zach's cue to follow. Addie was pleased to see that the tables had been situated to the sides and the center of the room cleared for dancing. Veronica had balked at the idea of having a dance as part of the celebration, but Serena, who loved nothing more than music and dancing, had obviously won this round.

"There you are," whispered Addie's old friend Catherine Lewis. "I've been looking everywhere for you. Did you see who was here?" She pointed with her drink hand to Lacey by the small bar in the dance area.

"Hi, yes, I saw."

"Does Serena know she's here?"

"She knows and is none too happy about it."

"What are we going to do?"

"We are going to keep them apart and let Serena have the best wedding party ever."

"I hope we can, but look."

"Oh no."

Lacey moved in on Preston, cooing and cawing all over him, until Annabel, in her slate-textured lace blouson gown, made a beeline across the dance floor toward them. She grabbed her husband's arm and swirled him toward her. They exchanged words Addie couldn't make out, but Preston gave Lacey a sheepish half smile and allowed his wife to pull him toward a table on the far side of the room.

"Lacey is in fine form tonight. I'd better go check on her," said Catherine.

"She has been drinking heavily so be prepared for her to take some offense."

"I can handle her. Remember, I used to babysit her." Catherine moved across the floor toward the woman. Addie admired Catherine, who since moving here had become like a mother to her after Addie discovered that she had met Catherine when Addie was a small child. It had shocked her to find out that Catherine and Addie's father had been involved in a love affair. But now Addie smiled easily as Catherine's shoulder-length brown hair swayed with each step she took. Her petite figure showed off her stunning sleeveless peacock-green and blue A-line midi dress, which accentuated the mature woman's proportions. Addie noticed she wasn't the only one watching Catherine.

The striking Captain Nevins and another distinguished-looking, silver-haired gentleman, whom Addie hadn't met, but understood to be Oliver's head of security, Felix Vanguard, sipped champagne and followed the elegant woman's swaying hips.

Felix set his glass down and started to go after Catherine but was stopped by Donna Camden, a meek little woman who worked as Veronica's personal assistant. More like her servant, though, Addie scoffed, having made that determination by observing their peculiar relationship this week, but now she boldly gestured toward the dance floor. Felix gazed longingly at Catherine as she made her way to Lacey's side. Then he glanced down at the dowdily dressed, middle-aged woman in front of him, nodded, and allowed her to steer him out onto the dance floor, where she positioned them directly beside her employer.

Addie shrugged, draining her champagne glass. Perhaps Donna was hoping some of Veronica's sequins would rub off onto her nondescript dark linen suit, which obviously had been chosen by her *Ladyship*, which except for Donna's skirt, was a similar style and cut to Oliver's formal-appearing suit.

For all of Veronica's objections to the dance portion of the evening, she did appear as though she were enjoying her husband twirling her around the dance floor. Another couple also appeared to be lost in the moment. Even though the music was upbeat, Serena and Zach huddled in each other's arms and appeared to be listening to their own tune, a slow waltz. The way they were nuzzled together on the dance floor made Addie wonder that in spite of their wanting to put as much distance been them and the Dragon Lady, it appeared that perhaps they hadn't thought the whole wedding night thing through. By the look of the two lovebirds, it might have been better if they had waited to leave on their honeymoon until the morning. She chuckled to herself at the sight of them wrapped in each other's arms, oblivious to everything going on around them, and she searched the room for Simon.

"Hey, you're missing all the fun," Elli shouted over the music as she and Curtis, the young police recruit she was dating, danced by her.

Addie shook her head and pointed to her still slightly swollen ankle. Elli made a pouty face and danced away.

Addie wasn't much of a dancer anyway, but the music was good and the sight of so many couples on the dance floor made her foot tap in time to the music. It would be nice if Simon were here to at least listen to it with her.

She spotted him in the lounge area. He and Marc were deep in a discussion, and by the looks on their faces, Addie didn't think either of them appeared as though they were recapping the events of the wedding. More than likely they were talking shop over this morning's events, a topic she felt had no place in Serena's celebrations, so she gingerly made her way through the crowd of people and edged up beside Simon.

"Hey there, stranger." she said, running her hand down his arm, clasping his hand in hers. "Are you avoiding me because you're afraid I'll haul you out onto the dance floor?"

"Not at all." He kissed her cheek. "We just had a few details to go over before we head out tonight."

"What do you mean head out tonight?" She glanced between Simon and Marc and noted the sudden flex of Marc's jaw.

"I'll go remind my officers who appear to be having too good a time that they are either working later or expected to be on shift by seven a.m." Marc glanced at Addie sheepishly and slipped away, disappearing into the crowd.

She heaved out a frustrated sigh. "So, you're going to work tonight and not stay here with me in that delightful stateroom?" She nestled into his chest and toyed with his jacket collar. "Is there anything I can say or do to change your mind?" She looked up at him, searching his eyes.

He clasped her hand to his chest. "I'm afraid not. There's a dead body lying on my table, and we don't know the first thing about him other than he was shot at close range by what appears to be a flare gun."

"Don't forget that torn corner of the book in his pocket. I'll need that as soon as you've lifted off any evidence you can find from it."

He glanced down at her questioningly.

"If I can touch the paper and smell it, I might be able to determine the age of the book, which would be a lead."

"It would be a start because right now we don't have a clue what any of it means, which is why I can't stay tonight." He kissed her softly on the lips. "No matter how much I want to," he whispered, and pulled her into his arms and kissed her deeply.

They both jumped when there was a crash and the sound of breaking glass behind them. Addie spun around to see Lacey weaving back and forth, a shattered crystal champagne glass at her feet.

"Oops." Lacey giggled and placed her slender hand

over her mouth. She strained in an obvious attempt to focus on Addie as she wobbled toward her. "Forgive the intrusion." Her words rolled off her tongue in a moist slur. "I just can't believe that the biggest book nerd I've ever known would tear a book."

"I didn't tear a book." Addie shot Simon a helpless glance. She studied the lanky blonde. "It's a case Simon is working on." Addie dropped her gaze. Getting into it with Lacey right now was the last thing she or anyone else here needed.

"What case?" Lacey's words held a warble of panic as her hand shot into her skirt pocket. Then her anxious brow relaxed, and she let out a short laugh. "Being a re- porter and all, I'm always open to a story." Her gaze held unyieldingly on Addie's.

"It's nothing," said Addie.

"It's police business," added Simon. "I suggest that if you're looking for a story, you speak to the chief."

Lacey glanced into the dining room. Marc and Ryley were wrapped in each other's arms, clearly enjoying a slow dance. Lacey brought her drunken-glazed stare back to Addie and Simon. "I guess I misheard. I thought you said something about someone dead," she gulped, "and a torn book page." She grabbed a champagne glass from the tray of a passing server and knocked back a mouthful. "Sorry, my mistake." She staggered toward the doorway to the outside deck.

"That was weird," said Simon, his eyes following her as she stumbled across the floor.

"Yes, I wonder how much she overheard, and more importantly, will she remember it and become a thorn in everyone's side as she tries to get a scoop on the story?"

Addie noted that as soon as Lacey was outside, she

tugged her cell phone out of her pocket and tapped out something on the small keyboard. "Oh dear." Addie glanced up at Simon. "It looks like she's making notes, so she doesn't forget what she heard."

"I'd better warn Marc to expect her to be snooping around in the case," Simon said, and then dashed into the dining room.

Chapter 7

"I think I've just opened a snake pit," said Addie to Paige, who'd slipped up beside her. Addie's stomach lurched at the sight of Marc and Simon heading back into the lounge. Their brisk stride told her neither was too happy with the results of her slip of the tongue, which in spite of all Addie's well-meaning innocence, had brought an unwelcome wrench into the works also known as Lacey.

"Given the fact I just saw you guys talking to Lacey and the look on your face now, I take it that witch is up to her old tricks again? Did you guys have an argument because of her?"

"No, not an argument, but it does involve her and something I said."

"I wouldn't worry about it. Judging by what I saw not long ago going on between her and Veronica in the dining room, she seems to bring out the worst in everyone. What did you say that made Simon run off and tell Marc?" Paige popped a crab cake into her mouth.

"Simon and I were discussing the piece of paper discovered in the dead man's pocket, and Lacey overheard us. Now she seems to think she has the scoop on a big murder story, and look at Marc's face as Simon is filling him in. He must be furious with me for being so careless about speaking openly about the case."

"Oh, pfft." Paige waved her hand and swallowed her bite-size morsel. "It's bound to get out sometime. A small-town murder really can't be kept a secret for too long."

"That's true, but her finding out about it tonight means Lacey will be sticking around after the wedding to investigate. Everyone's lives will be turned on their ears again. Remember last time she came to town?"

"Yes, but you won't be her target this time, and I'm pretty sure an ex-FBI agent can handle her." Paige gave a reassuring smile. "Well, I'd better go find Logan. He has to leave as soon as the bride and groom are off."

"It's too bad he has to work the day shift tomorrow."

"Tell me about it, but he's a rookie, and all the senior firefighters had the day off already. That's why I arranged ahead of time for Catherine to stay with me tonight. I thought it would be fun to have a sleepover for my big night on this fancy-pants yacht." She studied the room. "I know this will be a once-in-a-lifetime thing, and I wanted someone to share it with."

"You have me."

"Yeah, but you have Simon, and I didn't want to be a third wheel."

"No issue about that. Simon just told me he's heading

back to his lab as soon as Serena and Zach leave. Too much work to do on the murder case."

"Oh, well, then the three of us can hang out later. It'll be like summer camp." Paige said with a laugh.

"I was thinking of asking Kalea to stay in my state-room with me. She invited her new bestie"—Addie glanced over at Lacey, who was now pawing at Jean Pierre, the French chef, behind the buffet table—"and although Lacey is in no state to go far tonight, I don't want my cousin to have to deal with her boorish behavior."

"Good luck with that. From what I've seen tonight, Kalea is the only person here she hasn't been arguing with, so I doubt your cousin will listen to you. For some strange reason she actually gets along with that witch." Paige waved over her shoulder as she went in search of Logan.

Addie gazed around the lounge. She knew it would be no good to try to plead her case to Marc, and fingers crossed, Simon was doing just that as the scarlet coloring in Marc's face had finally returned to a normal sun-kissed shade of rosy red. Besides, her head was pounding, and her ankle was throbbing. It had been a long evening of having to run interference on Lacey and making sure she stayed away from Serena. She glanced into the dining room and decided that was the last place she wanted to be right now, crammed in there with the noise of people try-ing to talk over the band. Unfortunately, it appeared every seat in the lounge was occupied by guests, who like her were escaping the commotion in the other room.

Although, she had to admit, her evening of remaining vigilant had afforded her a few peeks into the lives of her friends and other guests. First, it appeared that Ida, her little birdlike friend from the book club, had finally been successful in catching the wormy captain's wandering eye, much to Martha's chagrin, as Ida and he had been dancing together for the past hour. Second, she couldn't help but notice what good friends Ryley and Mayor Bryant's wife, Zoe, were. Who knew?

She spotted Catherine and another of one of their fellow book club members, Gloria McBride, seated beside Martha on a sofa by the lounge entrance nearest the staircase. She wiggled her numb toes and hobbled over to them, plopped on the wide leather sofa arm, and heaved out a sigh.

"Hi, ladies, I hope you don't mind, but I can't stand for even one more second."

"Of course we don't mind." Martha smoothed imaginary wrinkles from her blue silky rayon skirt. "I was just telling the girls here that I am impressed with your cousin's dressmaking skills. This outfit has been so comfortable to wear, I feel like I'm at home in my caftan," she added with a chuckle.

"I wish now I'd gotten Kalea to make my dress." Gloria pulled at her underarm seam. "You'd think with all my trips as a travel agent I'd have learned by now to go for comfort and not buy something because it looked good on the rack," she continued to mutter while tugging at her waist seam. "I can't wait to get home and take this silly dress off."

"Well." Catherine smiled at her and glanced at her watch. "It shouldn't be much longer until the bride and groom head out, and then you can leave and we can start cleaning up."

"But they have staff for that sort of thing, don't they?" Martha glanced around the lounge. "I don't think it's something you have to worry about."

"We thought," added Addie, "that since Catherine, Paige, and I are staying on board tonight and Serena's mom looks exhausted, we should pack up all the gifts and store them in my cabin. Then we can load them into Wade's car tomorrow, and they can take them home for Serena and Zach to pick up when they get back."

"That was good thinking." Gloria sipped a glass of some fruity-looking cocktail. "I would offer to help, but I have to get home to Pippi. She doesn't take to being left on her own too long these days." She glanced at Addie a teasing glint in her eye. "I think you spoiled her rotten when I was laid up last winter and she had to stay with you. Now she expects me to take her everywhere I go."

"I don't think it was Addie who spoiled her to start with," smirked a giggling Martha over the rim of her glass. "I've never seen you out and about without that little ball of fur either."

"Well, I never," Gloria said, pointing her chin upward in defiance and then lowering her eyes in reconciliation. "Maybe I do spoil her just a little. It was heartbreaking to leave her this evening but that Veronica"—Gloria harrumphed with a snort—"had adamantly put her foot down to a dog being on board." A soft smile lit up her round face. "Besides getting home to her, Cliff told me he had a surprise for me when we leave, so I don't want to hang around too long after the bride and groom make their big exit."

"Ooo, what's Mr. Weatherly's surprise?" mocked Martha, obviously feeling the effects of her cocktail. "A moonlit buggy ride through the old town? I hear that's a popular romantic date these days." She poked her friend good-naturedly in the ribs with her elbow. "Maybe he'll even make kissy-face with you under the stars." She winked.

"After all, you've been waiting for him since high school, haven't you?"

"You stop that." Gloria gave her friend a playful swat. "You know darn well I wasn't waiting, and neither was he. We'd both moved on but now . . . well, I guess it was fated that we come back together, because this time it's different." A wistful look came to her eyes. "But I have no idea what he's up to tonight. He's been acting odd all evening. Speaking of him"—she hoisted her full-figured body off the sofa—"there he is, and here come the bride and groom."

Catherine jumped to her feet and darted toward a table of small baskets filled with rose petals on the sidewall beside them. "Quick, ladies, pass these baskets out to the guests as they file by you. When we get out onto the pier, we can all toss them at the happy couple."

"Phew, I don't know about you two, but I'm exhausted." Addie swiped unruly stray hairs from her face. "I can't believe that people were still dancing and carrying on until midnight."

"I know. Did you see Ida and that captain? I never knew she had it in her."

"Yes, by the end of the evening he seemed quite enthralled by her." Addie glanced at her friend, a teasing glint in her eyes. "Although, earlier in the night, I thought it was going to be you fighting off both him and that security fellow who works for Oliver."

"Me?" Catherine tossed her head back in a snorty laugh. "I must be getting old because I didn't notice any of that. But then again, chasing after Lacey all evening wore me out, and I was ready for bed hours ago."

"I thought she went to bed."

Addie glanced sideways at Paige. "Who?"

"Her." Paige pointed to the window. "Look who's outside on the promenade deck."

"I thought she had gone to bed, too," snapped Catherine. "I sent her down to Kalea's stateroom over an hour ago."

"She must have wandered back up here at some point."

"Yeah," said Paige, "looking for another drink, judging by the full one she has in her hand now."

"Who is she talking to out there?" Addie asked, moving closer to the window. "There are too many shadows to see clearly."

"I can't tell, either." Catherine shuffled up to her side. "Paige, your eyes are younger than ours. Can you make out who's standing in the shadows over there?"

"Nope, but it does look like a man. Wait, it's Wesley Harbinger."

"What? Veronica's lawyer?" Catherine squinted into the dim lights of the deck.

"What in the world would she be doing with him at one o'clock in the morning?" Addie glanced sideways at Catherine.

"Oh no, look!" Paige cried, her voice filling with panic. "He just grabbed her arm and spilled her drink all over her."

The three women gawked through the window as Wesley's hand forced Lacey back toward the railing. He leaned toward her, shouted something in her face, let her hand go with a jerk, and stomped off toward the stern.

"That's enough!" Catherine bellowed, already halfway through the lounge, as she marched toward the door lead-

ing to the outside deck. "She might be drunk and shooting her mouth off, but that's no way to treat a person."
She flung the door open and stepped out onto the stern of
the boat where Lacey had been. She stopped and scanned
to her right and left and swung around, looking questioningly through the window at Addie and Paige.

Addie shrugged. "Did you happen to see where Lacey
went?" she asked Paige.

"No, I was stunned by what I saw and then with
Catherine . . . she really is a no-nonsense type of person,
isn't she?"

"Yeah, I think my ex-almost-father-in-law has rubbed
off on her. The Catherine I first met a few years ago
would never have walked into an explosive situation like
that."

"What do you mean?" snapped Catherine from beside
her.

Addie jumped and patted her pounding chest. "Geezers,
where did you come from?"

"I came in the side door there behind the servers'
counter. I figured that could have been the only way
Lacey left, as she certainly didn't pass me outside to the
main doors."

"Did you find her?"

"No, she must have headed straight down to the
cabin."

"That's the same way Wesley went," piped in Paige. "I
hope she didn't follow him. She looked shocked then
really mad, and she's in no condition to confront him
about what he did right now."

"Look," said Addie, "why don't you two take these
last two boxes of gifts to my cabin, and I'll go down the
back stairs to see if she's there. She was so out of it, I'm

afraid she might stumble and hurt herself in the stairwell. Then I'll make sure she's not on Wesley's cabin deck, harassing him outside his door or something."

"Sounds good. Not sure my legs could take all that traipsing around right now," said Catherine. "Give me the key, and we'll just drop them off. Then I have to get to bed. If you're not back, we'll just leave the door open and your key on the dresser."

"Perfect," said Addie, limping toward the servers' door.

If Catherine's legs couldn't take all this walking, Addie wasn't certain hers could, either. Since her friend had twenty years on her, that didn't bode well for the condition she was in tonight. But it had been a long, tiring week and the run-in with the curb this morning certainly hadn't helped. *Yup, that's my story, and I'm sticking to it.*

After coming up empty-handed in the Lacey-search of all the decks except the engine room level, Addie stood, one ear to the door and the other plugged with her finger, straining to hear any signs of life from inside of what was supposed to be her cousin's stateroom. Kalea had made a last-minute decision not to stay on board for the night when she realized that her new bestie, Lacey, proved she wasn't here to make friends but to cause trouble. Her cousin, at least, had the common sense not to pursue that friendship any further. She confessed to Addie that sharing a room with a drunken virtual stranger was probably not the best idea she'd ever had and went home to sleep in her own bed. It had surprised Addie at the time, but it was one more indication that her harebrained cousin was finally growing up.

As far as Addie knew, Lacey had the king-size stateroom to herself. At least, by the last confrontation with
Wesley that she'd witnessed, she hadn't seen Lacey being
overly friendly with anyone at the reception that she
might have taken back to her room with her. So it stood to
reason that if Lacey had turned in for the night, there
wouldn't be any noises anyway. If Addie knocked on the
door to check on her and roused the very intoxicated
woman, there was a high risk another round of Lacey's
misadventures would be set off. It was far too late in the
night for her to deal with that. Best to let sleeping dogs
lie. Addie rested her ear one more time against the door
and then hobbled next door to her stateroom.

Chapter 8

"Good morning, Catherine, Paige." Addie dropped into a chair at the table and glanced at the vacant seat beside her. "I see Lacey hasn't made it yet this morning."

"After the show she put on last night, did you really think she'd be up by eight for breakfast?" Paige asked.

"That's true." Addie chuckled and scanned the Edwardian dining room. "I don't understand why last night we spent hours tidying the casual dining room upstairs so it would be ready for them to set up breakfast this morning and then Veronica moves it down to this monstrosity of a room?"

"I overheard her telling those people she and Oliver are sitting with that she was finally relieved to be able to show some decorum with the events this week, now that Serena has departed on her honeymoon."

"What? She doesn't think Serena has any class because she wanted to keep things casual? It was her wedding, and she should have been able to have the style of wedding celebrations she wanted."

"I know," Catherine said between sips of her coffee, "but remember, Veronica comes from a different world than we do. So, let's just eat, get through this, and then we can leave and get back to a normal life."

"Well, I for one," said Paige, "will be sad to leave the yacht. Especially now that I know Emma is having a blast with her five cousins at my sister's summer home in Cape Cod. This has been a free mini-dream vacation for me. Even that cabin on the lower deck that I thought was going to be small and dingy turned out to be five-star luxury, didn't it, Catherine?"

"Yes, there was nothing dingy about it. The window is huge, and the two single beds were very comfy—more so than my bed at home. I had to drag myself out of it this morning. The only thing lacking was a balcony like your room has, Addie."

"I will say the balcony was very nice, indeed. I even slept with the glass doors wide open and had a sea breeze all night." She glanced over the breakfast menu.

When she had made her decision, she glanced up at Catherine and opened her mouth to inquire as to what her choice was but snapped it shut when she spotted Marc in the doorway. It shouldn't have surprised her to see him. He was the brother of the bride and expected to attend this morning's breakfast. But the fact that he was wearing his full uniform didn't settle quite right. Then when Ryley, dressed in her usual workday dark pantsuit, and Jerry, in his lieutenant's uniform, joined him, Addie knew something was off.

"Ladies and gentlemen," Marc bellowed over the chitchat of diners. "Could I have your attention please?"

All eyes turned to the double-wide doorway, and a hush fell over the large room.

"There has been a slight incident in town this morning, and I have a few questions as we try to determine whether or not the situation is related to the wedding festivities last night."

"Excuse me?" Veronica shot to her feet and glared at Marc. "Are you actually implying that one of *our* guests caused a problem in town after the ceremony?"

Marc pinned the surly woman with his infamous detached gaze and then continued to scan the room, ignoring her declarations of protest.

Detective Brookes stepped forward, and in an authoritarian voice, which gave everyone the impression that she had never left the FBI, clarified the situation. "What the chief is asking deals with guests who did not stay on board overnight. What time did most of them leave?"

Marc nodded and rocked back on his heels as his eyes went from table to table, scrutinizing faces before coming to rest on a still-standing Veronica. "Care to begin, Mrs. Ludlow? You had a number of out-of-town guests here as I recall. Can you give us any indication as to what time each of them departed?"

"Well, I didn't take notes if that's what you're asking." She fanned her face with her hand. The seriousness of Marc's eyes obviously flustered this woman, who was not used to answering to anyone. "The Pettigrews and Colliers departed soon after your sister and Zach."

"The Reinholds left about then, too," piped in Oliver from his seat.

"And the Garveys left shortly after," chirped a small

pasty-faced woman from her chair across the table from Oliver.

"Kalea, Martha, Gloria, and Cliff left just before eleven," called Catherine from her seat.

"That's right, and a little later, so did Ida, Maggie Hollingsworth, and her mother, Vera," Paige added, and glanced at Addie. "But they wouldn't have done anything that would involve the police, would they?" she whispered.

"Probably not." Addie shook her head and suppressed a snort. "None of them are exactly known as town delinquents."

Marc's dark eyes bored into hers, and she shifted uneasily in her chair. He always had a way of making her feel as though he had just caught her passing notes in the classroom.

Marc cleared his throat and redirected his gaze to the group. "Perhaps it would be easier if you told us who of the overnight guests are missing this morning."

"Your aunt and uncle left about an hour ago to return to New Hampshire," said Wade.

"And the Stephensons went with them. They were their ride," added Janis.

Marc nodded and looked at Veronica. "Anyone else you can think of?"

She shook her head.

Catherine glanced toward the empty seat beside Addie. "Well . . . Lacey hasn't come in for breakfast yet."

Addie didn't miss the telltale tic of Marc's jaw, proving Catherine's words had struck a nerve. She knew right then this was more than a case of vandalism or delinquency that occurred last night after the reception. Something in his eyes and the look that flashed between him and Ryley confirmed that whatever had happened, Lacey had been involved.

"It's probably best if everyone continues along with breakfast. We'll be calling you out in small groups to speak to an officer," said Ryley.

"And," Marc added, "for the time being, no one will be permitted to disembark or board. In essence, we've locked down the yacht."

"What?" snapped Veronica. "Besides barging in here and asking questions about my guests as though they are criminals, you now have the audacity to say we are being held prisoner, too?" Veronica marched toward him. "I demand to know what this is all about."

"We can start with you," Ryley said, her tone rather curt.

Veronica gasped.

"If you could go with Lieutenant Fowley, he has a few questions for you."

"Well, I never!" sputtered Veronica as Jerry stepped toward her, indicating she should follow him.

She stared down her nose at him. "If you have any questions for me, then I want my lawyer present. That's my right. Wesley!" she hollered. "Come, now!"

"That's not necessary, ma'am," Jerry said. "We simply have questions for everyone on board to try to determine what might have occurred here last night, and being as you are the hostess, you probably are aware of more than most here."

Jerry shook his head when his protest appeared to fall on deaf ears and Wesley darted to Veronica's side.

"Very well then, follow me." Jerry led the duo through the formal Edwardian-styled lounge and out into the passageway where they turned left.

The minutes ticked by and Addie, Catherine, and Paige attempted small talk, but the questions racing through everyone's minds was evident, especially when Ryley, Marc, or Jerry came back into the dining room and took another wedding guest for questioning. When Addie and Annabel were the only two left in the dining room, Addie reflected that Lacey's seat at breakfast remained vacant. An unsettling twitch grew in her gut about the incident the police were investigating. Every once in a while, she'd catch a glimpse through the window of one of the other officers taking notes as they spoke to staff out on the outdoor deck. Then she'd glance back over to Lacey's vacant chair.

The other unsettling fact was that no one had returned to the dining room. Were they being detained elsewhere or released once they had offered any information they had regarding the times other guests came and went over the course of last night and this morning? Having that little tidbit of information would definitely give her a clue as to how serious the matter was that was being investigated. Her gaze flitted back to the empty seat, and her stomach churned.

When she was the last person left sitting and Marc appeared in the doorway, she knew she'd finally have at least a few answers and rose to her feet. He motioned for her to stay where she was, made a beeline for the coffee carafe, poured a cup, took a long, slow whiff, and stared out the window at the boats and islands dotting the horizon. Addie fidgeted with the napkin on the table beside her—the same one she'd been toying with for the last hour or so. She had rolled and twisted it into every shape she could manage, but Marc's stalling tactics were the final straw, and she brought her fist down hard on it.

He jerked and glanced over his shoulder, sauntered across the room, and took a seat opposite her. "Sorry, it's been a long morning, and I was just trying to clear my head."

"Yeah, it has been a long morning," she said, snatching up the napkin and twisting it like a corkscrew in her hands, "and one advantage you have over the rest of us is that you know what this is all about."

He blew out a deep breath, pulled a notebook from his inside jacket pocket, clicked his pen, and met her gaze. "Miss Greyborne—"

She rolled her eyes.

"Okay, Addie," he said with a slight twitch in his cheek, "it's my understanding that your cousin Kalea Hudson gave her stateroom to Lacey Davenport to use last night. She was then going to stay in your stateroom but changed her mind and left the reception?"

"True. She got bored once Jared left and decided to go home. She was working on a new dress design and wanted to get it finished before the client came in on Monday."

"What time was that?" he asked without looking up at her.

"It wasn't long after Serena and Zach left at ten. Why?" She pinned him with a look, but he didn't respond.

"And it's true that Simon left shortly after ten also?"

"Yes." She sat back in her chair. "You know that. He left the same time you, Ryley, Jerry, and Curtis left, because you all said there was too much work left to do regarding the investigation of the body you found on the beach yesterday morning."

He ignored her comment and continued to scribble in

his notepad. "Tell me, Addie, what time did you retire to your stateroom last night?"

"Um, it was after one a.m., I guess. Paige, Catherine, and I were tidying up. We were worried about all the wedding gifts being left out, so we moved them into my stateroom. By the time we finished running them back and forth, it was probably close to one."

"Did you happen to see Lacey at any time?"

Addie swallowed hard and nodded, recalling Lacey's argument with Wesley on the outside deck.

"Well?" He tapped the pen on the metal spiral.

"Yes, she was on the deck outside."

"What time was that?"

"It must have been close to one."

"Was she alone at the time?"

"No . . . the last time I saw her she was arguing with Wesley Harbinger."

Addie went on to give Marc a short recap of what the three had witnessed through the dining room window the night before. Marc stopped scribbling and glanced up at her.

"You're saying Wesley Harbinger left first and Lacey was still standing at the deck railing?"

"Yes. She was fairly intoxicated. It was more like leaning against the railing, but she was upright anyway."

"But you didn't see her leave? How is that when you were watching her?"

"Paige and I got distracted when Catherine went on a rampage about how he had just treated Lacey and set off to check on her. When we looked back out the window again, Lacey was gone."

"And you say you never saw Lacey after the altercation with Wesley?"

"No, we assumed she went down the back staircase to bed."

"Did you see Wesley after that?"

"No. We thought he'd gone down to his cabin."

Addie didn't miss the tightening in Marc's jaw. Was he offended by the fact that Lacey was drinking heavily last night or was it something else? Addie pushed back in her chair and studied Marc's face. He was good, very good, at masking his emotions, but there was something about his questioning that told her he was already aware of everything he asked her. This was only a matter of formality.

"Marc, it's obvious that whatever this incident is, it has something to do with Lacey, doesn't it?"

Marc dropped the pen and sat back, his unyielding gaze holding Addie's. "What makes you think that?"

"Because you barely even flinched when Catherine told you she hadn't come for breakfast, and I noticed you didn't send an officer to go find her. Also"—she leaned forward—"your entire line of questioning revolves around her state of mind and whereabouts. That tells me the incident you're investigating has something to do with her."

She didn't miss the tension in his jaw and the quiver of his Adam's apple.

"Did she track Ryley down at the police station later and cause a scene? Is that where she is, sleeping it off in a cell because she attacked the detective?"

Marc tapped his pen on the coil of his notepad but didn't look up at her.

"Marc, do you recall when we met and we discussed tells, and I pointed out your tell was a slight tic in your jaw when you try to not show emotion? Serena has a tell, too. It's her freckles popping out when she's angry or flustered. She might not say anything, but we all know when she'd been pushed too far."

He nodded.

"Well, I can read your tells, and they tell me you're holding something back about Lacey, and it might be more than a drunken rant she went on toward Wesley Harbinger or Ryley. Did she hurt Ryley? Or someone else? We all know she had altercations with at least four different people aside from Ryley last night."

Marc shook his head. "A fisherman," his voice dropped to a raspy whisper, "discovered Lacey's body entangled in seaweed in the dock pilings this morning." He paused and blinked away the tears forming in the corners of his eyes. "There was a large gash on the back of her head, and we're trying to determine if she bumped her head before or after she fell into the water."

Chapter 9

"Lacey's dead?" Addie tried to wrap her head around what Marc had just told her. No wonder he needed that coffee to clear his head. Although he and Lacey had ended their relationship a number of years ago, she had been his childhood and high school sweetheart. By Marc's emotional reaction that was what he was remembering now, not the fact that Lacey had basically left him at the altar and took off to go start her journalism career in Los Angeles. "I mean are you sure? She was drinking a lot last night, but I don't think enough for her to have fallen overboard."

"There's no question about it." Marc shoved his notepad back into his pocket. "Right now we're trying to determine whether she fell or if—"

"She was pushed overboard." Addie recalled the heated exchanges Lacey had with other guests the preceding night. "When will you find out if it was an accident or something else?"

"Soon, I hope. Simon called from the lab and said he was sending over a preliminary report."

A movement by the doorway caught Addie's eye, and she glanced up to see Jerry striding toward them, a large manila envelope in his hand.

"Sorry to interrupt, Chief, but the coroner sent this over with a message that it was urgent."

"That's fine, Jerry, thanks." Marc took the envelope and opened it.

His eyes scanned over the page. Addie studied his face for a tell, but he had masked it well, and she couldn't read him. He set the folder open on the table in front of him and rose to his feet. "Jerry, we need to talk," he said with a jerk of his head toward the door, and then turned to Addie. "I'll trust you not to touch that." He tapped his finger on the open file folder as he joined Jerry at the door, standing with his back to Addie, coincidently blocking Jerry's view of her. Or was it a coincidence?

He did know her well and knew that leaving a report wide open in front of her would be the same as inviting her to take a peek. Her gaze on his back, she reached across the table and turned the paper just enough to have a cursory read.

Preliminary Autopsy Report: No evidence of bloating or seawater found in the lungs. Conclusion: victim did not drown and was deceased prior to being placed in the water. A subdural hematoma was noted at the base of the occipital bone at the first vertebra of the spinal column and most likely

the cause of sudden death between one a.m. and
four a.m.—final results pending further investiga-
tion.

This meant Lacey hadn't accidently fallen overboard. Her death was no accident. Someone hit her from behind on the head and tossed her in the harbor.

Marc returned to his chair, glanced at the shifted papers, and then at Addie. She inwardly cringed, waiting for the scolding, but he simply closed the file and shoved it back into the envelope.

Addie struggled to find the words she knew she should say. As much as Lacey had been on the outs with practically everyone in town after her last visit, she was still someone whom he had once loved. The seconds ticked by, and she jumped when her phone vibrated a text alert. Out of habit, she reached into her smoky-blue, summer linen jacket pocket but discovered no phone. The vibration continued, and Marc glanced questioningly at her.

"Aren't you going to check that?"

"It can wait."

"It might be important."

"It's probably nothing." She tried to remember where she had put her phone, glanced down at her handbag on the floor, and frowned when the phone pinged again. Only the sound was much closer than the floor and not muffled as though it were in her purse. "Anyone who would be texting me today is still on the boat."

He raised his brow.

When the signal didn't stop, she relented, patted her sides, and pulled her phone from the deep side pocket of her flowery summer dress and smiled. "You know, my

cousin might be really onto something with her dress designs as they all have these handy-dandy pockets." Then
she recalled Kalea's envy of the summer dress Lacey
wore last night and how it too had pockets hidden in the
side seam. Or maybe her cousin merely copied the New
York designer who had created the dress line Lacey had
worn.

"Is everything okay?" Marc asked.

She glanced at the screen. "Um, yeah, it's Serena.
They've arrived in London and are on their way to the
hotel to sleep for a while before they start their English
castle and teahouse river cruise tour tomorrow."

"Don't say a word to her about any of this. After the
drama of the last few months, she deserves to go on her
honeymoon and be happy. It'll be tough enough for her to
deal with it when she gets home. We don't need to ruin
her vacation before that."

"I won't, but can you guarantee someone else won't
tell her what's happened?"

"No one is to know about any of what you may have
learned today, at least right now. Got it?"

"How am I supposed to do that? Everyone knows
something happened last night, otherwise why would you
all show up and start questioning us?"

"For now, we are only investigating an incident that
occurred after the reception." He leaned across the table,
and his voice dropped. "I hope you understand that we
are now looking for a murderer, and the longer we can
keep that bit of information to ourselves, the easier it
might be for someone to slip up and show their hand in
this."

"Okay." She shifted in her chair. "Who are you looking at?"

"Everyone who's on board right now."

"What about those who left last night or earlier this morning? Have you already excluded them?"

"Yes. Either they disembarked long before the estimated time of death, or, as my officers have established through interviewing them, they have airtight alibis for their whereabouts during one and four a.m."

"That still leaves a lot of people as suspects, doesn't it?"

He nodded.

That meant everyone still on board was now a potential murderer, and she didn't like the thought of that. The pool was just too big. It could be any one of them.

"Which is why," he said, "we've shut down the entire yacht until we know exactly what we're dealing with."

"For how long? The cruise ship arrives Tuesday, and *The Lady V* only has a docking permit until then."

"I am aware of that, and if need be, the yacht will be towed out to deeper water and anchored, but no one leaves. Jerry," he called, "could you please escort Addie to the billiard room?"

"If I'm going to be sequestered until you do some more digging around, could you make it in the library? I've been itching to get in there since I first came on board last week."

Marc shook his head in resignation. "Take her to the library." He pinned her with a look. "Remember, no matter who else is in there . . ." He pulled a zipper motion across his mouth.

She nodded and followed Jerry through the lounge toward the library and slowed her pace as soon as they were out of Marc's line of sight. "Jerry, before I go in, there are a couple of things I'm curious about."

"You know I can't discuss an open investigation with you."

"It's not about what happened to Lacey. I know I'm being detained as a suspect like everyone else until you can figure out what happened. It's regarding the man who was found on the beach yesterday."

"Well"—he paused—"I guess since Marc brought you in to see if you could identify him or the paper then . . . okay, I can tell you what I know, which isn't much."

"I was just wondering if you have managed to identify him."

Jerry shook his head. "As you saw on the photo, his hands were pretty burned, defensive wounds, Doc Emerson says, from the shot of the flare gun. He's trying dental records now to see if he can ID him." Jerry began walking again and then stopped and gazed down at Addie. "You aren't thinking the two murders are connected, are you?"

"It had crossed my mind. After all, flare guns are used on ships as a distress call. They really aren't in anyone's personal arsenal, and Lacey was discovered in the water after a night of partying on the yacht." She gazed up into his soft brown eyes. "But maybe it's just a coincidence that they both seem to involve boats."

"If I recall, you are the one who doesn't believe in coincidences."

Addie shrugged.

"But how or why would they be related?"

"That's what we have to figure out."

"What do you mean *we*?" Jerry gave her a side glance and pressed the button to the left of the library's sliding glass doors.

Chapter 10

Addie stepped across the threshold of the library. She couldn't help but notice the seals around the door and the perfect temperature inside the room. There had been a similar climate-controlled room like this in the archives of the British Museum when she worked there. Since the books in here would often be exposed to extreme temperature changes and sea air, Oliver had made the right decision, judging by some of the titles on the shelves. It appeared at first glance at the bindings and covers that he had collected a fair number of early editions. Her skin tingled with anticipation. Finally, she was going to be able to explore the shelves of books she had only seen from a distance. She stepped toward the bookshelf.

"Addie, over here," Catherine called out.

"Remember what you were told," Jerry whispered in her ear, and flashed her a warning glance.

"Yes, mum's the word," she said with a soft chuckle as he left. She strode over to Catherine and Paige, who were seated on a long leather sofa.

"I'm glad you're finally here," said Catherine. "Did you make heads or tails out of all Ryley's questions?"

"Actually, I was interviewed by Marc."

"Well then, you should have some answers," Paige piped in. "I met with Jerry, and he kept asking me what time everyone went to bed last night, who the last people I saw before I went downstairs were, and then when I asked him if it had something to do with Lacey not being at breakfast, he cut me off and the interview was over."

"If you ask me"—Catherine glanced at Addie—"our old friend Lacey has gotten herself into a bit of trouble drinking the way she was last night. It's no wonder. I was embarrassed for her, and I'm still mad at her for the last time she came to town."

Addie eyed Catherine and then glanced away. It was going to be harder than she thought not to spill what she knew. Hiding the truth from someone who was a good soul like Catherine, who, in spite of Lacey's shortcomings, still cared deeply for the woman, would no doubt be among one of the hardest things she'd ever have to do.

"Marc just asked me the same kinds of questions," Addie said. "I told him I went searching for her when we finished loading up the gifts, and when I didn't see her, I assumed she had gone to bed. So, I turned in myself."

"Yeah," Paige said, nodding. "I told Jerry you went looking for her, but he didn't say anything."

"I told Ryley the same thing, and I thought for sure

she'd send an officer to her stateroom to get her. But I haven't seen her yet this morning, have you?"

Addie shook her head. Catherine was too persistent to let the line of conversation go. She had to get away from her or Addie would let something slip.

"Since we have to wait in here until we get the all-clear to leave"—Addie scanned the large room—"I'm going to take advantage of the time. I see a number of books that have been calling to me from the passageway this past week." She practically dashed away from her friends toward the shelves trimmed with antique metal rods meant to secure the books in place when the yacht was on open water. In the center of the long wall of books was an iron grille door case. She made her way down the shelf toward it, glancing at the titles on the books' spines.

"You have a good eye for first editions," a rough voice said over her shoulder.

She glanced around and looked into Oliver Ludlow's gentle, cognac-brown eyes. His resemblance to the sweet Zach she had come to know was overpowering, and she couldn't help but smile at him. He was nothing like his current wife, and it was refreshing to be able to talk to him. Out of habit, she glanced over his shoulder for the always vigilant Veronica, who seemed to monitor every word the man uttered.

"My wife has been sequestered in the billiard room, if that's who you are looking for."

Addie hoped the relief on her face didn't give away the feeling that swept over her with his words, and Oliver proved what a gentleman he was when he turned the conversation back to the case in front of them.

"As you can see, I have been a serious collector for

some years now." A soft smile formed on his lips. "As a matter of fact"—he pulled a worn leather-bound book from the shelf—"this 1851 copy of *Moby-Dick* by Herman Melville was my introduction into book collecting."

Addie glanced longingly at the book he held to his chest.

"It's also the book that brought Melinda, Zach's mother, into my life." A wistful look came to his eyes. "She worked at a small used bookshop, not too different from yours, I imagine, in Annapolis when I was a first-year there. I had been into the shop on a few occasions and had spoken to her. She was delightful—so kind and full of a bubbly energy that I had never seen in a young woman before. She knew, me being from Connecticut and attending the Naval Academy and that I had done a lot of sailing and had a great love for the sea. One day I went in, and she was beyond herself with giddiness and pulled this very book out from under the counter. That day I not only fell in love with book collecting but also the young woman who remembered what I loved. The rest is history, as they say." He placed the book back on the shelf.

Addie was taken aback by the tenderness she saw in him as he spoke about his first wife and recalled the prickly man she had been in touch with this past week during the pre-wedding celebrations.

"From that single book, I have built this library, plus one in my home in Connecticut, and have never once regretted any of my purchases."

"I noticed when I came into the library that the air seemed climate-controlled, or is that just my imagination?"

"No, I learned the hard way about sea air and the damage it can do to books. If you take a close look at this one"—he plucked a copy of *Anna Karenina* by Leo Tolstoy from an upper shelf—"you can see where the salt air flocked the pages, and a small amount of mold was removed from the cover. I have been working on it slowly to restore it to its original condition, but I'm afraid it might be a lost cause."

"Have you tried freezing it?"

"Yes, that's how I managed to restore most of the cover but the pages themselves suffered too much damage and are permanently discolored, I'm afraid."

Addie ran her hand over the cover, and a sadness came over her. "Are there many of your books here like this that were damaged?"

"Not that many now. I sent a few away to be restored, and the rest I have currently in my home library. However, this one has been a special project along with the copy of *Moby-Dick.* They were my first acquisitions and are the dearest to me."

Addie smiled. She knew how he felt. They were his firstborn, and he felt responsible for them.

"That's when I got smart about having a library on the yacht and had this room built to maintain a hermetically controlled environment. When my wife"—he swallowed hard—"decided to redecorate a few years ago, I told her this room and the adjoining office were off-limits to her changes. Thankfully, she left them virtually untouched, making it possible for me, with the addition of the climate controls, to expand my collection in this library."

"Well, I must say, I am impressed." Addie slipped a copy of *Anne of Green Gables* by L. M. Montgomery from the shelf and laid it open in her hands. There was something about the feel of the paper and the color ink on the title page that made her take a closer look. She rubbed the corner of the page gently between her forefinger and thumb and then sniffed her fingers. Her face must have telegraphed what she was thinking because Oliver snatched the book from her hands.

"What is it? Is something wrong? Has the paper been damaged from the sea air?"

"Are you certain this is a 1908 first edition? The paper feels too smooth for books published in that era. Back then natural vellum was used in printing. Today we use a synthetic vellum bond that has a smoother finish and is not so porous. Also, the scent of this is slightly adhesive or vinyl. In older books the paper aroma is sweet, sort of like a vanilla-almond scent."

"My head of security, Felix Vanguard, who was an old Navy friend and onetime head of security at the Smithsonian, has introduced me to some very reputable buyers over the years. People he knew from the Smithsonian and has had dealings with in the past. Of course it's a first edition." He shoved the book back onto the shelf. "His reputation, as well as that of the dealers and brokers I work with, is above reproach."

Addie couldn't shake the feeling that the book was a reproduction or a later edition. She knew if she removed the book again now, it would insult not only Oliver but also his friend Felix, and she decided to let the matter go for the moment. Her curiosity had been piqued though, and she knew in her gut she'd be back later to have a closer look at the book in question.

Her gaze caught sight of a book that stopped her heart. She pulled a brown leather-bound book from the shelf. "You have a copy of *Tamerlane and Other Poems by* Edgar Allan Poe. It was the first book he ever published under the name, a Bostonian. It's very rare. Only about fifty copies were ever printed."

"Yes, that's one I'm particularly proud of owning. See here where it's numbered forty-five. I must say that Felix did a marvelous job finding that particular book dealer for me in London."

The only copy of this book she had ever seen had also been number forty-five, and it had been in the possession of a book smuggler, who dealt with black market books and antiquities. That copy was the real thing, but this particular book had an odd feel to the paper just as *Anne of Green Gables* had. Was it just her imagination, or did Oliver's collection require a closer look?

"Felix sounds like a real asset to you with his connections to dealers who have access to some very rare books, like this one for example." Addie pulled a copy of *The Mysterious Affair at Styles* by Agatha Christie from a shelf. "Did you know this was the very first book she wrote, and it's the book where she introduced the world to Hercule Poirot, who along with Sherlock Holmes, was probably the best fictional detective ever created."

"Yes, that one is a particular favorite of mine. I gave it to Melinda for our tenth wedding anniversary."

"Really, and she didn't claim it in the divorce settlement?" Addie chomped down on her tongue—*how rude of me.* "I'm sorry, I didn't mean that the way it came out. It's just that I imagine this book would have meant something special to her."

"Not at the time. When we divorced, things between us were not half as amicable as they are now. She wanted nothing to do with this yacht where Veronica and I had our . . . shall we say dalliances at the time. So no, she left it in the collection. I'm sure the sentiment meant nothing to her back then."

Addie flipped the cover open. The fine hairs at the back of her neck prickled, and she gasped when her chest squeezed tight.

"What is it?" Oliver grabbed the book and turned it toward him. "What the—"

"It's . . . it's . . . blood," Addie whispered. Her eyes scanned over the title page, and bile churned in her gut. The bottom right-hand corner of the page had been torn off.

Chapter 11

Addie clutched the book tightly in her hands, afraid to move her fingers even a smidgeon for fear she would contaminate the evidence even further. Marc donned his blue rubber gloves, carefully released it from her fingers, and dropped the book into an evidence bag.

She stepped back and forced herself to breathe. *Keep breathing. You need to think and to think clearly. You have to breathe.*

"Are you okay?" Marc studied her face.

She nodded and rested against the table behind her. "It was just such a shock to open the book and discover the blood and the torn page corner."

"I can imagine it was." He handed the bag to Jerry. "Get this to the lab right away and see what prints, besides Addie's, we can get from it. Also have Doc Emerson test the blood on the page. I want to know as soon as possible who it belongs to." He glanced back at Addie. "Who else saw the page?"

"Um, Oliver. He was standing beside me."

"What was his reaction?"

"Shock, I guess much like mine."

"Anyone else?"

"Paige, when I called her over to go find you."

"No one else who was in the room at the time?"

"Not as far as I know, but there was only the three of us and Catherine. Oh, and your parents and that couple, the Martins, who are friends of the Ludlows'. They were around the corner past the bookcase, chatting at the table by the window."

"Okay, sit tight. I'll have a few more questions after I examine the bookcase." He turned away and ran a blue light over the books on either side of where the Agatha Christie book had been shelved.

Addie hugged her arms to her chest and scanned the room. Not having been in here before today she really wasn't sure if anything looked out of place. She probably wouldn't notice anything that might help Marc with his investigation anyway, so she stayed put as requested.

Then her skin prickled. There was a distinct pattern on the floor under the small writing desk to her right. The area of wood was a different shade and suggested that at one time it had been covered by a small round area mat. Now the table sat clearly on the teak flooring. Odd. Teak floors were very prone to scratching and would show damage from the movement of the chair at the desk.

She glanced at Marc, his back to her, tiptoed over to the desk, and peered at the floor. There were no scratch marks. This would mean that a carpet must have been under the chair and table until recently. She started back toward Marc at the bookcase to tell him her theory, then she noted a lighter ring on the sofa table she'd been leaning against. It was the type of ring that would have been made by an object having sat there for some time and the wood around it would have darkened with the weather and sunlight changes. Even though the room was climate-controlled, the wood still would have darkened with age. Yet the ring indicated that something had sat there for a very long time and inhibited the natural darkening process.

Addie glanced at Marc and could tell by the expression on his face that his scan of the bookcase wasn't producing the results he had hoped for.

"Nothing?" she asked.

"No, the books are clean, and the shelf is clean except for the smear left when the book was replaced on the shelf." He glanced around. "I just don't get it. According to the splatter pattern on the book, there should be blood residue across this entire shelf and all the books on it."

Addie glanced over at the writing desk. She pointed to the reading lamp on top of it. "Unless the room was dark and whoever that blood belongs to took the book from the shelf over by the lamp and was struck from behind by something"—she glanced at the ring on the table—"that sat here."

Marc stepped over to the table and called for an officer to turn off the overhead lights and close the window blinds. He then shone the blue light over the table and the lamp shade. Unmistakable blue splatter patterns glowed across the shade, the top of the desk, and on the wall behind the desk.

"You're right. Whoever the blood belongs to was standing here when they were struck, and someone made a rough attempt to clean up after."

"Does the flooring under the desk appear to have been covered by a carpet at one time?"

Marc crouched down and scanned the floor under the desk. Addie could see that there was a large area indicating no blood spatter but a perfect circular edge where blood showed under the ultraviolet light. "Yes, and I'd say the area rug was removed after the injury was sustained."

"Could the weapon used have been something that sat over here on that table?" Addie pointed to the ring.

"Turn the lights back on," he said, rising to his feet and moving toward the sofa table. "I'd have to talk to Veronica to find out what ornament should be on this table but is no longer here, but I think you're right."

"In that case, Oliver is the one you should speak with. He told me this was his room and Veronica rarely came in here. If something is out of place, he'd be the one who would know."

"Good catch, Addie." Marc removed his gloves. His eyes narrowed as he studied the spot where something had been displaced and then glanced at the writing desk. "I'd say whoever was looking at the book took it from the shelf to look for something in it and went over to the lamp on the table to get a better look—"

"Which means the room was dark, and either the table lamp was on or the person had to turn it on to see the book . . ."

"Right, and someone came up from behind through that door—"

"Or the office door," Addie added quickly, "as they are both behind where the victim would have been standing."

Marc nodded.

Addie surveyed the scene. "My guess is that the object would have been heavy and brought down with a lot of force to cause a splatter pattern like the one on the page and floor and wall."

"Right, so where is it now?" Marc glanced around the room. "Jerry, I want you to take three officers and scour this boat from top to bottom, looking for an ornament of some kind that seems out of place." He looked at Addie. "I'll go find Oliver to see if he can help give us an idea of what we're looking at."

"Marc, obviously the paper in the mystery man's pocket comes from the book. Did the autopsy show that he also had a contusion on him anywhere that might have caused the blood?"

"I'll have to call Simon to see if he found evidence the mystery man was injured previous to being shot on the beach. He can run a blood screen to tell us if there's a match to the blood on the book to his." Marc raked his hand through his hair. "My guess now is the guy was a thief. You did say there are a lot of first editions in this library. Maybe someone caught him in here and assumed he was going to steal something and ran him off, catching up to him on the beach where they shot him."

"That still means the man was on board the night of the rehearsal dinner. Why doesn't anyone remember seeing him before or after?"

"Well, obviously someone did see him and lied about it."

Addie hugged herself and studied the empty slot where the book had been shelved. "You know, Marc, I think that's not the only lie being told."

"What do you mean?"

"I mean that when Oliver and I were talking about his collection, I came across a couple of books that didn't appear to be first editions that he said were."

"He is a collector. Wouldn't he know?"

"You'd think, but the paper on a few of them didn't feel like they were printed in the right era of publication, and the ink and typesetting on one, in particular, was from a Linotype machine that wasn't used during that publishing-date time period."

"So, what are you thinking?"

"I'm not sure yet, but I'd like permission, when you are finished in here, of course, to take a closer look at the books."

"It's now considered a crime scene."

"I know, but as the team goes through and clears some of the room, I'd like access."

"Addie, unless it has something to do with either body lying in Simon's morgue right now, I really don't want to hear about it."

"Maybe the counterfeit editions have something to do with the mystery man's murder. Why did he pick that book in particular, and why did he tear a corner of the page from it? There has to be a reason."

"Okay, when we're done here, and not a minute before, you can take a look at the books, but that's it. Got it?"

"Yes, thank you."

"But," said Marc, "I still think the man was a thief and got caught in the act."

"Then why did someone go through the trouble to cover it up? Why not report the incident to the police?"

"Because the man ended up dead, and someone didn't want to get charged with murder."

"Right, but if the mystery man was killed in the process of committing a robbery as you're suggesting and he was on board to steal something, why not a few rare books? Wouldn't that count as self-defense or defense of personal property, dismissing a murder charge?"

"Not necessarily, but for your own good, Addie, let it go. Leave the fact collecting to the police, so we can figure out what occurred here. As you know, we don't work on speculation."

"But my gut tells me that someone had something to hide that they felt was more important than squelching a robbery. And I think the first person you should speak to is Felix Vanguard."

"Oliver's security man?"

"Yes."

"Why?"

"Because according to Oliver, he was the middleman for the deals Oliver made with booksellers. If my suspicions about the counterfeit books are correct, he wouldn't have wanted that information discovered."

"What makes you think any of this is anything other than someone—the mystery man, most likely—getting caught while attempting to steal a rare and valuable book?"

"Because that copy of *The Mysterious Affair at Styles* isn't valuable. It's a copy. A very good copy, but the paper is all wrong for a 1920s edition. The binding technique is too modern, and there's something off with the gold gilt stamping on the spine and front cover. It doesn't fit the period. It's not flaked as it should be given the age of the book, so it was inked on, not stamped. And the smell of the paper is all wrong."

"The smell of the paper?" He scratched his head. "Okay, I'll take your word for that. You know about these things, but one mystery at a time. Let me investigate the two obvious murders we have, and then I'll look into your theory about counterfeit books. Officer Jefferies, can you open the door for Miss Greyborne? I want the integrity of my crime scene maintained." He added, muttering, "As much as it can be now."

"That's it? You're kicking me out?"

"Yes, Addie, you've been a big help, but now it's time for you to join everyone else in the lounge and let the police do our job." He fixed his gaze on hers. "Remember. Say nothing to anyone about any of this."

"What about Paige and Catherine? They were in here, and Paige saw the blood on the page of the book. They are going to ask questions. How am I supposed to continue to pretend nothing happened?"

"Say nothing about any of this. Do I make myself clear?"

"Marc?" Ryley stepped forward. "She's not wrong. Too many people are now aware that something serious occurred last night. Maybe it's time to make an official statement?"

Marc shot Ryley a look that would have made anyone else cringe in their tracks, but not her. She tilted her head and returned his glower with one equally as challenging. Addie took a step back. It was as though these two were circling each other, vying for dominance. Addie had the distinct feeling that the looks exchanged right now telegraphed much more than a subordinate calling into question the actions of her superior.

Had Ryley's conversation last night with the mayor and his wife put into play something else going on here? She knew Marc had not been happy about all the time the three of them had spent together at the reception. This outright questioning of his orders, in front of other officers in the room, was a direct assault to his authority.

Addie knew, regardless of their personal love relationship, that this power move by Ryley would not sit well with Marc. As much as she wanted to hang around to see how this played out, she knew better and nodded to Jefferies to open the door for her. She stepped into the passageway. *This day was just full of surprises, wasn't it?*

Chapter 12

Addie turned on her heel and headed toward the murmurs of voices in the Edwardian lounge. When she came to the grand entranceway, she spotted Catherine and Paige over by the far window chatting with Serena and Marc's parents, Wade and Janis. Addie zigzagged her way around the numerous tables and avoided making contact with the questioning eyes that looked to her for answers and slipped into last vacant chair at the table.

Catherine and Paige greeted her with the same questions in their eyes.

"Don't ask," she said with a wave of her hand before either could open their mouths.

"But Addie, you know something, and we have a right to know what happened."

"What makes you think I know anything?"

"Because I changed your diapers when you were a

baby, and I always know when something is bothering you."

"And," Paige added, "I work with you six days a week and have learned how to read you pretty well."

"I have a feeling that everyone will be told what's happening soon enough." She glanced around the room. "Please, just let it go, and we'll talk later, okay? Here comes Veronica, so just bear with me for a little while longer," she whispered as the woman approached their table.

"Addie, what on earth is going on now?" Veronica pinned her with a look that cried *I'm your superior; you will comply with my order.* "My guests are getting very tired of all this cloak-and-dagger stuff, and no one has any idea what it's all about. Do you see my poor husband anywhere?" She waved her hand around the room. "No, and that's because he was so distraught about something that occurred in the library that an officer had to escort him to our stateroom so he could lie down. I'm afraid all this has been far too much on him. I want you to tell me what happened in there that has us all held captive."

"I'm sorry, Veronica. I really don't know what to tell you."

"You're useless." She spun around and marched toward Wesley standing beside the bar. "I want you to go and speak to that police chief right now and find out why we are all being held prisoners." She flailed her hands wildly in the air. "It must be a violation of our rights or something legal that certainly my high-priced lawyer can sort out."

"Veronica, when they are ready to give us information," he said, exasperation clearly evident by his strained monotone voice, "they will."

A waiter came over to Addie's table and offered her a

coffee. With gratitude she accepted, and as she was stirring in cream, Marc and Ryley appeared at the entrance to the lounge.

"Ladies and gentlemen, if we could have your attention, please."

A murmured hush fell over the room as all heads turned toward the two officers.

"As you are aware, an incident occurred on board last night that resulted in the death of one of the guests."

Gasps filled the room.

"Unfortunately, I can't give you any details at this time, but we do ask for your patience as we try to sort through the chain of events leading up to this tragedy. You are free to return to your cabins or to go anywhere on board except the areas you see cordoned off with yellow police tape."

"Can we leave the boat now?" asked the balding gentleman, a friend of the Ludlows'.

"Unfortunately, not at this time. No one will be permitted to come or go until we find the answers we need." Marc raised his hands to squelch the growing protests. "Captain Nevins, if you would be so kind as to follow Detective Brookes to the office. We could use your assistance with some matters at this time. Everyone else, please continue to enjoy the hospitality of your hosts, the Ludlows." Marc glanced at Ryley, and Addie couldn't help but notice the smug expression on her face as the captain rose to his feet and followed Ryley out.

"It was Lacey, wasn't it?" Catherine grasped Addie's arm. "She's the person who died last night, right?" Her eyes filled with tears.

Addie glanced from one distressed face at the table to

the next. Even though Lacey, by the time she left last year, had not been a popular woman in this town, she was still a child of Greyborne Harbor. Despite personal feelings everyone had for her, she was dead, and they were going to grieve.

"Yes, Lacey died last night."

"Oh no," Janis Chandler wailed, and threw herself into her husband Wade's arms. "Poor Marc. He must be devastated," she sputtered between sobs.

Addie glanced over to where Marc had been standing and nodded. The tension she felt between Ryley and Marc could be due to his grief over the death of his one-time love and his current love's jealousy about those feelings. But Addie couldn't shake the feeling that there was more going on between the detective and the police chief than that, especially when the mayor's wife, Zoe Bryant, and Ryley appeared to be better friends than anyone ever realized. Had Marc been taken by surprise too last night?

It was no secret that Marc and the new mayor had locked horns more than once over the past twelve months. Serena told her that when he came into his position after the last election, the first duty he took on himself was to oversee the police department budget. After that he forced Marc to take his built-up vacation time and strongly encouraged him to take the FBI police training courses, which was where he met Ryley last year.

When Ryley showed up later with Marc, the mayor had been eager to take her on as a detective, a position the Greyborne Harbor police force had never had before. Had Ryley and the mayor known each other previously, or was he just impressed by her credentials? It also made Addie wonder if the mayor was grooming the former FBI agent for something else. Maybe Marc was on the outs. Ryley and Mayor Bryant definitely had their heads together on more than one occasion last night.

Addie shook it off. Marc and Ryley's relationship and his future didn't concern her. She had made her choice and was with Simon now and happy finally. Plus, there was a murder . . . no, there were two murders to solve.

Wade escorted Janis outside for some fresh air, and Addie understood that the news they'd just heard was bound to hit them hard. Lacey had been a part of their family for so many years, and she had been their future daughter-in-law at one time. Addie glanced from Paige to Catherine, who were wrapped in each other's arms, sobbing. Addie wasn't surprised at their outpouring of grief. Catherine had known Lacey her whole life and Lacey had been Paige's babysitter, and was her cousin, even though that family connection had been strained over the years.

Addie scanned the room. However, since whoever killed Lacey was still on board, someone here was not grieving her death. Addie had to find out who it was. She studied Veronica, who seemed more put out about the whole incident than upset that one of her guests had died. Wesley, on the other hand, was more concerned about placating his employer than he was troubled by the news of a murder on board, even though his altercation with Lacey made him a prime suspect, in Addie's eyes at least.

She glanced over at Preston and Annabel as they made a toast to each other and sealed it with a kiss. Now that was an unusual reaction to the news Marc had shared with the group. It made her curious to learn what they would be celebrating at a time like this. She rose from the table and made her way toward them but stopped when she heard Annabel proclaim that she was just happy to have him all to herself for another day without him being able to run off on work-related matters.

"Yes, but I'll have to call Björn to let him know there will be a delay in our next meeting."

"He makes enough money off you that I'm sure he'll be willing to wait an extra day or two."

"You're right. Cheers to our extended vacation."

Not exactly a grieving couple but given their hectic work schedules Addie decided a bit of a celebration was in order for them. She shook it off and went to the coffee table to get a fresh cup. Stirring in cream, she studied the faces of the guests. Someone in this room was a killer, but who? Then movement out the window on the deck caught her eye. Officer Jefferies was taking notes and talking to the young server who had brought Addie her first coffee. No, she corrected herself, not only someone in this room but someone on board and there must still be fifty people, including the staff in the pool of suspects. Her gaze danced from face to face, and she wondered how she was ever going to narrow it down to just one.

Chapter 13

Addie grabbed three strawberry scones from a server's platter, wrapped them in a napkin, and headed for Catherine and Paige still seated at the table. "We should probably eat something," she said, glancing out the window onto the deck where she noted that Officer Curtis Brewster, Elli's boyfriend, was interviewing another staff member. "I have a feeling this might be a long day."

"Thanks, Addie," said Catherine, waving off the scone, "but I don't think I can eat anything. I can't believe someone killed Lacey. Although I must admit, I felt like murdering her a time or two last night with all her antics. Someone actually did." Her voice caught in her throat as a sob overcame her.

"I know the feeling," Paige said. "But what scares me is"—she glanced around—"with the yacht in lockdown, whoever it is could still be on board. Any one of us could be next." She glanced from Addie to Catherine. "I'm scared. Aren't you?"

"Which is why we have to figure out who did it and why." Addie leaned toward her friends. "I have an idea. Do you two feel up to some sleuthing this afternoon?"

"Sure, what do you have in mind?" Catherine asked, bending toward Addie.

"Here, take my key and meet me in my stateroom. I'll be there in a few minutes. If anyone asks where you're going, just say to lie down for a while."

"Okay," said Paige, taking the key. "Be careful. It could be anyone." She glanced around the room. "We don't know half these people."

"I know, but that's going to change soon." Addie rose to her feet and headed toward the central staircase.

"Addie," Marc called from the stateroom passageway door. "Can I borrow you for a few minutes?"

"Sure," she said, coming to a halt. "What do you need?"

"Can you come up to the next deck with me? I want you to walk me through everything you were doing when you last saw Lacey and point out where she was when you last saw her."

Addie and Marc ascended to the above deck, ducked under the band of yellow crime-scene tape strung across the top of the stairway, and stood in the doorway of the lounge where the reception had been held the previous evening.

She strutted toward the table in the dining room beside the bar where the gifts had been. "It's like I told you before, Catherine, Paige, and I were packing up the gifts in boxes that one of the kitchen staff had brought us. I was bent over here," she said, pointing, "and we were all talking. Then Paige asked why she wasn't in bed. We looked out and saw Lacey back over there, standing under the deck light. I could see her face, and she appeared upset or furious about something. I couldn't tell at first who she was talking to because from where I stood there were too many shadows, but Paige said it looked like Wesley Harbinger. Then he stepped forward and we could all see him. He pointed a finger in Lacey's face, grabbed her arm, spilled her drink down the front of her dress, jerked her arm, and pushed her back against the rail. Then he turned and took off toward the stern."

"Come outside and walk me through what you saw."

They made their way back through the dining room and the lounge onto the promenade deck on the bow, turned, and walked back toward the stern. Addie eyed the dining room window and checked her position in line with the overhead light stand. "She was standing here."

"Did she hit her head when he pushed her back?"

"No, it didn't look like it. She just wobbled a bit and caught herself."

"Did you see where Wesley went when he left?"

"No. We got distracted by Catherine, who was already on her way outside. Paige and I assumed he went in that entrance behind the servers' station and headed down to his cabin. Catherine was already out here walking around from the bow coming here to where Lacey was. When Paige and I looked back out the window, Lacey was gone, and Catherine couldn't find her."

"Then none of you actually saw Lacey leave?"

Addie shook her head.

"Could she have fallen overboard in the time you say you last saw her and when you noticed she had vanished?"

"I don't know, I suppose, but look how high the railing is. She would have had to climb on something to get over the top of it."

Marc glanced around the area. "You're right. There's nothing here she could have used to boost herself up."

"And if there were, are you implying she went overboard on purpose?"

"No," Marc said. "At least the Lacey I knew wouldn't do that. But if not, then it means she just disappeared?"

"She couldn't have simply disappeared. When we were focused on Catherine's rant, she must have slipped into that nearby back staircase or took the elevator to head downstairs to bed, or . . ."

"Or," he said thoughtfully as he surveyed the deck, "she went around to the port side of the yacht and came in through that entrance. After all, you said you were in the dining room, and Catherine was outside, so you wouldn't have seen her come in there and head down the central staircase from where you were."

"I guess so . . . if she was running fast enough and that's why Catherine missed her, but in Lacey's inebriated condition, I doubt she was capable of a sprint. No," said Addie adamantly. "She must have used the back entrance. It's the closest."

"Did any of you check on her later to make certain she was in her cabin?"

"I did . . . well, sort of. Catherine and Paige took the last load of gifts down to my cabin. I think they took the elevator. I took the stairs behind the servers' station and then searched the three decks below. I wanted to make certain she hadn't gone looking for Wesley or tripped and lay hurt somewhere." Addie glanced at the pinched look on Marc's face. "I listened outside her cabin door and didn't hear anything."

"Did you knock to make sure she was in there?"

Addie shook her head. "Today I am kicking myself for that, though. I just assumed she'd passed out, and I didn't want to risk waking her and starting round three of the Lacey show."

"Round three?"

"Yeah, Catherine had sent her to bed earlier. That's why we were all so shocked to see her outside with Wesley at one."

"Yeah." He brushed sweeping strands of windblown chestnut hair from his eyes. "After something like this happens, hindsight always raises the what-ifs and I-should-have questions, doesn't it?"

Addie dropped her gaze and nodded.

Marc jumped at his ringing cell phone and fished it out of his pocket. He glanced at the screen. "It's Simon. I have to get this." He stepped away out of Addie's earshot.

Addie turned her face to the warm midday sun and took a deep sea-air breath. She turned and smiled at Jerry, who had the black crime-scene bag and was scanning the deck surface and railing with the blue light. Two other officers worked farther down the deck, scanning the area around the back door to the dining room and the elevator entrance. Addie conducted her own sweep of the deck and slowly traced Lacey's possible steps until she reached the bulkhead door leading into the elevator and stairway entrance at the far end of the dining room. She reached out to open the door and stopped when a voice barked over her shoulder.

"You know better than that."

She pulled her hand back.

"Sorry, Jerry, I wasn't thinking. Of course I know better," she said with a soft laugh. "I was just trying too hard to get into Lacey's head, I guess, and I wanted to follow what she must have done after we lost sight of her last night."

"Well, no damage done, I guess." Jerry gave her a wry smile as Marc joined them.

"Did Simon have any updates?" Addie asked hopefully.

"Yes, as a matter of fact, he did."

She eyed him with anticipation.

"You told me earlier that you witnessed Lacey drinking heavily last night, is that right?"

"Yes, we all did and were concerned. She always had a drink in her hand all evening and was falling over and staggering. Even Simon tried to convince her to slow down, but she lashed out at him, too. Why?"

"Because"—his gaze darted from Jerry's to Addie's—"according to her autopsy report, she only had a very small amount of alcohol in her system. Definitely not enough to make her intoxicated, and there was no indication of drugs."

"What?" gasped Addie. "That doesn't make sense. We all saw her, she drank—"

"Did she?" Jerry piped in. 'Or did we all just assume she was drinking because she carried around a glass?"

"You saw her too, Marc," Addie said, wide-eyed. "You even expressed concerns over her behavior."

"Her behavior, yes, but it's clear now she was not in an altered state when she was acting like that."

"Was it all an act?" Addie frowned and glanced at Marc and Jerry.

"It seems so, but the real question is why?"

"Yeah"—Jerry scratched his head—"why would she pretend to be drunk, pick arguments with everyone she spoke to, and then end up dead?"

"Surely the dead part wasn't her intention when she undertook her little charade."

"No, Chief, I was just . . . trying to make sense out of it."

"Well, have the team continue to comb this deck. There has to be a clue here somewhere as to why and what happened."

"Yes, sir." Jerry picked up the case and returned to the railing.

Addie gazed out into the harbor. Her mind raced trying to put all this information into some perspective, but it didn't fit into any boxes she could think of. Why would Lacey fake being intoxicated, argue with anyone and everyone even to the point that she staggered off at the end of the night?

Addie fixed her gaze on Marc's. "Could it have been something so petty that she was jealous of the attention Serena was getting because it was her wedding? We all know Lacey loved to be the center of attention. Was it her way of making sure people focused on her?"

"Except that Lacey liked to be adored and acting drunk and obnoxious wasn't going to win her any points in that department."

"No, you're right." Addie tried to think of another reason someone would feign being out of control. "Perhaps she was trying to cover up for the fact that she and Ryley had words. She lost the battle of wills with Ryley, so maybe she pretended to be intoxicated so people wouldn't think your new girlfriend bested her."

"What do you mean she and Ryley had words? When?"

Addie looked at him in surprise. "Ryley didn't tell you what happened?"

"No."

"When you went to the bar to refill your drinks, Lacey lit into her."

"About what?"

"It started off with a few jabs about Ryley's dress looking second hand, and she said Ryley must like her men the same way because heaven knows you'd been around with plenty of other women, even some in the room, and then looked point blank at me."

"What?" Marc's face turned cherry red. "She said that?"

"Yeah, but it didn't stop there. She told everyone listening some rather"—Addie's gaze dropped—"personal things about you. Things that only someone who you had been intimate with would know—"

"Stop!" Marc said, throwing his hands up.

"I'm sorry. I just assumed that Ryley told you about the incident."

He shook his head. "No, but things are adding up now."

"About Lacey? Do you agree that maybe she pretended to be drunk to save face?"

"I don't know, but Ryley told me I should recuse myself from the case because I'm too close to it."

"She did? I noticed the tension between the two of you earlier, but I had no idea she thought you should step down from the case."

"Yes, and if I didn't know her better now, I'd be inclined to agree with her, but . . ."

"But what?"

"I know the mayor and his wife think the world of her,

and when she first came to town, I did, too, but lately . . .
well, I'm not so sure what her true ambitions are."

"There's nothing wrong with a woman being ambi-
tious."

"No, except when that ambition is vying for your job
and will stop at nothing to get it. If I recuse myself from
this case, she'll step in and take over with Mayor
Bryant's blessing, and I'll never get it back."

"Are you sure? She really seems to love you. Maybe
she's just concerned about you and your past relationship
with the victim."

"She's concerned all right. She's concerned that she
won't make chief and fulfill her ambitions."

"Marc, are you sure? Since Ryley came into your life,
you've seemed happier than I've seen you in a long
time."

"I was at first, but . . ."

"But what?" Addie placed her hand on his arm.

"Nothing."

"Marc, you and I are still friends. Something is obviously bothering you. What is it?"

"Addie, we might be friends, but once we were more
than that, and talking to you about problems Ryley and I
are—"

"So, there is an issue aside from one of the victims
once having been close to you."

"Please leave it, Addie." His fingers whitened as he
squeezed the deck rail.

"I will, but whatever it is that's tearing you apart, you
need to talk to someone about it."

Marc nodded without looking at her. "What time was
the altercation between Lacey and Ryley?"

"The last one was right before you left, why?"

"What do you mean the last one? How many times did she and Lacey argue?"

"There was the first time when you went to get a drink, and we were all standing over by the door. Then just before you left, Lacey stumbled into her and said something rather rude. Ryley hauled her outside, they had words, and Ryley came back in. You came over and you left."

"I saw her chatting with the mayor not long before that."

"Actually, she was visiting with him and Zoe quite a bit throughout the evening. Catherine said Ryley and Zoe have become great friends recently."

"I bet they have."

"What did Ryley say to you when you left and went back to the station?"

"Not a word about spending so much time with the mayor and his wife or either of her run-ins with Lacey."

"Even though the two of you were working all night on the mystery man case, she still didn't mention Lacey?"

"No, I could tell something was bothering her, but she only said she had to go home because she had a headache and left around quarter to one. What was the last time you saw Lacey, again?"

"About one, just before we went to bed."

"I got home about four, and Ryley was sleeping."

"Then you don't know if she went straight home after leaving the station?"

"No, no, I don't."

"What was the time of death?"

"Between one and four a.m." He released his white-knuckle grasp from the railing and shored himself up. "The question is why didn't Ryley tell me about the words exchanged between them?"

Addie didn't know what to say. Two years ago she would have wrapped her arms around him and told him everything would be okay, but maybe he was right. Possibly there was another reason why Ryley hadn't been straight with him. "I'm just throwing it out there because *everyone* is a suspect at this point." Addie winced and took a deep breath. "Perhaps there's another reason why Ryley wants you to step away from the case."

Marc looked down at Addie. "Thank you. Our conversation has made my decision whether or not to recuse myself much easier."

"Wait, does this mean you're going to?"

"Not a chance now," he said, and marched back into the lounge.

Chapter 14

Addie raced down the central staircase to the lower deck bulkhead door to the pier ramp, which she knew would be closed and guarded to keep anyone from exiting or entering. She smiled and nodded at the young officer who was seated on a stool beside the wide doorway.

"May I help you?" he asked, looking up from the morning edition of the Greyborne Harbor newspaper he'd been reading.

She spotted the target of her search over his shoulder. "I'm just here to collect that poster for my friend Serena. She's going to want to keep it as a souvenir of her big day."

He glanced at the wedding announcement that sat on an easel by the door. "Sure, I can't see why not."

Addie had seen him around but couldn't recall his

name, so she simply said, "Thanks," and grabbed the poster board. She dashed back up to the main deck, down the passageway to her stateroom, and flung the door open.

"What took you so long?" asked Paige from her prone position across the far queen-size bed.

Catherine glanced up from the box of wedding gifts she'd been sorting and placed her hands on her slender hips. "The way Marc took you out of there, I thought perhaps you had been arrested. So, what's going on?"

"Look what I have." Addie flipped the poster board toward them. They glanced at it and then blankly back at Addie. "It's our makeshift crime board. Perfect, right?" She placed the blank white side forward on the dresser top and leaned it against the attached mirror. "Now all I need is a pen. A marker would be best, but I'm not sure I packed one of those," she said as she sorted through her handbag.

"I think I can help with that." Paige grabbed her bag off the end of the bed and dug through it. "I happen to have a couple." She held up a small vinyl pen case. "I always carry these mini-markers for Emma because wherever we go she insists on coloring."

"They're perfect," squealed Addie with delight.

"You are a good mom, that's for sure." Catherine smiled.

"My motto is to always be prepared because you never know what mood your four-and-a-half-year-old child will be in when you take her out in public," Paige added with a soft laugh.

Addie eyed the blank side of the poster board and glanced over at Catherine and Paige. "Now, where do we start?"

"I'm guessing," said Catherine, sitting on the edge of

the bed, "the two of you do this often, but this is a first for me. So please explain exactly what it is we are starting."

"This is Addie's thing," said Paige. "I've tried to help in the past, but it's generally Serena and Simon who work with her on stuff like this."

"Well, Simon is in the lab, trying to find the evidence needed not only to determine who the first victim is but also exactly what happened to Lacey and how she ended up dead in the water."

"But I'm afraid I'm not much use when it comes to deciphering clues," said Paige. "Remember the last time I tried to help? I got all muddled and couldn't think straight."

Addie glanced at Paige, and her eyes softened. "That's only because we were investigating your family. This will be different. I promise."

Paige relented and moved over beside Catherine.

"Look, I need other eyes on this to see what I miss and both of you have a great eye for detail. I'm sure we can work through this and get a picture of the puzzle we're trying to solve."

"Is that what this is? I do like puzzles," said Catherine.

"That's exactly what it is. We need to start by writing down everything we know in relation to the events leading up to the murder. Then whatever clues we come across that can point us in the direction of the killer and give us the completed picture."

"If I remember correctly," said Paige, "there's a lot of guesswork involved."

"Yes, and we don't discard anything. No matter how trivial it appears on the surface, it could mean something to the big picture in the end. The only thing is, you can't tell anyone what we're doing, and we don't share any information with Marc or any of the police until we have evidence and proof." Addie glanced from one woman to the other. "That is something I've learned over time. Marc will only follow evidence and doesn't want to hear our speculations."

"Well, I think this is exciting," Catherine said. "I have read enough of those Agatha Christie novels now, and of course, given the line of work my Jonathan is in—" Her hand slapped over her mouth. "Oops, I don't think I should have said that."

"It's okay. Between us, I'm very aware what my ex-going-to-be father-in-law does for a living. I didn't for all the years David and I were together before he was killed, but I got the picture now. Anyway, getting back to the board." Addie primed a blue marker in her hand. "What do we know about Lacey's death?"

"As far as I know, that's it." Catherine shifted on the bed. "You know, what Marc said when he came into the dining room."

"I do know a bit more."

"How? Marc doesn't like to share information with you." Paige leaned forward and fixed her eyes on Addie. "Or have you already been doing your snooping thing?"

Addie chuckled. "No, you might say I just happened to be in the right place at the right time. Some important information came to Marc while he was questioning me." She began writing. "Now, some of this might shock you, but it is what it is, and the only way we can find out who killed Lacey is to go through this process."

Addie wrote *Lacey* at the top of the board and then underneath it wrote,

Dead before she went in the water, and *head injury cause of death not drowning.*

"What? Someone knocked her out and killed her and then tossed her overboard?" cried Catherine.

Addie nodded and wrote,

Time of death between one a.m. and four a.m.

Catherine fanned herself and sniffled. "I had no idea, the poor girl. No matter what I thought of her lately, she didn't deserve that."

"You're right, so now we have to figure out *who* would have thought Lacey needed to end up dead and *why*." Addie circled *who* and *why*. "We all saw her having altercations with a number of people last night. Paige, what did you see and overhear?"

"I saw her arguing with that chef."

"Really," Catherine said, turning to her. "Why in the world was she arguing with the chef?"

"I have no idea, but I was going over to the buffet table, and she was behind it. At first, I thought she was flirting with him, but the closer I got, the more I realized she was questioning him about something that happened in England."

"What?" Addie focused on Paige's words. "Why would she be bringing up England? I know from what Serena told me, Veronica was married to a lord at one time, but he died over five years ago, and then she left and met Oliver and . . ."

"And what?" Catherine gazed up at her.

"And what if Lacey was working on a story about Veronica?"

"Why would she be doing that?" Paige sat upright. "She said she was here to see her oldest friend married even though she wasn't invited. Did she discover something about Veronica and her past while she was here to make her want to find out more?"

"Or was her coming to the wedding the cover for a story she was already working on?"

"What would be in Veronica's past that would be newsworthy?" Catherine glanced from Addie to Paige.

Addie looked at the little bit she had written on the board. "What do we know about the mystery man and his murder?"

"Less than we do about Lacey's, I'd say," said Paige. "You were asked to identify a scrap of paper found in his pocket, he was killed on the beach not far from here, and he had no phone or identification on him. Oh, and don't forget you found the book in the library with the torn page corner, which matches the scrap of paper he had."

"And," said Addie, "it was covered with blood, so I'm guessing someone found him in the library and hit him with something and then mystery man took off and was killed on the beach."

"Which," Paige added, "means he was probably a thief and used the cover of the crowds coming and going for the rehearsal dinner as a way of gaining access to the yacht."

"We know that for sure by the torn book page"— Addie scribbled under *mystery man*—"he was on board the yacht." She tapped the pen on the board. "I don't think it was a coincidence that these two murders happened a day apart. My gut tells me they're related somehow, especially because of this last line." She tapped the board. "As my father, who as you know before he became an insurance artifact and rarities retriever, originally worked as an NYPD detective, always told me, there is no such thing as coincidences in a crime. Everything is related if you dig deep enough."

"But how?" Catherine chirped in. "The man had no ID, and Lacey made it clear she was here for Serena's wedding."

"Or was it a cover?" Addie said with a quizzical lilt to her voice. "Did she know something about Veronica or someone else on board that got her killed to keep the secret quiet?" Addie looked at Paige. "What else did you overhear between Lacey and the chef?"

"Nothing really. As I said, she was behind the buffet table when the chef was torching the crème brûlées. He turned the torch off. They spoke for a few minutes. I was making my way down the table, so I couldn't clearly hear anything they were saying over the noise in the room, but I did clearly hear the word 'England.' Then he waved the torch in her face, and she stormed past me on the other side of the table. I asked her what that was about, and she said, 'My crab cake smelled off.'"

"Oh dear," said Addie. "I hope no one gets sick, that's all Serena needs on top of all this."

"I wouldn't worry about that because the weird thing is, as long as I've known Lacey, she's been allergic to shellfish."

"That's true," piped in Catherine. "I remember that from when she went to a lobster fest on the beach as a teenager, and she ended up in the hospital."

"So why did she have a crab cake?" said Addie. "Or was that just something she said to brush you off?"

"That's the only thing I can think of," said Paige. "What would they have talked about that she didn't want me to know?"

"Good question." Addie glanced at Catherine. "Did you witness any of the incidents she was involved with?"

"A few, when I was talking to Serena's mother, Janis, I saw Lacey having a chat with Preston and his wife. It was in the dining room where the dance was."

"Did they look like they were arguing?"

"No, I don't think so, but Annabel did look upset about something Lacey was talking to Preston about." Catherine shrugged. "I just figured Lacey was up to her old tricks and playing the part of the flirt."

"What did Annabel do?"

"Nothing, but when Lacey moved on . . . toward the bar again . . . now that I think about it, Annabel followed her with her eyes. If looks could kill, Lacey would have been dead right there and then."

"She did overhear you and Simon talking about the scrap of paper in his jacket pocket," Paige said weakly.

"Yes, she did, didn't she?"

"And before that, you and I were talking over by the hors d'oeuvre table, and I asked you what happened when Marc dragged you out of the bookshop. You told me about him wanting to know if you could identify a book, and then Serena called you over. When I turned around, Lacey had been standing behind us."

"Why didn't you tell me this?"

Paige shrugged. "I didn't think it important at the time, and I wasn't sure she heard because she didn't say anything to me and went to the bar and ordered another drink."

"It's interesting isn't it—how we all saw Lacey going or coming from the bar all evening."

"Not to mention," said Paige, "when she stumbled into Ryley and spilled her glass of champagne all over Ryley's dress."

"I saw Ryley haul her outside after that," said Addie studying Lacey's name on the board.

"I saw the whole thing from start to finish," Paige chirped. "Lacey stumbled and fell into her, the drink went flying. Ryley was drenched, and then she—"

"Grabbed Lacey and took her out onto the deck and they had words, I saw that part." Addie tapped the marker on the palm of her hand. "The only thing is, Lacey wasn't drunk." Addie wrote *low alcohol blood level* on the board under Lacey's name.

Catherine snorted. "You have to be kidding. You saw her as well as I did. She was stumbling drunk for most of the evening. Even later when she had the run-in with that lawyer fellow and he spilled her full glass all over her dress."

"But did any of us overhear what was being said between the two of them?"

Catherine and Paige shook their heads.

"That's right. We have no idea what went on and what they were talking about. But one thing I do know for sure is this." Addie pointed to the low alcohol notation. "Her blood work came back when I was with Marc upstairs, walking through the time we last saw Lacey on the promenade deck. She wasn't drunk or drugged."

"Then what, she was faking it?" Catherine asked, her eyes wide. "I can't believe she would do something like that."

"But why?" asked Paige.

"That's what Marc and I were trying to figure out. I suggested that perhaps it was because Ryley had bested her in their two run-ins, but Marc didn't want to hear about it. As I said before, he's not interested in guesswork, but if we look at what we do know for certain, maybe we can come up with a reason why she would fake

128 *Lauren Elliott*

being intoxicated." Addie scanned the board and then
looked back at Catherine and Paige. "Any ideas?"

Catherine's eyes narrowed. "What if . . . she *was* here
working on a story of some kind and used intoxication as
an excuse to behave badly and push some people's buttons? She was probably hoping they would think she was
just inebriated and let something of interest slip."

"Maybe what she overheard about the book and the
mystery man being found dead gave her a story idea, and
she was trying to get to the bottom of it?"

"That makes sense." Catherine rose to her feet and
stretched out her shoulders. "She might have come to the
wedding for all the reasons she said but then got a story
lead when she overheard you two talking and ran with it."

"Maybe," Addie said, scanning the board, "and maybe
she found out who killed mystery man, and it got her
killed, too."

"But," Paige said, "if the guy was a thief and was killed
in the act of stealing a valuable book, why wouldn't the
killer just report it as an act of self-defense or something?"

"That's a good question." Addie snapped her fingers.
"Unless he was killed for another reason."

Chapter 15

Addie paced back and forth in front of the dresser. "Please sit down," said Catherine. "You're making me dizzy."

"Sorry, I need to move to think, but I'm stumped."

"Look," Catherine added. "We've been at this for over an hour and have nearly filled the board. We're running out of room and still have nothing to take to Marc. What do you say we break for lunch?"

"Yes, I'm starving," echoed Paige. "We've only had a scone and coffee today." She glanced at her phone clock. "It's twelve thirty, and lunch should be being served in the dining room now." She pushed herself off the bed. "If I'm going to get an extra holiday on a five-star yacht, I want to take advantage of all the perks before I have to go back to reality."

"You're right," said Catherine from the door. "Are you going to join us?" She glanced at Addie.

"Yes, I'll be along in a few minutes. I just want to try to get a feel for some of these points."

"Okay," Catherine said with a laugh, "but you aren't going to solve this today."

"I know, but I just need to make some sense out of it before I take a break," she said.

After the door closed, Addie plopped down on the edge of the bed and stared at everything they had written. It all looked like gibberish.

"I need Simon's eyes on this. He's so good at seeing what I'm missing." She glanced at her phone. Still no message from him. She hadn't heard from him since he left just after Serena and Zach did last night.

Miss you, she typed on the small keypad. *Wish you were here. If I'm going to be trapped on a multimillion-dollar yacht, you're the person I want to be trapped with. XXXXX*

She waited . . . no reply. She shoved her phone back into her jacket pocket and scanned the board. None of this sat right with her. First off, she didn't know enough about the other passengers on the boat, and second, she hadn't overheard all the conversations Catherine and Paige had relayed firsthand. She couldn't be one hundred percent certain of the events that had transpired between Lacey and the people she had altercations with. All in all, she had an uneasy feeling in her gut that the mystery man's murder and Lacey's were related. *But how?*

She looked at each clue on the board, and nothing jumped out at her. Perhaps Marc was right. Mystery man was a thief and got caught in the act and was chased off the boat. Maybe he and his chaser had a physical altercation on the beach and mystery man was killed and the killer, although in self-defense, was too scared to admit to it. Then she looked at Lacey as the next victim. Marc could also be correct in assuming that she had pushed someone too far with her drunken behavior and snide comments. Someone could have lashed out at her, delivering what turned out to be a fatal blow, and then pushed her overboard. Maybe they didn't know she was already dead when she hit the water. Could these two deaths be as simple as all that?

Addie tossed the marker on the dresser, turned the board to face the wall to hide what was written from any housekeeping staff that might enter to refresh her room, and headed down the passageway to the dining room to join her friends.

At the dining room door, she came to an abrupt halt when she spotted Oliver and Felix sitting with Catherine and Paige. Not wanting to interrupt what appeared to be an enjoyable conversation between the four, Addie glanced around the room for another table to join for lunch but turned at the sound of her name.

"Addie," Oliver called. "Please join us." He rose to his feet and pulled over a fifth chair from a nearby table. "There's someone here I'd like you to meet. This is my oldest and dearest friend, Felix Vanguard, and the head of my personal security team."

Addie extended her hand in greeting, which Felix shook. He gestured with his head. "Oliver here has told me so much about you, and I have seen you on board all this week, Miss Greyborne. Sadly, we never had an opportunity to meet."

"Please, call me Addie," she said with a smile as she took her seat. "Yes, it's nice to finally meet you. Oliver was just telling me this morning that you're an old Navy friend and used to be the head of security at the Smithsonian, is that right?"

She waved the server over and gestured toward the coffee carafe. The young woman poured her a cup and re-filled the other coffee cups at the table.

"Yes," he said with a hearty chuckle, "this old-timer and I go back a lot of years." He glanced at Oliver. "I believe we met as wide-eyed plebes the first day on campus when we were what, eighteen years old?" Oliver laughed and nodded. "Then spent a number of years working in different departments in the Navy, but me being in Naval intelligence, our paths always seemed to cross." He sat back and crossed his arms over his chest. "That was until my friend here"—he gave a short laugh—"decided the private sector was more lucrative and left the service."

"Yes, but it didn't take me long to convince you to do the same." Oliver let out a chesty laugh and slapped his friend on the back.

"You're right, and with that position you had on the board of directors, you got me that great job as head of security at the Smithsonian. Something I will always be grateful for."

"What about the job you have now? Doesn't that count for anything?" Oliver said, feigning insult, his smile the only thing giving him away.

"Yes, yes, my friend. Who doesn't love chasing around after you all day and doing your bidding like a personal butler?" Felix gave Oliver an exaggerated eye roll and took a sip of his coffee. "After all, someone"—he glanced over his shoulder—"has to watch your multibillion-dollar back for you."

Oliver's jaw tensed, and he glanced at the table where

Veronica sat with Preston, Annabel, and Wesley. "Yes, you're so right, and I thank you every day I wake up," he murmured, and took a drink from his coffee cup.

Addie didn't miss this exchange between the two men and glanced over at Veronica's table then back at Oliver. His eyes darkened as he gazed at his wife, his head shaking ever so slightly. He slurped up a spoonful of his soup. Addie toyed with her napkin and considered the exchange. Perhaps there were secrets here after all that Lacey had discovered and ones that got her killed. She shook it off and ordered a Waldorf salad for her lunch from the server who had returned to their table.

Once the lunch orders were completed, Felix leaned forward and pinned his gunmetal blue eyes on hers. "My friend here tells me you are somewhat of a rare book expert and have questioned the authenticity of some of the books in the library."

He certainly didn't mince words, and by the tone in his voice, he'd set up a challenge, one that Addie wasn't about to back down from. "That's correct," she said, and placed her cup on the saucer with a rattle and a bit more force than she'd intended. "I am questioning whether a couple of the books I had the pleasure of browsing this morning are in fact the first editions Oliver believes they are."

His eyes held fast on hers. "Then perhaps after we finish our lunch, you wouldn't mind joining me in the library to point out the books in question."

"I would be happy to." She caught sight of two officers on the outside deck. "That is, of course, if Chief Chandler permits our intrusion into his crime scene."

"Don't worry. He will," Felix said, his voice firm in the conviction.

Addie studied the man, who appeared to be as comfortable in his own skin as he was in his buff-colored linen day suit. He easily chatted through the rest of their lunch with Catherine, Paige, and Oliver.

It was clear by his actions and the focus of his attention that he was quite taken with Catherine. As any normal man would be. Catherine was absolutely striking today in her 1960s sleek wiggle sundress that Kalea had created for her. The shades of peach brought out the sun-kissed glow in Catherine's cheeks and highlighted the sparkle in her soft hazel eyes. Her brown bobbed hair swung easily whenever she turned her head or laughed at something Oliver said. The exchange between them made Addie recall Jonathan, another silver-haired fox, whom Catherine had become involved with. Addie wondered what it was about these dashing men that made them such flirts.

Oliver chatted with various guests as they passed their table on their way out. Soon they were the last remaining group seated in the large dining room. Without the hum of background voices, Addie had a better opportunity to hear what Catherine and Felix were discussing for the first time during their lunch.

"Dinner would be lovely," Catherine giggled softy. "However, you should know I am seeing someone right now."

"Anyone I know?" Felix looked around. "Is he on board? I certainly hope I haven't offended him."

"No, he doesn't live in Greyborne Harbor, and his work wouldn't allow him the time to attend the wedding as much as he would have liked to."

Felix took a sip of coffee. "What kind of work would

he be in that wouldn't give him the weekend off for a friend's wedding?"

"He's an antiquities insurance reclamation broker."

Felix's brows rose. "Really? Perhaps I know him. I have a lot of friends in that line of work with all my years at the Smithsonian."

"Well, perhaps you do then. His name is Jonathan Hemingway."

Felix's Adam's apple quivered as did his hand when he set his coffee cup down.

"Jonathan Hemingway?" He clasped Catherine's delicate hand in his and gave it a slight squeeze. "Well, he is a very lucky man." He released her hand and turned his full attention to the other conversation at the table, never glancing in Catherine's direction again as he stuffed the last of his chocolate cake into his mouth and drained his coffee cup.

It was clear to Addie that Felix either knew Jonathan Hemingway or at least had heard his name before. Either way it was enough for him to pull back. Catherine caught Addie's eye across the table and gave her the *what did I say?* look. Addie shrugged her shoulders and glanced at Felix, who rose to his feet.

"If you'll excuse," he said, glancing at Addie, "I will go and speak with the police chief about allowing us entrance into the library and meet you there. Let's say in about thirty minutes?" He glanced at a very expensive-looking white-gold wristwatch. "I am most curious as to your suspicions." He strolled across the empty dining room and out the door.

Oliver dropped his napkin on the table and rose to his feet. "I should be off now, too, ladies." He smiled from one woman to the next. "It has been a pleasure, but I do have to go and find my lovely wife now."

"Yes, it was a pleasure. Thank you so much for introducing us to your friend, Oliver." Catherine held out her dainty hand.

Oliver bent to kiss the back of it. "Yes, I do believe Felix enjoyed it himself until he discovered that his rival for your attentions was also a onetime business rival of his."

Catherine's mouth dropped, and Addie fixed her gaze on Oliver. "So, you know Jonathan?"

"I don't know him personally, only by reputation, but I do know that my friend there"—he motioned to the empty chair—"has had a dealing or two with him over the years. Now, if you'll excuse me."

"Yes, thank you again," Addie said, and glanced at Catherine. "Well, that makes sense that Felix knows Jonathan. After all, Felix was Navy intelligence and the head of a security detail that is more like the Secret Service."

Catherine sat with her chin in her hand and a wistful look crossed her face. "Do you think there is an unwritten code that only dashing men with silvery hair and voices to match can apply to work in secret government organizations?"

Chapter 16

Within thirty minutes Addie stood outside the library door. There was still a lot of police activity beyond from what she could tell. Jerry had obviously finished his scan of the outside decks, and his blue light now hovered over the wall across from the bookcases. She had anticipated a resounding no from Marc on entering the crime scene and was shocked when Felix came up behind her and pressed the button to open the door. "Shall we?"

They stepped into the crowded room, and the door shut automatically behind them. "Now, Miss Greyborne, please show me the books you questioned the authenticity of."

She glanced nervously at Ryley, who loomed in the doorway of the small office. Ryley appeared absorbed with a report in her hand and didn't even give them a second glance as they made their way past her toward the bookcases. Jerry, on the hand, stopped what he was doing and plucked two sets of rubber gloves from a box in his case and shoved them in Addie's hands with an instructional nod of his head at them.

"Yes, thanks." Addie handed a pair to Felix. She pulled her gloves on and reached for one of the books she'd seen earlier. "This Poe book caught my attention. You see it's inscribed as number forty-five in the first edition run—"

"Yes, we were lucky to have come across that one. Very rare indeed," Felix said as she flipped it open to the title page.

"Yes, but I know for a fact that this book number was taken into evidence in another case two years ago. There is no way it could be here in Oliver's collection."

"I beg your pardon," Felix said, his voice filled with insult.

"Look at the paper and the binding. It's not correct for the period in which it would have been printed. Plus, the edges of the page show no flocking, meaning the paper has a synthetic additive which didn't come about until years after its 1827 print run."

Felix slipped the book from Addie's hands and turned it over and examined the stitching in the binding. "Hmm, you say this numbered edition is in police lockup?"

"It was, and as far as I know, it still is. It was evidence in a large-scale smuggling ring that the FBI eventually took over investigation of."

"I'd have to go over Oliver's records with him to see who the broker was that we used for this particular book, but I can guarantee that all the books Oliver has in his collection were authenticated by a reputable source."

"That's what Oliver said, but look at these." She pulled *Anne of Green Gables* and a copy of Agatha

Christie's novel *Curtain: Poirot's Last Case* off the shelf. "I discovered the same thing on these books along with half a dozen others." She pointed to the shelves.

"Jerry," Ryley called from the office, "can you come in here?"

Jerry dropped his swab kit into the black case and sauntered toward the door. His body language suggested the dictatorial tone of Ryley's voice had not been well received. Addie could hear nothing but a muted woman's voice from where she stood, but her PI radar was working overtime. She shuffled crablike along the bookcase, pretending to check book titles until she was as close to the office door as she dared.

"So, the mystery man on the beach was a New York City reporter?" Jerry asked.

"It appears so. According to Simon, he has identified him as a Todd Brown, a freelancer. Since he wasn't affiliated with any of the major news outlets, we don't know why he was in Greyborne Harbor. Given that he was most definitely murdered, it must have been something big that brought him here."

Ask her if he had any connection to Lacey, Addie screamed in her mind.

"Do we know if Lacey Davenport and this fellow were connected?"

Thatta boy, Jerry. Addie smiled.

"Not as far as I know," Ryley said, her voice faltering. "Why do you ask?"

"It just seems funny that they were both reporters, and they both ended up dead."

Yes! Addie did a mental fist bump. *Way to go, Jerry. Show the ex-FBI agent that two and two doesn't make five.*

"I thought Lacey was here for Serena's wedding?"

"I know, but—"

"When we get more information, I will update you. For now, we work on the premise that the man was on board, was injured in an altercation here in the library, was chased off the boat, and then was shot later on the beach. We don't speculate. We work with the facts we have. Got it, Lieutenant?"

"Yes, ma'am," Jerry replied, and returned to his black case.

Felix shoved a book he'd been examining back onto the shelf. "Well, I don't know enough about fraud detection of counterfeit books, but I've found about ten more that I am questioning. I won't be able to verify their authenticity until Oliver and I go through the sale documents and see who the appraisers were that did, in fact, verify them."

"Are those records here or back on the estate in Connecticut?"

"I'll have to talk to Oliver," he said, turning on his heel. "This is most distressing," he muttered, and darted around the end of the bookcase to the door leading out onto the open deck.

Addie watched him go, the words she had just overheard Ryley share with Jerry rushing through her mind. The mystery man was a reporter from New York City. *Okay, Addie, think.* She glanced at the spot where the copy of *The Mysterious Affair at Styles* had been located, to the desk, and then to the sofa table where there was a missing ornament. She then moved slowly from the bookcase to the deck door and pressed the button. Once outside, she squinted and shielded her eyes from the bright sunshine and made her way toward the bow of the yacht. Deck chairs were scattered in conversational groupings at intervals along the sidewalls, but nothing out of the ordinary stood out to her. She crept around the bow, noting a lifeboat in its hanger. A quick examination of that didn't provide any apparent clues or evidence.

When she reached the other side of the bow, she came to the outside metal staircase that joined this deck with the ones above and the engineering deck below. At the bottom of the stairs was a metal box marked *Emergency*. She lifted the lid. It contained a whistle, what appeared to be a signal mirror, a small handheld LED light, a small laser pointer, a small whiteboard and pen, a number of glow sticks, a survival manual, a small first-aid kit, and an orange flare gun.

She dashed up to the above decks, peeked inside each emergency box, and saw the same assortment she'd seen below on the main deck. All the flare guns in the boxes were yellow. Why then was the one in the emergency box on the deck off the library orange? What reason would there be in it not matching the rest of them?

Addie tried to picture what had taken place the night before the wedding. Everyone was on the deck above, enjoying the dress rehearsal. Following dinner, as far as she knew, this deck would have been deserted except for the odd person out for a deck stroll under the stars perhaps.

Todd Brown had obviously come on board under the pretense of being a guest . . . or a staff person. Was that why he was wearing a jacket similar to the other staffers' jackets? Addie knew she needed to find out if that night was his first trip on board or a return trip because he had discovered something of interest previously.

At some point during the evening he must have slipped downstairs from the promenade deck to the main deck and into the library. Someone either followed him or stumbled across him in the library, saw him going through the books, picked up an object from the sofa table, and struck him, causing the book to fall but not before he tore the corner of the page, accidentally or on purpose. Even though he would have been stunned by the blow to the head, he was with it enough to start running. The person who attacked him probably chased him out onto the outside deck and around the bow of the boat, where Todd most likely descended the stairs here.

She glanced to the deck below and where it came out off the main foyer by the gangway, which is where he would have exited the yacht. Whoever was chasing him grabbed the flare gun from the emergency case as they gave pursuit and caught up to him on the beach.

Did Marc know one flare gun didn't match the others? Had they looked for a trail of blood on these stairs or on the decks, because if Todd had been struck first, as the blood splatters on the book indicate, then there would have to have been some blood residue left behind, wouldn't there?

Addie dashed through the double doors into the empty lounge, except it wasn't empty. Just past the doorway into the dining room, she spotted Veronica and the chef Jean Pierre, locked in a passionate embrace. The tenderness and intimacy of the kiss they shared was of two people who had been engaged in a long-term affair, and not exactly the raging passion of a onetime fling.

Addie backed out onto the deck and crossed her fingers that they hadn't seen her. Now she needed not only to find Marc to talk to him about the different flare guns she discovered and ask him about a blood trail. But she also had to find Felix to ask him what, if anything, he knew about the two lovers she'd just seen. Could it be that their affair might have been one that someone would be willing to kill a couple of reporters for to keep quiet? After all, Veronica was married to Oliver, a billionaire, and an affair with their chef could mean her total ruin.

Chapter 17

Addie watchfully made her way around the outside deck to the doors to the port-side entrance into the foyer off the lounge and slipped down the passageway toward the library, hoping she had evaded detection by the two lovers. She peered through the glass door and waved to get Marc's attention, but it was no use. He and Jerry had their backs to her as they stood reviewing evidence bags.

Her phone pinged a text alert. She fished it out of her jacket pocket, glanced at the screen, and breathed a sigh of relief. Simon, finally. She hoped she'd be able to get an answer to her biggest question, if Todd's autopsy showed any indication of a head injury. She began reading Simon's text then grabbed for the door. Marc turned around, and when his eyes locked with hers, he darted for the door. "Addie, what's wrong?"

"Is it true?" she said, gazing into his concern-filled eyes.

"Is what true?"

"That the blood in the book I found this morning was a match for Lacey's and not the first victim's, Todd Brown."

"How in the world do you know that?"

"I get around," she said with a shoulder shrug, and discreetly slipped her phone back in her jacket pocket.

"I can see that." He glanced down the passageway to his left and right. "Get in here," he ordered, and marched to the office, closing the door behind her. "Now, tell me what you do know."

"I only know that the blood on the title page is a match to Lacey and not Todd." She wrung her hands in front of her. The look on his face told her she was in for a scolding. She raised her head high and met his intense glower and decided to throw all caution to the wind—after all, she'd come this far. "I'm guessing that's why I didn't hear anything about the crime-scene investigation team finding a blood trail leading from the library out onto the pier?"

"You know I would never discuss that with you anyway, but the question remains. How do you know the first victim's name?"

"I . . . um . . ."

"Who have you been talking to?" His gaze bored into hers.

"It doesn't matter how I know any of this, does it? I just know."

His jaw clenched, and he opened his mouth.

"Did you know that there's an emergency box at the bottom of each outdoor staircase?"

"Yes, that's a requirement of a boat this size with as many decks."

"Did you know that the flare gun on this particular deck is different from any of the others?"

"We've checked them all. None appears to have been fired recently, and all flare shots are accounted for."

"Think about it, Marc, the ones you checked probably are all clean and not been fired, at least recently, but who's to say they are the ones that were originally in the box before Todd Brown was shot with a flare gun."

"That means that someone might have replaced the one used with a new one."

"Bingo." She grinned.

Marc pursed his lips together and studied Addie's face. "Is that all?"

"What do you mean 'is that all'? I just gave you another lead. Check the marina and boat shops and see if they have recently sold a gun to someone."

"What makes you think that we haven't?"

"Well, I just . . ."

"You just assumed we don't know how to conduct an investigation?"

"No, but I just told you about the gun differences, and you didn't seem to know about it before."

His brow rose and a sly smile touched his lips. "Addie, give me more credit than that. As soon as the murder weapon was identified, we checked with every boating house supplier in a fifty-mile radius to see if one had been recently purchased."

"Oh right." Her gaze dropped. "I guess I didn't think about that." She glanced back up at him. "So, you don't think Todd was shot by a flare gun from this yacht."

"I didn't say that. I only said we checked purchases in the area."

"So, you are looking into the possibility that he could have been shot by one of the guns on board. Does the one that was originally in the deck box on this level appear to have been replaced?"

"Addie, go back to your cabin and stay out of trouble, and if I discover who's been feeding you information, then I'll be firing—"

"It was Ryley," she added quickly as she didn't want Marc suspecting any of his officers.

"Ryley?" His face paled. "She wouldn't."

"No, she didn't directly. I just overheard her talking about the first victim and she named him, and . . . I might have also overhead that he was a reporter from New York."

Marc didn't take his gaze off her.

"And . . . well, don't you think it's weird that two reporters were killed in a matter of two days?"

She didn't miss the tic in Marc's jaw.

"Have you found a link between Lacey and Todd? Maybe they were working on a story together?"

"Addie, please leave the investigating to us." He pointed to the library. "As you can see, we are on top of the evidence."

"Okay, I'm just throwing that out there because it seems a little too coincidental, and you know what they say about—"

"Yes, I know, in a murder case there are few coincidences. Now, please let me get back to work."

She started for the door and stopped. "Were you aware that Veronica and the chef, Jean Pierre, I think his name is, are having an affair?"

"What?" His face radiated disbelief. "Who told you that?"

"No one. I saw them kissing with my own eyes."

"When?"

"Just a few minutes ago in the dining room. From what I could tell, it was fairly passionate. I'm pretty sure this is something that has happened before."

Marc ran his hand through his hair, sending it up in chestnut tufts. "What did they do when you walked in?"

"They didn't see me. I caught myself from intruding just in time, and there was no one else in the room."

"Thank you, but I find it hard to believe. Veronica has a lot to lose."

"That was my first thought." Addie turned away and then glanced back at him. "Do you think either of them would kill to keep that affair secret?"

"I just know it adds a couple of more names to my suspect list."

Addie nodded and opened the door to the library and stopped short when Felix caught her eye.

"Addie," he said, rushing over to her. "Oliver told me some of the purchase agreements and receipts are here in the office. I've been waiting to ask Marc if I can go in to check for them."

"We're done in there for now," Addie said, "so go ahead and ask him."

"Thanks," Felix said, sweeping past toward the open door.

"Oh, Felix." She grabbed his jacket sleeve. "Before you go in, can I ask you about something?"

"Sure, what?"

"How long has the chef worked for the Ludlows?"

"As long as Veronica has been around, about five years now. Why?"

"Do you know where he worked before that?"

"Yes, he worked for her in England. He was her personal chef for about fifteen years before that."

"So, he came over with her?"

Felix nodded. "What makes you ask?"

"I just saw something I was curious about, that's all."

"Look," he said, glancing at Marc, who was gathering files from the small office desk, "I better catch Marc before he heads back to the station. He told me earlier he has a meeting with the mayor."

"Yeah, sure thing. If you find the purchase agreements and authenticity certificates, I'll be in my cabin."

"Thanks." He smiled and headed over to Marc.

Addie scanned the police activity in the library and then glanced at where the Agatha Christie book had been. Of all the books in the library, why was Lacey drawn to the exact same book that Todd had torn a corner out of, and why that particular book? They had to have been working together and communicating with each other prior to her becoming a murderer's second victim. Where were Todd's and Lacey's cell phones? Addie knew she had to find at least one of them. It would prove that these two murders were connected just like her gut told her they were. There was no doubt in her mind that Lacey's crashing Serena's wedding was a convenient cover, but her real intent was to investigate a story.

"Jerry, do you mind if I take a closer look at a few of the books? I have a hunch."

Jerry's gaze darted from Marc chatting with Felix in the office to Jefferies making notes on a pad. "I guess since the chief let you in here already, it would be okay. As long as you wear the gloves and don't remove anything from the scene."

"Thanks, I won't."

"Are you looking for anything in particular?"

Addie glanced at Jerry then at Marc and Felix and whispered, "Have you not wondered how that scrap of paper from one of the books on this shelf ended up in Todd Brown's pocket and then the next day Lacey's blood is discovered all over the same page the paper was torn from?"

Jerry stood erect and met her gaze. "As a matter of fact, that has recently crossed my mind. I think I'm of the same mind as you." He glanced toward Marc. "These two knew each other before they came to Greyborne Harbor and were looking for something particular on this yacht."

"Exactly," said Addie. "Now we just have to figure out what it was." She scanned the books. "But from what I discovered earlier, I think I might have a pretty good idea."

"The books?"

"Yes, some of them aren't what they appear to be, and I think someone was trying to keep that a secret."

"Oliver Ludlow?"

She glanced at Felix. "I'm not sure, or someone very close to him."

Jerry followed her gaze. "I see. Just be careful and make sure you bring anything you turn up to one of us immediately."

"I will, don't worry," Addie said, and removed a copy of Margaret Mitchell's 1936 edition of *Gone with the Wind* from the shelf. After inspecting the cover, she returned it to its place on the shelf.

Her fingers tapped over various spines as she made her way down the row. Every once in a while, she'd remove one, examine the paper and binding, and replace it. The ones she needed to analyze closer, she left sticking out by an inch. She hoped no one would notice so she could return later and take a proper look when the police had cleared the scene.

Chapter 18

"Thanks for letting me take a look, Jerry," Addie said, and as she started toward the door she caught sight of Marc and Felix in the office sorting through various file folders in the cabinet. She hoped that meant Marc took her thoughts about the books seriously. She slipped out into the passageway and made her way to her stateroom. There was a lot of new information she needed to add to her makeshift crime board, and with so much coming at her, she was afraid she'd forget it all. She reached into her pocket for the key.

"Addie."

She spun around, a wide grin spread across her face.

"Simon," she cried, dashing toward him and flinging herself in his outstretched arms. "You have no idea how much I've missed you."

"Me too," he murmured, and softly kissed her. "This

has been a couple of crazy days, and I'm not nearly done. But I needed to see you if even for only a few minutes." He nuzzled her cheek.

"You're just in time. I was about to make some new notes on my crime board, and I could use your help deciphering them."

"I don't have much time. I still have fiber samples to test, but I'm all yours until then." He grinned and pulled her back into his arms and kissed her again.

She looked up into his eyes, and the same feeling as when she first met him swept through her. It was as though a peaceful wave washed over her, caressing her, consuming her. "I'll take whatever I can get right now because my head's swimming." She laughed softly. Yes, this was exactly what her heart needed.

She turned and fit the key in the lock and froze when the door opened freely in her hand. "I know I locked this when I left earlier."

"Perhaps housekeeping was in?"

"Maybe, but they are pretty good about locking up."

"Let me go ahead," Simon whispered, and skirted around her as he slowly pushed the door open. A deep chuckle rumbled in his chest.

"What?" Addie cried, peering around his arm.

"Hi, Addie, Simon." Paige laughed and gave them a sheepish finger wave. "I hope you don't mind. We came looking for you when the housekeeper was here, and well . . ." She glanced at Catherine beside her on the bed.

"We had some things to add to this." Catherine grinned and held up the makeshift crime board.

"Of course I don't mind. It just took me by surprise." Addie took the board from Catherine's outstretched hand.

"Wow," she said after reading what they'd written.

"Veronica's second husband, Lord Alfred Easton, died under questionable circumstances?"

"Yes." Paige leapt off the bed and pointed to the next line. "See here? According to Melinda Ludlow, so did Veronica's first husband, Preston's father, Jason Buckley."

"Melinda told you this? When?"

"We saw her in the spa," said Paige, "and joined her in the steam room to chat. Let me tell you, she was more than willing to shovel the dirt on the new Mrs. Ludlow."

"We asked her," piped in Catherine, "what the deal was with Veronica calling herself Lady Veronica Ludlow."

"She told us the story as best she knew it from Oliver and added"—Paige glanced at Catherine, a flash of mischief in her eyes—"that she'd had Felix check into it. Apparently, he discovered that Lord Easton's three children from his first wife believed Veronica was a gold-digger and questioned whether the hunting accident really was an accident. It was also rumored that through the course of their marriage, Veronica was involved in an adulterous affair. However, no one could ever discover the identity of the man in question or prove foul play in Lord Alfred's death."

"Now, that's a motive for killing a couple of reporters, isn't it?" Catherine said, glancing from Addie to Simon.

Addie glanced at the board. "If it's true that there was something to Lord Easton being murdered and not dying of a hunting accident as reported, then yes." Her gaze caught Simon's. "And I think I know who the mystery lover was."

"Who?" cried Paige and Catherine in unison.

Addie laid the board on the bed, plucked a pen from Paige's fingers, and wrote *Jean Pierre*.

"The chef?" Simon looked at Addie in disbelief. "How did you come to that conclusion?"

"I just saw them in the dining room, kissing, and let me tell you, it was not a friendly kiss on the cheek that the French are known for. No, this was"—she shrugged—"something a lot more personal."

Simon glanced at the board. "But could he have been with Veronica in England and be the same mystery lover his children suspected?"

"Felix confirmed it when I asked him about Jean Pierre. He told me he came over to the States with her about five years ago."

"But he has to be what, about ten years younger than her, doesn't he?"

"All I know is that the intimacy of the kiss they shared makes me suspect that the two have a longtime romance that one or both might be willing to kill for."

"Hmm," Simon said. "It makes sense that if Lacey and Todd were digging up history on the Ludlows and discovered those two were involved with each other . . . Yeah, it might be motive for murder."

"My only question is what *The Mysterious Affair at Styles* has to do with it. That's the book both victims were interested in." Addie set the board on the dresser and studied it.

Catherine edged toward the poster board. "From what I remember of that book, the evidence pointed to one character, but another was arrested. Hercule Poirot wasn't completely convinced of the second man's guilt, though, because through his investigation he had discovered all sorts of shenanigans going on in the household."

"That's right," said Addie excitedly, "including a very seedy affair."

Simon studied the notes on the board. "Does that mean they used the book to leave a clue to all the sordid entanglements that appear to be going on here?"

"That's a good question, but maybe." Addie picked up the pen and wrote:

Veronica affair with Jean Pierre
England, fifteen years
Husband #1 and #2 die under questionable circumstances
Children and stepchildren England, + Preston, Zach

"You can't seriously think Zach had anything to do with it," cried Paige.

"No." Addie stopped writing. "He wasn't here for Lacey's murder, and he was far too busy with the dress rehearsal the evening before for Todd's. I'm just writing a list of who would have motive to keep something like Veronica's affair secret."

"I think you can take off the English lord's children then, too," added Simon. "They aren't here, and it seems to me, they would like nothing better than having Veronica's secrets revealed."

"You're right. So . . . if we look at this from the perspective that the affair is the motive behind the murder, then who in here would have the most to lose by that secret being exposed?"

"Preston, for one," Paige piped in.

"Yes, and Veronica herself," added Catherine.

"What about Preston's wife, Annabel?" said Paige. "If her husband lost his future inheritance, she would, too."

"Yes, and if Veronica was cut off from inheriting anything from Oliver by the disclosure of her infidelity, Wesley and Donna would also be unemployed and stand to lose a great deal, too," Addie added, writing their names on the list.

"That's all true," said Simon, glancing at his watch. "I have to get back to the lab."

"Really?" Addie said, hoping her disappointment wasn't too evident in her voice. "But you just got here. I thought we'd have more time."

"Sorry, but the work is piling up, and I also have a surgery scheduled this afternoon. I'll let you know if anything else turns up in my tests." He kissed her cheek. "See you later, ladies." He nodded at Paige and Catherine. He pointed his gaze directly at Addie. "Promise me that you all will stay out of trouble and take any evidence you turn up directly to Marc."

She nodded and had begun to close the door behind him when she heard muffled laughter coming from the stairwell entrance crisscross the passageway from her room. Sure that Simon had left, she crept down the hall, placed her ear against the door, stuffed a finger in her other ear, and strained to listen as the voices drew closer. Whoever it was, was obviously on their way either upstairs or down. But she couldn't make out what was being whispered between a woman's giggles. The pitch sounded too high and common for Veronica, and the whispers were too deep for it to be two of the female staffers having a laugh together. No, it was definitely a man and woman. But who, and what was with the long pauses between giggles?

"Are you coming back in?"

Addie jumped and spun around, patting her rapidly pounding chest. "Yes, sorry, Paige. I'll be right there."

"We were afraid you tried to smuggle yourself off the yacht under Simon's shirt," Paige said with a short laugh.

"I wish," Addie chuckled. "I thought I heard something." She started back to her stateroom, stopped, turned around, and pressed the elevator button. "You know what, I'm just going to run down to the kitchen for a minute and see if they have any snacks we can have while we work."

"That lunch didn't fill you up?" said Paige.

"You know me, when there's a French chef cooking for us, I'm going to take advantage of it."

Paige stood in the doorway of the stateroom and eyed Addie. "Something tells me French pastries aren't the only thing you're going to the galley for."

"I'll let you know." Addie gave her friend a sly smile and stepped into the elevator as the door opened.

Chapter 19

Addie stepped off the elevator at the staff passageway and turned left into the large galley. From around the end of a baker's rack, she spotted Maggie Abbott, Jean Pierre's personal assistant and sous-chef, whom she'd had the pleasure of meeting earlier in the week. Judging by the amount of diced vegetables on the large island cutting board, Addie doubted that the woman's voice she'd heard was Maggie's. She also appeared to be completely alone in the kitchen.

"Excuse me," Addie said, popping out and making herself visible.

The young woman jumped, dropped her knife, and spun around. "Miss Greyborne, sorry, you gave me a start." She patted her chest and took a deep breath. "I must have been lost in my own little world." She wiped her hands on her white apron. "What can I do for you?"

Addie quickly scanned the kitchen and then the ruddy-faced young cook. "It's quieter down here than I would have thought with all the people there are to feed in a few hours."

"They'll be along soon. I like to start prep early because Jean Pierre, I mean Chef Gagneux"—her face turned a darker shade of red—"will need assistance with this evening's dessert creation."

"Does Chef have something special in mind?"

"It's a secret." Maggie pressed her fingers to her lips and laughed.

"I won't tell anyone," Addie said, stepping closer. "Can you just give me a little hint?"

"I can't. He'd kill me for ruining his surprise for Lady Veronica," she said with a soft laugh. "You'll see in a few hours along with the other guests." She gave Addie a wink and picked up her knife from the cutting board. "Now, what was it you were looking for down here?"

"Right," Addie blurted, "a snack. Yes, that's what I came down for."

"Of course." Maggie set the knife down and opened the large walk-in refrigerator door. "Salty or sweet, fruit or pastries? We have a little of everything in here."

Addie poked her head around the door and scanned the wall of racks displaying trays of prepared food. "You aren't kidding, are you?"

"No, and if it's fresh fruit you're looking for, we have another cooler beside this one, and if you want ice cream, we have a large walk-in freezer, where I'm sure we could find a flavor to your liking."

"Some of those pastries and scones from this morning would be perfect. You know, just to keep us going until dinner." Addie eyed a tray in front of her. "Speaking of dinner, can you give me one little hint what Jean Pierre's surprise menu item will be?"

"Not a chance," Maggie said with a grin. "Chef likes his secrets and loves to surprise her Ladyship."

"I bet he does," said Addie, recalling the passionate exchange between the two in the dining room. "Are these secrets and surprises a regular occurrence?"

"Chef has worked for her a long time. I guess they've come to share a few inside jokes."

Amongst other things. "Yes, I imagine they do. Say, how long have you worked with Chef Gagneux?"

"Um, about six years now, I guess," said Maggie, standing on tiptoes to peer at a tray just above her head. "Yes, here are some more scones. I'll pull these down for you, too."

"That would be perfect," said Addie, her mind reeling to find a way to stay on topic. "I assume you came over from England with Jean Pierre and Veronica? Is that why you still refer to her as her Ladyship?"

"Why, yes, I guess. That's who she was when I first went to work for Chef, and I suppose the title has stuck in my mind."

"I imagine in all that time you've come to know her and her personal staff quite well."

"Oh yes," she said, balancing the tray on her arm. "You'd be shocked to hear some of the things that have gone on in my years of service."

"Like what?" Addie said, feigning innocence as she fixed on Maggie's flushed face.

"Well, I'm not one to gossip, but there were rumors right after I arrived, to be exact."

"Rumors?"

"Yes, about her Ladyship and Lord Easton's death."

"What kind of rumors?"

Maggie's gaze dropped. "I really shouldn't say, but I tell you if anyone knows the truth about what went on, it's that Mr. Wesley Harbinger or her Ladyship's assistant, Donna Camden. Those two know a whole lot more than I do. But never mind all that. I could lose my job for speaking out of turn. If you want to get a plate from the plate rack around the corner, I'll put some goodies together for you."

"Thank you," Addie said, hoping her disappointment in the abrupt change of subject wasn't noticeable. She spotted the rack around the corner from the cooler and scanned it for the perfect-size plate. It needed to be big enough not to rouse suspicion that this was an excuse to try to discover whose voices she had heard in the stairwell, but also the plate couldn't be so big as to give the impression she was a piggy, although the thought of gorging on French pastries all afternoon was tempting. Heavy footsteps around the corner caused her to pause as she reached for a plate.

"Maggie, my love, I've been texting you for the last five minutes."

There was no mistaking Jean Pierre's silky voice as it drew closer to the cooler. "Ah, there you are. Come here, my little nymph," he murmured. "I have an itch that only you can scratch, and I need it scratched now. . . ."

"Shh," Maggie snapped, and then whispered something Addie couldn't make out.

Addie gulped. The murmurs, the whispered reply, his itch could only mean one thing. Addie peeked around the side of the cooler and saw Jean Pierre, arms wrapped around the sous-chef. Maggie struggled to release herself from his embrace. She pressed her finger to his lips, stood back, smoothed her ruffled hair, and gestured with her head toward where Addie was hiding around the corner.

Addie pulled back, pursed her lips, and sucked in a deep breath to calm her racing heart and then called, "I think I found the perfect size." She grabbed a dinner plate and stepped out into the main galley. "Oh, hello, Chef," she said, attempting to sound surprised. "I hope you don't mind my intrusion. I only came down here looking for an afternoon snack, and Maggie has been most helpful."

"Guests aren't generally permitted in this area," he said in a clipped tone.

"I understand that, but I was so hungry and desperate for more of your amazing French delicacies. They are the best I've ever had," Addie said with the most innocent smile she could muster, and handed Maggie the plate. "Just a few of each of this morning's treats would be perfect."

"Yes, right away." Maggie, obviously flustered, seized a set of tongs from a hook on the wall and arranged an assortment of pastries on the plate, covered the plate with a snug sheet of plastic wrap, and with a shaky hand, gave it to Addie. "I hope this is enough."

Jean Pierre snorted and peered down his nose at Addie. "Perhaps call the next time you're in need of something, and we'll have someone bring it to your cabin."

"Yes, yes, of course. Again, sorry for the intrusion into the galley." Addie grabbed the plate and dashed through the kitchen to the elevator door. Behind her there wasn't a sound, and when the elevator door opened, she stepped back, waited for it to close, and tiptoed back into the galley. Using the baker's rack as a shield, she peered past it to see what was happening now that they thought they were alone. Jean Pierre had Maggie pressed against the outside of the cooler door, his hands embracing her body as his lips caressed her face.

"I need that itch scratched. Shall we go to my cabin?" he cooed in her ear, and pulled the giggling woman toward Addie's hiding spot.

Addie's chest tightened, and she glanced around the rack and crept to the backside as they passed her. She held her breath until her lungs screamed in pain, but not until she heard the clank of the door leading to the staff quarters close did she dare let it out. Addie gripped the plate, dashed to the stairwell door, and raced up the stairs taking them two at a time. She bolted out into her stateroom deck and flung her room door open.

Catherine let out a little squeal as she jumped, and Paige dropped the pen she held in her hand. Both stared wide-eyed at her, their mouths open, but no words came out.

"I'm glad you're both still here," Addie cried, and raced over to the bed. She dropped the plate of goodies and grabbed the pen. "I've come across some new information, and I think it tells us a lot more than we knew before." She scribbled on the board and held it up for her friends to read.

Beside *Veronica affair with Jean Pierre*, she had written *AND Maggie Abbott*.

"What?" Paige plopped onto the bed.

"I just saw them kissing, and he took her to his cabin."

"You're kidding," Catherine said, fanning herself. "That means . . ."

"That means the chef is not only having an affair with Veronica but also his sous-chef. She's worked for him for six years, so I doubt this is something new, either."

"Do you think Veronica knows?"

"It's hard to say, but wouldn't that give Jean Pierre a motive for wanting to shut up two nosy reporters?"

"Yes, something he certainly wouldn't want either woman to find out about."

"Especially Veronica Ludlow, his employer. He'd be out of a job."

"This list of suspects just got a whole lot longer, hasn't it?" said Catherine, eyeing the board.

"It's about to get even longer because before Jean Pierre showed up in the kitchen, Maggie told me there were rumors about Veronica's husband's death in England."

"Didn't we already know that?" said Paige, taking the board from Addie's hand.

"Yes, but she said Wesley and her assistant, Donna, knew more than they were saying about that."

"So, we need to talk to them and find out what they do know."

"Look at you, Catherine, thinking like a detective, and you thought you wouldn't have a head for this." Addie laughed.

"I guess all those murder mysteries I've read have helped," Catherine said, chuckling.

"Okay, how are we going to get that information?" Paige asked, glancing from Addie to Catherine. "We just can't go right up to them and say, 'Hey, I hear Veronica might have killed Lord Easton. What do you know about it?'"

"You're right." Addie studied the board and snapped her fingers. "Catherine, you said Melinda Ludlow was willing to dish the dirt. Can you speak with her again and find out everything you know about Veronica's previous husbands? I'll talk to Felix and see what else he knows and find out about the books because I have a feeling that they are in some way related to this. Paige, you can talk to Donna and see what she knows about Veronica's past? We will meet later to see what we've all been able to add to this."

"All right, but what does that have to do with Jean Pierre having an affair with two different women?"

"Maybe somehow it's all related. Maybe he poisoned Lord Easton for Veronica, and she is forcing herself on him, and if he doesn't comply, she will turn him in, but he's secretly in love with Maggie?"

"Like blackmail?"

Addie shrugged. "All I know is we have a long list of suspects and a growing number of motives. We have to figure out which of these people"—she tapped the board—"are worth keeping on here, and who had the most to gain and the power and influence to cover up the murder of two reporters."

Chapter 20

Addie stopped outside the library door. From her vantage point, she could see Marc hunched over the desk and assumed by the arm of a buff-colored suite jacket that he was standing behind Felix. She hoped that meant they had found some of the paperwork regarding the book purchases.

Paige and Catherine continued up the passageway toward the Edwardian dining room to seek out their targets for interrogation. Addie mentally crossed her fingers that her two friends would be able to handle their assignments discreetly as to not raise any suspicions. No one needed the impression that they were suspects on a homemade crime board.

Addie knocked on the glass. Marc glanced over from the office and then returned his focus to whatever it was he was reading at the desk.

Addie knocked again, this time with more force, and Jerry, who was seated on the sofa, packing evidence bags into his black crime-scene case, strode to the door.

"What can we do for you?" he asked as the door slid open.

"I was hoping to speak to Marc if he's not busy."

"That's fine," Marc called, and waved her in. "I think we could use Miss Greyborne's eyes on this, too."

Excitement built in Addie's chest as she sauntered into the library. This could only mean they had found something. Finally, a few answers to help eliminate a few of the motives piling up on her board.

"Ah, Miss Greyborne," said Felix, removing his dark-framed glasses and laying them on the desk. "I was just going to come to find you."

"Did you find some of the authentic certificates and bills of sale?" she asked hopefully.

He sat back and grinned as his gaze darted from Addie to Marc. "We have, and I feel as though I have been vindicated by them." He turned a printed copy of a spreadsheet toward her. "As you can see, many of the books in question are listed here not only with the broker's or bookseller's name and contact information but also with the corresponding certification numbers and provenance documentation of many of the books."

She scanned the papers in her hand. "So, according to this, all the books we discovered were originals when purchased?"

"Correct." Felix pulled a folder from the bottom of the papers still on the desk. "Here are the corresponding certificates."

"We matched the certificates to the line entries on there, and it all looks like it's in order," said Marc. "I guess your theory about some of the books not being original first editions was incorrect, and we have to work another angle on this investigation."

Addie focused on the line entries on the page. How could she have been so wrong in her assessment that many of these books were not originals? "Yes, it looks like everything is here." She read one entry after the other. "I must say that Oliver has kept very detailed records."

"When he's dealing in the dollar amounts that his collection is worth, it's necessary, and it's a good thing, too, for when something like this arises."

"Yes, yes." Addie read farther down the page. She recognized many of the brokers listed as the supplier broker. Broker after broker and the next one and the next—they were all reputable, and some were even ones she'd had dealings with, in the past. This didn't make sense. How could she have been so wrong? She froze. One name jumped off the page at her.

She swallowed hard and glanced at Felix. "Did you arrange for this transaction between Oliver and Björn Svensson?"

Felix frowned and shook his head. "I'm afraid that name doesn't ring a bell. Who is he?"

Addie let out a deep breath. Her mind raced, trying to recall what she could about the man. "He's a Swedish bookbinder, a very good one. He was contracted from time to time by the British Museum, as well as many others worldwide, to restore rare and valuable books that had been damaged. When I was doing my internship in London some years ago, he was arrested and charged with book forgery."

"What's the date of the transaction with him?" Marc asked, coming to her side and peering over her shoulder.

"Two years ago," she said. "About a year after he disappeared if I remember correctly. His case never did go to trial. From what I heard later, he had simply vanished."

"So that means this Poe book was purchased *after* he went on the run?"

"Yes, but that's not the only weird part." She fixed her gaze on Marc's. "This is one of the books we discovered in that smuggling ring bust you made about two years ago."

"How is that possible? Those books are still in evidence."

"I know," said Addie, "and the one we found then was in fact the original as verified by not only me but Dr. Albert Finch, and he's a renowned book appraiser the FBI often uses in their antiquities cases."

"So how did it end up here?"

"It couldn't have, which means that at least this Poe book that Oliver purchased was a forgery from the beginning and the appraisal certificate and provenance are fakes, too."

"Would this Björn fellow have known that at the time?" Felix rose to his feet.

"It's hard to say," said Marc. "I don't think that bust made the news right away as there were other players in the ring the FBI had to track down. But if this guy is as well connected as you say he is, Addie, then maybe he did know about it."

"Yes," she said, "and most likely, he thought his forgery would never be discovered because he knew the original was in lockup and didn't think it would ever emerge." She glanced at Marc. "I'll call an old associate of mine at the Boston Library. She might know if there are rumors that Björn has resurfaced and is back in business."

Felix glanced hopefully at Addie. "But even if he is, only one of the books you questioned is a forgery, right?"

"Not necessarily. If my hunch is right, and Mr. Svensson is back in business, the ones I've questioned could still be copies, very good copies. He is the best in the business, but they're still copies."

"How can that be?" Felix ran his hand through his silvery hair. "The books were all purchased from reputable buyers. It says so right here." He stabbed his finger on the page clutched in Addie's hand.

"Yes, they *were*, but that doesn't mean they weren't swapped out at a later date."

Felix's eyes widened as he glanced from Addie to Marc. "You're not implying I had something to do with that, are you?"

"We're not implying anything at this point," said Marc, "but what Addie is saying makes sense. We just have to figure out who would have access to these books and who had the opportunity to swap them for copies."

"Provided, of course, that we can track down the whereabouts of Björn Svensson," Addie added.

"Yes," agreed Marc. "If he's gone into hiding from the FBI, I image it's also an Interpol case now, too, and he must be in deep cover to avoid their detection."

"Let me reach out to a few of my contacts," said Felix. "They might have heard of this fellow or have a lead on him."

"Sure," said Marc, eyeing Felix as he headed for the door. "Remember not to arouse suspicion. Only make general inquiries."

Felix met Marc's gaze. "I think you're forgetting, Chief, that I was in national intelligence for a good number of years before private security. I'm pretty sure I haven't forgotten all my basic training." He winked and left the library.

"Do you trust him?" asked Addie, watching him go out into the passageway.

"I ran a check on him, and yes. He's everything he claims to be and has received a number of commendations over the years. I think we can trust him, as much as anyone right now."

"I know. It's tough though, isn't it? The pool of suspects seems to be growing by the minute."

"Why? Who else have you added to your list?"

"What list?" Addie said, not able to hide her smile. "And what would ever make you think I've been doing any of my own investigating?"

"Oh, Addie, Addie, Addie," said Marc, taking the spreadsheet from her hands. "I know you too well, and I have a feeling you've come up with some names that I haven't even considered yet."

"Moi?" She laughed and patted her chest.

"Yes, you." He sat on the edge of the desk. "So, who have you come up with since the last time we spoke?"

She proceeded to tell him about what she saw and overhead in the galley between Jean Pierre and Maggie, but by the look on his face, he didn't seem surprised.

"Did you already know about them?"

"I suspected as I've seen a few exchanged looks between them and discovered them more than once in a position that looked like they were more than employer and employee. I guess all you've done is confirm that."

"But don't you think that's a secret one of them might not want exposed, especially since Jean Pierre is also having an affair with Veronica?"

"Probably, but we need proof, and so far, that's exactly what's missing from any of this. It's all pure speculation."

"All right," Addie said, twisting the ends of her pony-tail in her hands. "I can at least try to find out some information on Björn Svensson. It's the weekend, but I still might be able to reach my contact in Boston. I'll have to go to my stateroom though and look her up on my contact list on my laptop."

"You brought your laptop to Serena's wedding?"

"You have no idea of the maid-of-honor list I had to check off before the festivities," she said, with a chuckle. "Remember, your sister had turned into a Bridezilla and kept us all hopping."

"You're right," said Marc with a snicker. "She did that . . . and you're certain you think these books have something to do with the two murders?"

"I think it's one of the many possibilities. If nothing else, it might help confirm or erase one of the motives that led to two murders."

"You don't think the affairs are the ones?"

"I'm not sure at this moment. The fact that Todd tore a page out of the Agatha Christie book only for Lacey's blood to be on that very same page gives me pause. Although, we have come up with a couple of other secrets someone might want to keep. Who knows what they could have done feeling threatened by two dogged reporters sniffing around?"

Chapter 21

Addie wasn't certain she'd receive a reply from her friend Barbara at the Boston Library on a Sunday evening, but she hoped she would hear something back by morning.

She glanced at the clock in the bottom corner of her laptop screen, closed the lid, and changed from her afternoon dress into something a bit more formal for dinner. She spun slowly in front of the full-length mirror and admired the job her cousin did on this dress design, too. It fit her like a glove on top and flared out from the waist just enough to flow off her hips and create an hourglass image. It really did make her appear ten years younger and a few pounds lighter, not that she had gained a lot of weight in her early thirties, but she wasn't eighteen anymore, either. However, the sleeveless, wide-shouldered, square-neck wine-colored floral print made her feel as though she was.

Addie dashed down the passageway and into the Edwardian dining room. Catherine and Paige were seated with Serena's parents near the front. At the table next to theirs was Veronica and Oliver, the older couple from New York—she could never remember their names—and Preston and Annabel. As she took the seat Catherine gestured to, she couldn't help but notice that Wesley and Donna, Veronica's assistant, were huddled together in what appeared to be a serious conversation at a table by the serving station near the backroom elevator entrance.

"Any luck there today?" she asked, motioning with her head to Paige.

"No, I couldn't find Donna when I went looking, but I did manage to learn a few other things from Melinda," she whispered.

"Great, we'll meet after dinner."

Paige nodded and sipped on her water.

"Addie," said Serena and Marc's mother, Janis, "I was just telling Catherine and Paige that Serena called this afternoon. Well, it was late evening for her, and we didn't talk long, but she sounded so happy and relaxed. They absolutely love their river cruise."

"That's fantastic. I know she was excited to explore all those real English teahouses and looked forward to getting some ideas to use in her shop. I only hope they remember there's more to the country than tea, and it's not just a working trip for her."

"Oh no, they've taken in some castles, old abbeys, and the markets. Well, she went on and on about those and says she has some great ideas for our town markets and events, too."

"That's fantastic," said Catherine. "We keep doing the same old things, and it might be nice for some refreshing ideas."

"You can't mess with tradition," barked Serena and Marc's dad, Wade, gruffly as he waved for the server to refill his water glass. "I always say, if it's not broke, don't fix it."

"Nonsense, dear," chirped Janis. "There's something to be said for new ideas. It might be just the thing to bring in fresh tourist traffic, too."

"You're going to have a tough time convincing some of the celebration committee people to make any changes." He glanced at Addie. "It seems that the ideas your aunt Anita came up with all those years ago when she chaired those boards are written in stone."

"You do know how persuasive your daughter can be when she sets her mind on something." Janis laughed and placed her hand over her husband's, giving it a gentle squeeze.

He chuckled. "Yes, she is very persuasive. When she talked herself out of every grounding and punishment as a teenager, I always thought she'd be a great lawyer."

"That sounds like our Serena." Addie chuckled softly and dropped her gaze. "Say, you didn't say anything to her about what's been going on, did you?"

"No, Marc gave us strict orders not to let her know. He doesn't want her honeymoon to be tarnished." Janis dropped her gaze. "It's going to devastate her when she gets home though."

"You know," piped in Wade, "she and Lacey weren't the best of friends this last year."

"I know, but up until . . . that incident with the money"—Janis took a sip of her water—"Serena idolized Lacey most of her life. This news is going to hit her hard."

"As it has Marc, I'm afraid." Wade opened his napkin and placed it on his lap as he took a bread roll from the basket.

"I hope Oliver got the message from Marc, too," Addie added, toying with her water glass. "It would be horrible for Zach to find out through his family. Serena would feel so deceived by us all."

"You're right, and that's exactly what I said to Marc, and he assured me he was going to speak to Oliver and Veronica," Janis said, picking up the evening menu. "Although, I don't think Veronica even cares about what happened the way she's been carrying on."

"What do you mean?" Addie glanced over the top of her menu.

Janis lowered her voice. "I mean she's so busy playing the role of her Ladyship and entertaining her guests that I'm not really certain that any of what happened has even fazed her."

"Yeah," said Catherine, glancing over at Veronica's table, where Veronica chatted freely with her dinner companions. "It's more like a simple annoyance to her, if anything."

Addie ordered shrimp cocktail from the young server but was disappointed there was table service tonight instead of the usual buffet. These last few days she'd found that mingling in the room and on the buffet line offered its advantages in overhearing tidbits of information. Her gaze darted to Wesley and Donna's table. She was dying to hear what they were talking about. They both appeared tense, but they weren't arguing from what she could tell.

There was something about their body language, though, that told her they weren't simply two coworkers discussing work.

As her dish was taken away and her main course of prime rib was served, Addie kept trying to come up with a reason to go to the servers' station behind Wesley's table. Maybe she could overhear their conversation now, because it appeared that he had Veronica's assistant near tears. Then an idea struck her. She discreetly removed one of her pearl earrings, the bridesmaid gift she had received from Serena, tucked it into her palm, and made a mad dash over to her server, who was scraping plates and putting them in a plastic bin to be taken down to the galley.

"Stop, please," cried Addie. "I seem to have lost one of my earrings and am afraid it landed on my plate."

The young woman ceased clearing the plates and looked in horror at Addie. "Oh dear, I hope not." She glanced at the garbage in the bin and then back at Addie. "What does it look like?"

"This." Addie pulled her free-flowing hair away from her right ear to show the other earring still in place.

"Hmm, pretty small. It might be tough to find in here." She stuck her nose up at the discarded food in the trash.

"Can you please look, we have to find it. It was a gift from the bride, and I wouldn't have the heart to tell her I'd lost it."

The server wrinkled up her nose again and with a long-handled salad fork began gingerly poking around in the garbage.

"Thank you. I'll look over here, in case it rolled off the plate onto the floor." Addie feigned peering under the servers' counter and around the area behind Wesley and

Donna's table, careful not to cause too much of a distraction from their conversation. But it didn't seem to matter as they appeared oblivious to the goings-on around the room, except for Veronica's table. While they spoke, Donna didn't take her reddened eyes off them, and Addie edged closer, keeping low in search of the phantom lost earring.

"How many times do I have to tell you, Donna, that I've done my best with the situation? She's married into the family now, and that should give you some comfort."

"But Wesley, she looks so miserable."

"Her happiness isn't my concern. She's exactly where we wanted her. She is Veronica's daughter-in-law, and you know what that means for all of us."

"I know, but Preston and she really don't appear to have a good marriage."

"It's not about a good marriage; it's about marrying for convenience. You seemed to be fine with it when we first discussed it. Why the change of heart now?"

They were talking about Annabel, but why? What connection did she have to the two of them? Addie swallowed hard, crouched lower, and crept closer to the table.

"I guess I thought she might grow to love him, but the way she's been carrying on with . . . Well, I see that's not going to happen, and you know what that could mean."

"Look, I made sure that a special clause was included in the prenuptial, so she's still going to be set up financially just as long as that dimwit of a husband doesn't discover what's going on. But I don't think that's what we have to worry about, I made sure of that." Wesley's voice dropped. "Damn those reporters for snooping around."

"Wesley!" Donna gasped. "You didn't—"

"Let's just say that whoever did . . . Veronica should

be rewarding them." Wesley leaned closer to Donna and then jerked and glanced at Addie questioningly, her hind end wagging in the air as she crouched over having expanded her search to only a feet from their table.

"Found it!" she cried, and stood upright, calling out to the server still digging through the garbage can. "See!" Addie frantically patted her chest and held the pearl stud out for the server and Wesley to look at. "It did fall off the plate when you brought your armload of dishes back here. Phew, what a relief. I was starting to think it was lost forever." She smiled her appreciation at the server. "Thank you for your help." She then flashed Wesley and Donna a wide celebratory grin. "Sorry to interrupt your dinner." She spun on her heel and headed back to her table.

"What were you doing over there crawling around on the floor like a dog looking for scraps?" asked Catherine as Addie plopped back into her chair.

"I lost my earring and thought it landed on my plate the server took, so I tried to catch her before she dumped the trash."

"Did you find it?" asked Janis with concern. "I know Serena would be heartbroken if you lost one. It took her forever to pick out a gift for you that she knew you'd never buy for yourself."

"I found it on the floor. It must have rolled off the plate," Addie said, holding out the pearl stud.

"And . . . it just happened to fall beside Wesley and Donna's table?" whispered Paige, plopping her last piece of lobster dripping in melted butter in her mouth.

"Look at your chin." Addie laughed as she picked up Paige's napkin and wiped her friend's mouth. "I got big news," she whispered between unmoving teeth as she patted Paige's chin. "There, now it won't drip on your dress."

"Thank you." Paige plucked the napkin from Addie's hand and gave her a sly smile as she finished wiping her own face.

"Your dinner's going to be cold. Perhaps the server could have it warmed for you," said Catherine, looking around for the girl.

"No, it's fine, really," said Addie, digging into a piece of her prime rib. "Actually . . ." she said between bites, "it's still warm and so delicious . . . num, num, num . . ."

Addie pushed her plate away when she'd polished off every last morsel and then waved off the slice of mile-high chocolate cake presented to her. As it passed by her and was set in front of Paige, Addie couldn't help but notice that the top was covered with what appeared to be gold flakes sprinkled across the icing. As her dinner companions dug into theirs, Addie felt a pang of jealousy over their oohs and aahs. However, she was stuffed, and unless she wanted to split the seams of her dress right here and now, there was no way she could indulge . . . but it sure did look good.

She recalled Maggie telling her Jean Pierre had a special treat for dessert tonight, and aside from the decadence of the gold leaf, she wondered what made this cake so exceptional. Well, aside from it standing seven inches high and dripping with oodles of caramel sauce. She glanced around the room and not seeing him, she decided she might have to make another reconnaissance trip to the galley. She'd justify her snooping by asking about the special ingredient.

She'd started to rise to her feet when Wesley got up, tossed his napkin on the table, and stomped across the dining room out into the lounge. Veronica immediately rose, made an excuse for her abrupt departure to her table companions, and rushed out after him. Donna rose to her feet and fled through the servers' door. A few moments later Addie saw her standing by the outside deck railing, her shoulders shuddering as though she was crying.

Catherine glanced at Addie, shrugged her shoulders, and tipped her glass in the direction of Addie's stateroom. Addie nodded her understanding and sat back down.

"I can't eat another bite," said Wade, pushing his half-eaten cake away. "I think we'd better go for a walk, or I'll be up all night after this meal. What do you say, dear?"

"I think you're right, but all I know is that whatever is in this cake is the best thing I've ever eaten." Janis stuffed the last bite into her mouth and scraped her plate with her fork. "But I agree, we need to walk this off, or you'll be rolling me into bed tonight," she added with a chuckle.

Serena's parents took their leave and headed out the same door as Donna had fled. Addie noticed through the window that Donna took no heed of them as they strolled past her, hand in hand. She felt a spark of envy. She missed Simon and yearned to spend the evening walking the decks with her hand tucked securely in his. However, given that she hadn't heard from him since he went back to the lab earlier, the moonlit deck walk was out of the realm of possibilities—for tonight, at least.

She tugged her phone out of her skirt pocket and silently thanked her cousin for incorporating pockets into her dress designs. She tapped out a hurried text to Simon as Paige and Catherine groaned and pushed their cleaned cake plates away from them.

"Janis won't be the only one having to be rolled into bed tonight. After this meal and dessert and the long day we've had, I'm about done," said Paige, licking the last bit of chocolate with her finger off her plate as she shoved it farther away from her.

"Not so fast. I think we have a bit of work to do right now." Catherine glanced over at Oliver's table, which was now free of not only Veronica but also Annabel. She leaned closer to Addie and whispered, "We found out some interesting information this afternoon."

"Right, I forgot for a moment I wasn't on vacation and that this was a working trip," said Paige with short laugh. "Yes, it seems like yesterday, but we did have a rather productive afternoon. How did you do?" She glanced at Addie.

"I think we should take our coffee back to my room and compare notes." Addie glanced at Donna, who was still at the railing. "I've found out a lot of information, too, but I can't make heads or tails out of it yet. We all need to talk. Maybe our puzzle pieces will fit together better then."

Chapter 22

Addie drew a circle around Wesley's name and glanced over at Paige sprawled out on the bed. "You said Wesley has been Veronica's personal lawyer since before the death of her first husband, Jason Buckley?"

"Yes, Melinda said Wesley and Veronica met when he was Jason's band's lawyer. I guess Jason was a big deal at the time and a real up-and-coming rock star."

"Did she say what happened to him?"

"Yeah, he died in a freak accident."

"That's interesting, isn't it?" said Addie glancing at the board.

"It gets even more interesting," chirped Paige, propping herself up on her elbow. "Melinda said Veronica was pregnant with Jason's baby when he died and right after that, Wesley orchestrated the marriage between her and

Jason's *very* elderly grandfather, George Buckley, a very wealthy pharmaceutical tycoon."

"Which means," gasped Addie. "Lord Easton was actually her third husband, not her second, making Oliver her fourth?"

Paige and Catherine nodded.

"That also means Preston's natural father was Jason Buckley but when he was born his father on paper would have been his great-grandfather?"

"Yeah, but Melinda said it definitely wasn't a marriage out of love and she didn't think anything went on between Veronica and George since he was extremely elderly and had a bad heart among other medical conditions and was also wheelchair-bound."

"Really?" said Addie, as she tried to keep up with what Paige was sharing and scribbling notes on the board.

"I guess," added Paige. "When George died in his sleep, the police had questions about his sudden death because Veronica stood to inherit billions even though they were only married for a couple of months."

"But they never found any evidence to prove foul play?"

Paige shook her head.

"And he had no prenuptial or other family to contest her getting everything?"

"No," said Catherine. "According to Melinda, he was all alone after his grandson, Jason, died and apparently left everything to Veronica and Jason's baby boy."

"It sounds like between these two deaths and then the death of her husband in England, Veronica has made out fairly well, at least financially."

"Oh yes," added Paige, sitting upright and crossing her

legs. "I guess having Wesley as her longtime lawyer through all of these marriages"—she waved toward the board—"was a good way to make certain that she inherited some pretty tidy sums after their deaths."

Addie stood back and studied the board. "Yes, and it makes me wonder if Mr. Wesley Harbinger knows more about the deaths of Veronica's three preceding husbands than he lets on."

"I think you're right," said Paige. "From the beginning of Oliver and Veronica's affair, Melinda said she was suspicious of the woman's background and that of her entourage. She had Felix check on them all then, but he came up empty. He told her if there was anything Mr. Harbinger was, it was an excellent lawyer as he had covered their tracks well."

"Really?" Addie's eyes narrowed as she scanned their notes on the board.

"Yes, and then she said later, when it appeared her marriage was really over, and Oliver was going to marry Veronica. Melinda hired a private investigator, because she was concerned about Oliver's future given Veronica's history of husbands, but he couldn't find any evidence of foul play in any of their deaths either. Although, he did tell her, it didn't mean they were"—Catherine wagged her fingers in air quotes—"accidents or natural causes as reported."

"Yeah," said Addie. "Felix confirmed much the same thing earlier, too. Say, where did you find Melinda this afternoon? I haven't seen her around since breakfast."

"Same place we found her this morning," said Paige. "At the spa."

"She told us," added Catherine, "that although her

presence on board was tolerated for her son's wedding, that tolerance hadn't been extended into our lockdown, and she's been made to feel very unwelcome by her *Ladyship*."

"You have to admire her resilience though," said Paige. "She decided to bide her time by working out in the gym and enjoying the full benefits of the spa. She said she's even taken to eating her meals in her cabin to avoid creating more conflict."

"I feel bad for her. Being the ex-wife, but still Zach's mother and required to be here for her son's wedding, must be a difficult situation to be in," said Addie.

"I get the feeling," added Catherine with a sparkle in her eye, "that she's waiting for Veronica's past to come back and bite her. Then Melinda, by remaining close to Oliver but not too close, will be in the position to rightfully regain what she sees was hers before Oliver was seduced away from her. Plus, I get the feeling she wants to keep an eye on Oliver."

"Why," said Addie, "is she worried about Oliver?"

"She's terrified," said Paige, "that Veronica is only with him now because he's a successful venture capitalist and financer. Although, that part went right over my head, but when she said he'd been named in *Forbes*'s list of the top twenty richest men in the country, I took notice as I know that's a big deal."

"She's afraid he, too, might have an untimely death," Catherine chimed in.

"It certainly looks like it could be a possibility, doesn't it," said Addie, underlining Oliver's name on the board.

"What?" Catherine fixed an astonished gaze on Addie. "You don't think our sweet Zach's father is involved in the murder, do you? Did you hear what Paige said? Melinda is afraid *he* might be the next victim not the murderer."

"Yes, but who knows what secrets his empire has been built on and whether the buying and selling of rare books on the black market is part of it?"

"But that's like putting Wade's and Janis's names on the board and underlining them," Catherine all but spat out.

"Just because he's Zach's father doesn't mean he's lived the same moral life that we know Zach has. Even Zach spends very little time with his family, which I always found odd."

"But I think that's because of Veronica and Preston. According to Melinda, before the divorce and Oliver taking up with her *Ladyship,* the family was a pretty tight threesome."

"Is that why Zach spent his life in boarding schools?" Addie pinned Catherine with a questioning look.

"No, but at least he went home for holidays. He hasn't done that for a few years now." Catherine fluffed a pillow and leaned onto it.

"Does he see his mother now very often?"

"No, she said she generally spends her holidays in Europe."

"Which is where she spent most of Zach's young life, too, I assume, and the reason why he was, for the most part, raised by nannies and private school administrators."

"Look, Addie, I like Melinda. She seems real with us, and both times we've talked to her, she has been a wealth of information."

Addie sat down on the side of the bed and took Catherine's hand in hers. "Have you asked yourself why she's been so ready to dish out all this information and implicate everyone around her but says nothing about herself?"

"No," said Paige. "She seems genuine."

"Yes, but you have to consider where she's getting all the money for her travels and to maintain the same lifestyle she had pre-divorce."

"I'm sure she got a very good settlement," said Catherine. "After all, Oliver is on the *Forbes* list. I'm certain him having an affair and kicking Melinda out of the company at Veronica's request came with a pretty hefty payout to her."

"Maybe." Addie glanced at the board propped up on the dresser. "Although, all of this is interesting, especially when we add it to what I told you about the kisses I caught Veronica and Jean Pierre exchanging. Plus, he later shared the same thing with Maggie in the galley. And don't forget the weird conversation I overheard at dinner between Wesley and Donna. It just all seems—"

"Like there could be a dozen reasons why two reporters were killed," Paige said.

"Yes," said Addie, tapping the pen on her knee. "Add in the fake first editions I discovered in the library, and we have—"

"A very tangled web of deceit and lies," said Catherine, "and we still don't have a clue what secrets two reporters would have been killed for."

"There's just so many motives," groaned Paige, flinging herself back on the bed. "I'm exhausted. This has been the longest day *ever*."

"You're right," said Catherine, "and I don't feel like we're getting any closer to sorting this out. I must say, Addie, when you said it was like doing a puzzle, I had no idea the pieces would be so numerous and tiny. Come on, Paige, time for bed."

Paige didn't argue with her older friend, who took it upon herself to get Addie's young assistant's shoes on and collect Paige's handbag for her before they headed out the door to their cabin.

Addie flung herself on the bed and pounded her fists into the pillow. "Why is this so difficult?" She slammed the pillow harder. "I want to go home. I want Simon."

She lay there for what felt like an eternity, her mind taking in every clue she had on the board, and it all came back to the books. There might be a dozen other secrets happening, but it all came down to who had access to the library and who would have had the knowledge to switch them out for fakes.

Felix! She leapt off the bed, fluffed her hair in the mirror, and checked the time on her cell phone. After scrolling through for a possible missed message from Simon, she shoved her phone into her dress pocket and headed down the passageway to the library. She knew it was nearly eleven but hoped that Marc might still be around. The yellow crime-scene tape still across the door told her they weren't done in there yet. The library itself was dark, but from the passageway door she could make out a desk lamp on in the office. She raised her hand to knock when her cell phone dinged out a message alert. *Simon?* She excitedly fished her phone from her pocket and checked the screen. Her heart fell. Much to her surprise, it was an e-mail from Barbara. Addie clicked the message open and read,

*Hi, Addie, sorry about the late-night reply, I was
at my daughter's for dinner. As soon as I got home,
I did a bit of research for you and discovered that
Björn Svensson disappeared over three years ago
when an Interpol arrest warrant was issued for
him. From what I could find out, through some of
my contacts here, he was last seen in Cuba. Since
they don't have extradition there, the authorities
can't do much about it to arrest him. If you're looking at well-crafted counterfeits, I'm guessing he's
your man unless it was one of his apprentices.
When I get back in the office tomorrow, I'll see
what I can find out about them, who they were, and
where they are now.*

Miss you, much love, Barbara

Addie raised her hand and frantically knocked on the
glass door. Marc poked his head out of the office and ambled toward the door. She couldn't help but notice how
worn and taut his face appeared, and she realized it had
been a long day for him, too, made especially difficult by
who one of the victims was.

He flipped the switch, and the door slid open. "Addie,
I'm surprised to see you this late."

"I couldn't sleep. There's just too much buzzing
around in my head tonight."

He raked his hand through his chestnut-brown hair and
nodded in agreement. "Yeah, it has been one of those
days, hasn't it?"

"Can we talk for a few minutes? I have something to
run by you."

"Sure, Felix and I are still going through the inventory
for the library. Maybe you can help."

"You're still working on that?"

"Yes, I think you might be onto something when you pointed out the fake books and asked why Todd Brown would have torn a corner from that one book and why Lacey's blood was discovered on the same book."

Addie dropped her voice and glanced at the library door. "Do you think that Felix is the best person to help you with this? He's the only one on board I can think of who has a background in rare books and antiquities. He's also the one who introduced Oliver to the brokers and sellers he dealt with."

Marc leaned into her. "Do you really think," he whispered in her ear, "that I would have enlisted his assistance without checking him out thoroughly? Plus, Ryley also ran a background check on him through her FBI contacts. He's as clean as they come." He stood upright. "Now, do you want to help or not?"

Chapter 23

It was just as Addie thought. She eyed the stack of . . . ten . . . twelve . . . fourteen . . . sixteen . . . eighteen . . . twenty . . . twenty-one books as she placed them on the sofa table behind her. There were far more than the couple in the bookcase that she'd suspected initially as being fakes. For the past few hours, she'd been calling out the titles, and then Marc and Felix would sort through the paperwork in the office until they came across the corresponding purchase records and provenance, if there was one. They then matched it to each of the book titles she had pegged as frauds. It was a slow task, and her head ached and her arms hurt.

There were numerous counterfeits here, definitely not the first editions that Oliver believed he owned. Through her past work, she knew that the bookbinder who created these facsimiles would have to have been a highly skilled professional like Björn Svensson. To the untrained eye, these counterfeit books would have possibly gone unnoticed for years or would have never been detected.

However, her old friend Barbara raised an interesting point. Björn could have had an apprentice who joined the book forgery business when his master went into hiding. Her comment made Addie wonder if it that could possibly be someone on this yacht.

That question and the other one she couldn't get out of her head dealt with Oliver. If Oliver was aware of this, he could run his own kind of resale scam. He could be claiming the purchases of the books as a business investment and then reselling the originals on the black market and keeping the money for his personal use while keeping his library intact with the fakes just in case the IRS decided to audit him. However, for the life of her, she couldn't wrap her head around that idea. But it was after two a.m.—according to the last time she checked the clock on her cell phone—and maybe it was a theory she needed to sleep on.

"Guys," she called, "I have to take a break and get some fresh air. I can't even see straight anymore."

"I think we all need a break," Marc replied, and stepped out into the library. "I think if we can muster up another hour here, then we'll call it a night."

"Okay, but I need a brisk walk around the deck if you want me to keep at it."

"Yeah, me too," Marc said. "Felix, let's take five then get back at it. I'd like to get as much done here as we can tonight because tomorrow is going to bring a new set of challenges."

"How so?" asked Addie.

"We're going to have to start interviewing all the staff

again and some of the guests who are frequent visitors. I need to find out who would have access to these books on a regular basis and the opportunity to take the originals off board and replace them with the fakes."

"Then you are working on the premise that the books are the key to the murders?"

"I have to follow the evidence, and right now the evidence says the books are the best lead we have so far. I don't see with the blood and torn book page how the murders were random, and I can't ignore that."

Addie did a mental high five to Marc. In the years she had known him and crossed paths with him on cases, she was fairly certain that this was the first time that he didn't poo-poo her theories. It felt good, and she couldn't stop the smile she felt from spreading across her face.

Marc's gaze dropped. "See you in five." He turned and abruptly left through the door out onto the outside deck area.

Addie followed, but as Marc staked himself out on the railing, she took advantage of the light nighttime sea breeze that wisped strands of her disheveled hair across her face and set off on a quick pace to get a lap of the deck in before she resumed scanning books.

She rounded the stern by the dining room and paused when she thought she saw a shadow through the window on the far side of the room. Squinting into the room only illuminated by the security lights, she didn't see any other movement and decided it must have been a shadow of her walking past—or a figment of her overly tired mind—and she plugged on. As she rounded the stern and began a hurried pace along the deck that faced the town of Greyborne Harbor, she slowed her steps and took in the dramatic view of the distant twinkling lights of the town in the night sky. Was one of those lights Simon still working in his lab? She hoped he wasn't, but she was starting to become somewhat concerned that she hadn't heard a word from him since he left that afternoon. Was that only today? Wow! It felt like an eternity ago since she had last seen him or spoken with him. Her bottom lip quivered. There wasn't even a good-night message. Very unusual.

She pushed it from her mind, lifted her chin, and relished in the gentle breezes that caressed her cheeks. He was no doubt up to his eyeballs in work with the two murders, and she felt certain she'd wake in the morning to an apology and lots of virtual kisses.

When she came around the bow and headed back toward the library entrance, she hesitated when she saw Marc still standing at the railing, staring out into the blackness of the night seascape.

"It's beautiful, isn't it?" she said softly, sliding up beside him. "All you can see forever is the stars against the blackened water with the odd twinkle of lights from boats harbored in the bay."

"Yes, very calming," he said with a sniffle.

She glanced at him. Had he been crying?

"I guess we'd better get back in there so we can finish up for the night," he said matter-of-factly, but his voice was brittle and faltering. "I don't know about you, but I'm exhausted and can't wait to hit my bed."

"Is that where Ryley is?"

He glanced sideways at her.

"I mean, I haven't seen her around at all since late this afternoon and thought . . . well, perhaps she had called it an early night." She couldn't help but notice his fingers whiten as he grasped the rail. "Marc, is everything okay?"

"Yeah," he said, nodding. "She took some samples from the library over to Simon just before dinner."

"Oh, I see, and did she come back afterward?"

He shook his head. "No, she texted me and said they were going out to dinner to discuss his findings and would let me know what he said."

Addie had to squelch the rock that formed in her tummy. Did he just say that Simon went out to dinner with Ryley? All her fears raged through her overly tired mind, and a wave of panic surged through her. She shook her head. *Don't be silly, Addie. They are coworkers, and it's normal for them to discuss a case.* "What did she say he'd found? I know you don't like to share case information"—she noticed his knuckles growing increasingly whiter—"but I do kind of have a vested interest since I am helping with the books and all."

"I never heard back from her."

Okay, Addie, now you can panic. "What do you mean?"

"I mean the last I heard they were off to dinner at Lombardo's on the waterfront, and that's it." He turned to her. "Does it bother you?"

She fought the worries that threatened to overtake her. "No. Not in the least." She hoped she sounded convincing enough for her answer to win an Academy Award. "You?"

"No." His fingers wrung the deck railing as though it were someone's neck. "I know Simon loves you." He glanced at her then quickly away. "That's not bothering me."

"Then what is?"

"I shouldn't."

"Look, Marc, we might not be"—she swallowed—"together anymore, but we are still friends. You can tell me what's going on. I know right now after all this that you need someone to talk to. I know I do, and I wasn't even fond of Lacey, but it's been hard on all of us."

"Believe it or not, I did my grieving for Lacey. I know that sounds cold, but she and I have been done for years, and well, I feel bad what for happened to her, but . . ."

"But what?"

"It's Ryley."

"Okay?" Addie's gaze did not waver from his face as she waited to hear what made one of the most emotionally detached-appearing men she'd ever met appear so dejected.

"Over the winter things started to change between us. She began to question every decision I made and second-guessed my orders in every investigation. Today she told me she knows it must be hard working as chief of police in a small town when someone gets killed because the investigations generally involve people I've known my whole life. I even overheard her say that to the mayor last night." The deck lights reflected off his whitening knuckles. "Ryley has proven that she's a career law enforcement officer, and anything else I thought we had was merely a hiatus until she felt strong enough after San Diego and her departure from the FBI to step up and take over. Now she appears to be making her next move, and that's what's got me worried. She seems to have gone rogue with the mayor's blessing, and I feel like I've been sidelined."

"Oh, Marc," Addie whispered, and placed her hand on his arm. "I'm so—"

"Marc! Addie!" Felix called from the library door. "I found something, and you're not going to believe it."

Addie and Marc dashed toward him and followed him to the office, where he had piles of papers laid across the desktop. "Look, here's the purchase record of the Poe book and the purchase record stating it is number forty-five. But, look, it's dated a year ago."

"Wow," said Addie, "so that definitely proves it is a fake like we suspected."

"Exactly, because you both said the number on it is in police lockup as evidence in another case. Look what I found in this old binder at the back of a drawer." He pulled a large black binder closer. "It's a purchase agreement dated fifteen years ago for the same book but numbered forty-six not forty-five, and it's a different broker and a different signature on the certificate of authentication from the one we've been working with."

"How can that be and why?" Marc asked, as he studied both documents.

Addie's mind ran through different scenarios, and then she snapped her fingers. "Because the person switching out the original books for the fakes couldn't find the original purchase information. Whoever created the counterfeits knew that number forty-five was in police custody, so it wouldn't be showing up on the market, black or otherwise, and they probably felt that if they gave it a number long gone, it would never raise suspicion."

"Not realizing someone who was involved in the first case would also be the person to discover the forgery," added Marc.

"It makes sense," said Felix. "The forger had to create a realistic-looking document in case of an audit, and it would satisfy anyone digging into the collection."

"That also means," said Addie, "that whoever is responsible for exchanging the books made this one happen last year." She pointed to the date on the document. "Now we just have to figure out who in Oliver's circle would have been anywhere near Cuba during that time."

"Cuba?" Felix and Marc asked in unison as they glanced questioningly at Addie.

"Why Cuba?" Marc asked.

"Because I have it on very good authority that's where Björn Svensson fled to and is hiding out now."

Chapter 24

Addie bolted up in bed the next morning, pushed her tousled hair from her eyes, and stared at the contraption on her nightstand that wouldn't cease its incessant vibrating. As her dream fog lifted from her mind, she realized what it was and fumbled her phone like a football, catching it only before it hit the floor.

"Hello," she yelled, finally placing the phone to her ear. "Simon? . . . Well, good morning, stranger . . . what do you mean I should look out into the passageway? . . . Okay, just a minute. Hey, it's not something gruesome, is it? . . . Okay, but I really couldn't take gruesome right after I wake up . . . all right, hold on . . ."

Addie shoved her feet into her slippers and grabbed her robe from the foot of the bed, tying the belt as she stumbled to the door. She opened it a crack and jumped back with a screech when a dark figure blocked her view.

"Now, that's what I call a welcome," said Simon with a soft chuckle, as he snaked his arms around her and hugged her so tight she struggled to breathe.

She nestled into his arms, overwhelmed by the subtle musky fragrance he wore, which always had an effect on her that she couldn't explain. Oh, how she'd missed his smell. She closed her eyes and drew in a deep breath, and then wondered if Ryley had noticed his heady scent last night.

Simon tilted her chin up so his lips were in line with hers, but he seemed to notice the angst in her eyes. His own filled with concern. "What is it? What's wrong?"

"Nothing," she said, praying her voice remained neutral. "It's just that I must look like such a sight." She pulled away and ran her hand through her tangled mass of hair. "I was . . . just not expecting such a wonderful wake-up call, that's all." She stepped back and tightened the tie on her robe. "Come in, please. We can order coffee and catch up."

"That sounds perfect." Simon swept his lips across her hot cheek as he sidestepped her into the stateroom. "Say, what's up with Marc?"

"What do you mean?"

"I mean that I just ran into him downstairs, and he's back to treating me like he did when I first came to town, like I was his rival or something." He eyed her warily. "Has something happened between the two of you that I should know about?"

"No!" Addie's hand flew to her chest. "Definitely not. We've been working on some clues together, but that's all. There's nothing . . . I know he's struggling a bit with Lacey's murder, but that shouldn't affect how he feels toward you. Unless . . ."

"Unless what?"

"Unless your dinner with Ryley last night has him—"

"Stop right there. That was strictly a professional dinner meeting, and . . . wait . . . you found out about that before I could tell you this morning, and that's what's bothering you, too, this morning."

Addie turned her gaze from his and feigned straightening her robe belt.

"It is, isn't it?" He swept her into his arms. His lips did not back away this time, and kissed her hard—this time, she really couldn't catch her breath for a moment. "I love you and only you," he whispered. "Last night was work, and that's it. I'm sorry I didn't call if that's what made you think the worst, but when I got back to the lab, it was late, and I didn't want to wake you."

"Just be quiet and kiss me again," she said, her voice soft and breathy as she grabbed his collar and tugged him to her, his lips eagerly responding to hers.

He laid his damp forehead on hers, and she didn't miss the wide grin that spread across his face. "Now, that was more like the reunion I was looking for when I arrived," he said with a soft laugh, and pulled her down on the bed beside him. "So, Ryley was right. This case isn't one Marc should be leading, then?"

"What are you talking about?"

"You said he was having a tough time because Lacey was one of the victims, so I assumed that Ryley taking over the case was because of that."

"What?" Addie jumped to her feet. "Since when did Ryley take over?"

Simon stared at her. "Why, last night. She told me that and said I was to give all my reports to her."

"Then that's what you picked up on from him this morning, his resentment toward her, not you."

"Why would he resent her for stepping in to investigate his old fiancée's death?"

"Because she's also apparently after his job and—"

"And what?"

"And I have my suspicions that she could also have been the last person to see Lacey alive."

"When?"

Addie relayed to him what Marc had told her about his suspecting Ryley was after his job and how close she had become to the mayor and his wife. Then she shared the information he had told her about the night Lacey was killed. How Ryley left the station early when they were working on the mystery man's murder and said she had a headache, but he didn't get home until four a.m. "Don't you see? There's a four-hour window there that he can't place exactly where Ryley was, and just before they left the party, Lacey and Ryley had words."

"That is interesting, isn't it?" Simon gazed at the wedding announcement poster propped up on the dresser. "Have you managed to add any more since yesterday?"

"As a matter of fact." Addie flashed him a grin and turned the board around to show the writing on the board.

Simon let out a low whistle. "My, my, you have been busy, haven't you?"

"I can't take all the credit. Catherine and Paige have proven themselves a couple of very worthy sleuths in their own right."

Simon scanned the board. "What's that about the chef and Veronica and Maggie, the cook?"

Addie explained how she'd seen him kissing both

women, and how intimate he had appeared with both of them.

"Then I think you can add one more to his list of conquests."

"What? Who?"

"Annabel."

"When?"

"Just now. When I was coming up the back staircase, the two of them . . . were . . . well . . . only as far apart"— he measured with his hands in front of him—"as the two cups of coffee between them."

"Maybe I'm still half asleep, but I don't get what you're saying."

"Jean Pierre was holding two Styrofoam cups of coffee in front of him, and that was the only space between them. When they saw me, Annabel's face turned so red, I was afraid she was having a stroke. Jean Pierre thrust the two cups in her hands, opened the door for her, and said, 'Have a good day, Mrs. Buckley.' Then he trotted down the stairs past me as if it were nothing."

"Maybe it was? Maybe he was just helping her carry her coffee to her room."

Simon's brows quivered. "Yeah, along with some fairly close contact between them, and her body language told me she wasn't objecting."

"But you actually didn't see anything, right?"

"No, I didn't, but it sure was implied."

She tossed a pillow at him, laughing. "Dr. Emerson, you've become an old gossip and way worse than Martha. Have you been going to her bakery daily now that I'm not around to make your meals?"

"Of course not, we both know you don't know how to

cook anyway." He laughed and pulled her down on the bed beside him. His lips grazed over her neck and nuzzled her ear. "I just know what it looks like when I see two people in love." His warm breath wafted over her cheek.

Addie pushed him off her and sat upright. "There's another motive!"

"What?" Simon blinked at her and raked his hand through his thick black hair. "As you say, I really didn't see anything happen between them. I just found it interesting, that's all."

"Interesting is right." Addie sprang to her feet, spun around, and studied the board. "What if Jean Pierre is having affairs with Veronica"—she pointed to a line on the board—"Maggie, his sous-chef, *and* Annabel, Veronica's daughter-in-law? That's a pretty good motive to knock off two reporters snooping around, isn't it?" She glanced at Simon still sitting on the bed. "And you didn't think to lead with this tidbit of information when you knocked on my door?"

"I didn't knock." He rose to his feet and placed his hands gently on her shoulders. "And besides, I wasn't thinking about what they *may* have been doing before I arrived. When I saw you looking all morning-dewy fresh"—he nuzzled into her neck—"I was only thinking about my own kisses that would be waiting for me."

She placed a glancing kiss on his lips. "You weren't completely wrong," she said with a light chuckle as she wiggled herself free of his tight embrace. "But don't you see? Now we definitely have another good suspect to keep on the list." She glanced past his arm at the board and bit her lip in thought. "After all, I did see Lacey having words with Jean Pierre at the wedding, too. Maybe she told him or hinted that she knew what was going on and threatened to write a story about his dalliances. That would be a strong motive to kill her, wouldn't it?"

"What about Todd?"

"He and Lacey must have been working together. Maybe he, after hanging out the week before the wedding, discovered the affairs the chef was having and told Lacey. Then she came here under the pretense of attending her old friend's wedding only to discover her partner had been murdered."

"That alone might have given her motive to pretend she was drunk and push everyone's buttons at the reception, wouldn't it?"

"Yes," said Addie, "she'd be devastated herself and grieving the loss of her friend, so maybe she really dug her heels in to discover which one of these high society types killed Todd."

"And in the meantime, she got too close to the truth and wound up dead herself." Simon fixed his eyes on the clues Addie had written on the board. "It makes sense."

Addie picked up the pen from the dresser and circled *counterfeit books*. "Except what does the Agatha Christie book have to do with it and all the other fake first editions we've found in the library?"

"There has to be a link."

"Yes, but to Jean Pierre and his affairs with three women? What does that have to do with the fraud?"

"Could he also be behind replacing the original books with fakes and pocketing the money he makes off selling the originals on the black market for himself?"

She tapped the pen on her hand. "Maybe. I'll have to try to find out if he has a background in rare books."

"Would he need to know much about them? It could be

that he just saw a good opportunity and knew a good scam when he saw it. He's already leading on at least three women we know of, so there has to be something in that for him, too."

"You're right, and perhaps that's also a connection to the books. Veronica might be the one passing on information about Oliver's new acquisitions, and he puts in an order with the forger."

"So, they could be in it together?"

"Yes, or he's plying her for the information under the pretense of their affair, and she unwittingly tells him."

"What about the other two women?"

Addie shrugged. "Maybe he's just a womanizer on top of everything else."

Chapter 25

It took Addie forever to shoo Simon out the door so they could go in search of coffee. The fact that she needed to shower and dress before she could go anywhere made him even more reluctant to leave. However, he eventually relented but only after her promise of meeting him soon in the lounge was punctuated by a long, lingering kiss. It made her think that perhaps a few days of separation from each other had been worth it in the long run because reunions were so enjoyable.

She took one last look in the mirror at her two-piece halter-topped and billowing knee-length skirt, another beautiful creation from Hudson's Creations on Main. Pride surged through her at her cousin's amazing talents.

Unfortunately, it was the last wardrobe option in her bag. When she had packed it, she hadn't expected to be sequestered indefinitely after the wedding. She fluffed her hair, which she had left loose again today. She was almost out of shampoo and other toiletries and wondered if she could trust Simon enough to bring her more. She chuckled. If anything, it would be interesting to see the wardrobe choices he made for her.

Satisfied with her reflection, she surveyed the room for anything she didn't want the housekeeper's prying eyes to discover. To her horror she noticed the makeshift crime board was still on the bed where it had fallen when Simon tossed it aside and swept her into his arms. Snatching it up, she started to prop it, announcement side front, on the dresser and paused reading over what was written on the back. She shook her head. So many what-ifs, but there wasn't one concrete answer to any of the umpteen possibilities that were emerging.

They had discovered far more skeletons in Veronica's family closet than Addie would have thought possible. Everyone from Veronica, to Annabel—provided Simon's hunch was correct—to Veronica's personal assistant, Donna—based on the conversation she'd overheard—to the philandering French chef Jean Pierre, and the ever-loyal Wesley Harbinger. They all seemed to have a secret they probably wouldn't think twice about killing to keep out of the news. And all these people listed on her board had been seen having verbal confrontations with Lacey only hours before her murder. Not to mention Ryley. Now, she was one Addie wasn't sure about, given the detective's stellar reputation, but still . . . it did leave itself open to question given that Ryley was apparently now in charge of the case.

Addie dropped the announcement board into place and

headed down the passageway to the Edwardian lounge, turned right, and stuttered to a stop. Speak of the devil. Ryley and Simon were in a deep conversation over by the coffee bar set along the far windows. Judging by Ryley's close body language, she was making full use of her new-found status as his supervisor.

The Me Too movement also applies to men! Addie fumed as she marched past the twosome and grabbed a cup from the tray on the table behind Ryley, making sure it clattered against the others as she seized it in her hand.

Ryley glanced over her shoulder at Addie, nodded, and laid her hand on Simon's forearm as she impressed on him the importance of keeping lines of communication between their offices open.

That's not all she wants to keep open by the look of it. She glared at Ryley's dark silky hair swaying gently with every word she uttered as she leaned in a little closer to Simon.

Addie snatched the coffeepot off the warmer, touched the pot, and scowled. It was barely warm. It appeared as though someone had turned the warming burner off. Better than nothing. She poured herself a cup, and before she could enjoy the first sip of tepid coffee, she caught sight of Ryley giving Simon a light shoulder bump as she simultaneously tucked her hair behind her ear.

That was a typical woman-on-the-manhunt maneuver and Addie swung around, the cup and pot in hand, ready to bring both crashing down on Ryley's head. She remembered as she lifted her arms that she was supposed to be an adult. Still, she needed to end this exhibition. Not only for poor Simon's sake because he appeared to be oblivious to the wiles of a woman on the prowl, as were most men, but also for Marc's sake. This woman had already done enough to hurt him.

With her cup full, she set the pot on the table and swirled around in front of Ryley and gave a stumble worthy of an Academy Award. Lukewarm coffee splashed all over the front of Ryley's white blouse.

"Oh, no!" cried Addie. "I'm so sorry. The rubber soles on my sandals seem to catch on this teak flooring all the time." Addie set her cup on the table and grabbed a napkin. "Here, I really hope no damage has been done. It didn't burn you, did it?" Addie mustered all the concern she could for this woman, who now seemed to have set her sights on Simon since she'd obviously gotten what she wanted out of her relationship with Marc. There was no way Addie was going to let that happen. Not now, not ever.

"No," Ryley said, blotting the napkin over the front of her blouse, "but it does look like I'll have to go get my blazer from the library to cover this." Her darkened gaze met Addie's. "I'll be back later, and Simon"—she turned to him with a slight smile edging at the corners of her lips—"we can finish our discussion then." Her eyes narrowed as she glanced back at Addie, made a wide arc around her, and marched across the lounge and out into the passageway.

Simon stroked his chin, and his brow arched in question as he gazed firmly at Addie.

"What?" she asked.

"Somehow, I don't think that was"—he glanced down at her sandals and then met the most childlike gaze she could muster—"a shoe issue."

"Seriously? You think what just happened was . . ."

He nodded.

"Well . . . I had to do something. Don't you see what she's doing?"

He placed his hands gently on the tops of her arms. "Addie, do you have so little faith in my love for you?"

"No, it's her I don't have faith in. I mean, she just screwed Marc over, and now she wants to be all friendly and such with you. I tell you, she's up to something, and I don't trust her."

Simon smiled. "I agree, and I plan on discovering exactly what that is. Remember, keep your friends close but keep—"

"Your enemies closer, I know." Her gaze dropped. "She's not exactly an enemy though, is she?"

"No, but like you said, she had an altercation with Lacey, and there are four hours of that evening unaccounted for. So, I figure that until proven otherwise, she remains a suspect like about thirty other people on board right now."

She looked back up into his eyes. "Please, be careful around her until we can figure out what's going on."

"I promise." He kissed the tip of her nose. "But I'm afraid as much fun as this morning has been, I really have to get back to the lab. I've been running an analysis on fibers right now, and the final results should be ready."

"Could you do me an incy-wincy favor?"

"Sure."

"Could you go by my house and pack some clothes and toiletries for me?"

"Anything else you need?"

"No, I'm good for shoes." She glanced down at her

sandals. "So, I think just some clean . . . undies." She felt her cheeks grow warm. "And a few outfits for daytime activities. I have nothing else for evening in my closet, so I will have to make do with what I have. But I do need more shampoo, conditioner, and toothpaste."

"You got it." His lips softly grazed her cheek, and he turned to leave.

"Oh, and maybe you could swing by the bookstore and make sure everything looks okay. You know, no broken windows or anything."

"I hear Martha has been a vigilant protector, so I don't think you have to worry about that."

"I know. She told Paige, but I just feel so helpless stuck in here."

"Don't worry. I'm sure this will be over soon, and then we can all get back to normal."

"You're right. The murderer is bound to slip up sooner or later, and besides, we have to be out of this slip by to-morrow when the cruise ship arrives."

"Didn't Marc tell you?"

"What?"

"If they haven't cracked this by morning, the yacht will be towed out to deeper water and anchored in the harbor."

"I know, but let's hope at least some of us will be re-leased before then. Right now my attachment to Grey-borne Harbor and you being able to come and go at will is one of the only things keeping me sane. If we get towed out to deeper water, that means no more drop-by visits from you."

He titled her chin so she had to look him in the eye and placed a fleeting kiss on her lips. "I can't see him keeping you, Catherine, Paige, or his parents much longer. I think holding most of you is a show for the few who are on his actual suspect list."

"Let's hope you're right, but I guess it's Ryley's suspect list now. We can only hope she feels the same about releasing some of us when the time comes."

He squeezed her hands, and his departing smile gave her the confidence she needed.

Chapter 26

Addie gazed at Simon as his long, lithe body ambled effortlessly across the lounge and down the central staircase. A contented sigh escaped her throat. When he disappeared down the stairs, she scanned the room for Catherine and Paige. She spotted them seated on a love seat by the double door that led out onto the outside deck. Addie clutched her cup of cold coffee and scurried toward them.

"Good morning," she said, and took a seat in one of the two chairs across a small coffee table from them.

"My, my, aren't you late coming for coffee this morning?" Catherine asked with a teasing lilt to her voice.

Paige softly tittered as she picked up her coffee cup from the table. "Yes, we were about to send out a search party for you. That is until we saw Simon, and then we

figured the two of you had a bit of a reunion." Her cheeks
grew flushed. "But imagine our shock when Ryley made
a beeline for him at the coffee bar. And you were nowhere
in sight."

"I had to shower and dress," Addie said, glancing to
the spot where Ryley and Simon had stood. "I guess my
half-hour delay opened all kinds of windows to a door
that had been opened last night, by the way."

"What do you mean?" asked Catherine over the rim of
her cup.

Addie set her cup on the table and leaned forward. "It
seems that last night Ryley took Simon out to dinner
under the pretense of discussing the case."

"You're kidding!" Paige's cup clanged against the
saucer as she brought it down on the table hard.

Addie shook her head. "Then when I walked in and
saw her getting a little too cozy with him this morning—"

Catherine let out a snort. "You mean the coffee incident wasn't an accident?" She slapped her knee, her
laugh overtaking her.

Addie feigned an innocent expression and fanned her
cheeks. "Why, Miss Catherine, are you actually accusing
me of doing something childish and underhanded?"

Catherine tossed her head back and let out a howl.

"Yes, I think we both are," Paige coughed out with a
throttled laugh.

Addie waved them both off and glanced around the
room. "It looks like everyone on board is getting a case of
cabin fever and feeling the need for human companion-
ship. Even Melinda has joined us this morning." She nodded in the direction of the table where Melinda was deep
in conversation with Serena and Marc's parents.

Addie studied the woman. Melinda was far more attractive than the current Mrs. Ludlow. Her mid-shoulder, blond, under-curved bobbed hair held a glimmer of gray just around the hairline. She appeared to be the type of woman who wasn't trying to hide her natural color and pretend to be someone who hadn't earned every one of her gray hairs. Addie decided that even though Melinda was likely to be in her late fifties, she could easily pass for a woman in her early forties. Her fair skin appeared to have natural tautness and glow that definitely didn't come from the assistance of a surgeon's scalpel or Botox injections unlike Veronica's flawless complexion. Addie glanced at her friends. "You guys have gotten to know Melinda fairly well. What do you think of her as a suspect?"

"Not much," said Catherine, swirling the last of her coffee in her cup. "She's provided some very insightful information regarding Veronica and her previous husbands and has inferred that their deaths might not have been accident, or in the case of her second husband, natural causes. But, if you ask me, the poor old soul was helped to an early grave either by a medication overdose or perhaps even suffocation in his sleep. At least, that's what Melinda thinks."

"And Veronica's third husband, the lord?"

"As we discussed last night," said Catherine over the rim of her coffee cup, "it seems pretty suspicious according to what Melinda could learn from the private detective she hired." She sat forward on her seat and lowered her voice. "The week before he died, he had met with a lawyer. A divorce lawyer, mind you." She pushed herself back on the sofa, a glimmer of smugness on her face. "A week later he suffers a fainting episode while on a hunt, falls off his horse, and breaks his neck. Now you tell me that isn't at all suspicious."

"A divorce lawyer? Is she sure?"

Catherine crossed her arms and nodded.

Addie set her gaze on Veronica chatting freely with her New York City friends. "Not suspicious at all. Did Melinda hear what led up to the accident that killed husband number one?"

"Yes." Catherine peered at Addie over the rim of her cup. "She said he also suffered a dizzy spell and fell off his motorbike and crashed."

"But she said there was no evidence of poisoning in either case," added Paige.

Addie sought out Veronica's lawyer seated in a chair, sipping coffee and reading the newspaper. "And Wesley was working for her then, too."

"So was Donna. She started working for Veronica with her second husband. The one who died in his sleep." Catherine drained the last drop from her cup. "If you ask me, had Melinda wanted to kill anyone, it would be Veronica out of fear for Oliver, not the two reporters who might be working on a story that could crash Lady Veronica Easton-Ludlow's empire."

"I think you might be right, especially given that there is so much speculation surrounding her husbands' deaths?" Addie scanned the room again and took note of Donna sitting beside herself and reading a book. However, by her constant glances over the top of the page at Wesley seated not far from her, her mind was definitely elsewhere.

It made Addie wonder exactly what their relationship was. By the conversation she had overheard at dinner the night before, they seemed to be close but not friendly. "Did Melinda she say if anyone ever investigated Veronica's staff?"

"I think once the police found no linking evidence, it was only the lord's adult children who pursued the notion of foul play. They never trusted Veronica and felt there was something off with the timing of their father's death, given how bad the marriage had become. But Melinda said nothing conclusive came out of the private investigation they launched, either."

"Has Melinda mentioned how Donna came to be in Veronica's service?"

"She mentioned," Catherine said, "that Donna was her second husband's caregiver, and after he passed away, Veronica asked her to stay on as Preston's nanny. When Veronica shipped him off to boarding school, Donna then became Veronica's personal assistant. Why? Do you suspect Donna of being part of any of this?"

"Do you?" asked Paige. "Because from what I can see, she's a meek, mild little thing that keeps mostly to herself, and when Veronica says jump, she says how high."

Catherine laughed softly. "Well, you do know what they say about the quiet ones."

"She sounds very loyal though, doesn't she? Plus, she would have been there when hubby number two died." Addie gazed intently at the woman across the lounge.

Donna glanced up at Wesley again and then caught sight of Addie, and their eyes met. A light blush rose up Donna's cheeks, and she resumed reading. Except in the few minutes Addie had been watching her, she hadn't turned a page.

"Interesting, isn't it? She was the old gentleman's caregiver. He dies, and she gets the job of a lifetime, working for an extremely wealthy woman. At least she was after his passing, right?"

"Yes, but Veronica's first husband was extremely well off, too. According to Melinda, he was worth millions when he died."

"And then an English lord, who was most likely very well off, too." Addie studied Veronica with a new eye. She didn't just dislike her for the manner in which Veronica had treated Serena through the wedding planning, but now after hearing all this, Veronica could possibly have the biggest secrets here, ones she wouldn't want two reporters to disclose. But how did the books fit in with all this? She had to be missing a connection. Or was Jean Pierre the link?

Paige leaned forward and whispered, "I'm worried about Oliver and what Veronica might have planned for him."

"I am now, too." Addie's gut tightened at that thought. "I hope for Zach's sake we're wrong though." Addie's gaze flittered from Melinda to Veronica. "To be honest, I don't see the attraction Oliver has for the plastic woman over the natural beauty of his first wife."

"That's some men for you," said Paige. "They want the flattery and conquest of a fresh face. Just look at the way Simon was carrying on this morning with Ryley."

Addie's gaze shot back to Paige.

"Oh, Addie, I'm sorry. I didn't mean . . ." Paige hung her head. "I shouldn't have said that."

Catherine sat back in her seat and took a deep breath. "I think all this confinement is getting to all of us. I'm sure Paige wasn't implying that Simon would—"

"I'm sure she didn't." Addie laced her fingers together in her lap. "As a matter of fact, Simon and I discussed something similar, and he assures any attention he bestows on Ryley is only to discover her true intentions of taking over the case. Besides, she's still a suspect on the board because of her argument with Lacey that night and the four hours between the times she left the station and when Marc got home. It's only her word that she was at home in bed. In essence, she really doesn't have an alibi for the time of Lacey's murder."

Paige reached across the table and grasped Addie's hand. "I feel horrible for what I said and apologize. I wasn't thinking."

Addie nodded and sniffled back the tears that loomed behind her eyes. "It's okay." She didn't want to admit that Paige's words had hit home with her because she was beginning to fear the same thing even though she tried not to.

"I don't know about you two," said Catherine, rising to her feet, "but I could use another cup of coffee. I think there's enough left for half a cup each in that last pot."

"It's cold. Someone turned off the warmer," said Addie. "That's why I didn't feel too guilty about what happened earlier."

"I'm glad there was no risk of her getting scalded, but what you did do sure sent her hightailing it out of here fast enough. Funniest thing I've seen in days." Catherine laughed.

"Perfectly executed." Paige chuckled and lifted her cup in a toast.

Catherine glanced around the room. "Speaking of coffee, I haven't seen one staff person since we came in."

"Neither have I," chirped Paige. "The coffeepots were all full on the warmers and the trays of pastries were laid out, but there's been no one buzzing around like normal refilling our cups."

Addie looked around the large lounge. "You're right. I wonder where everyone is. It's unlike Veronica to allow her guests to go without." She pressed down on the arms of her chair and rose to her feet. "Something isn't right. I'll be back in a minute."

"If you find more coffee, bring it back with you," called Catherine.

Veronica's head swiveled and she glanced disdainfully at Catherine, then went back to the guest at her table.

Addie strode through the lounge, into the dining room, and headed for the back servers' counter. There was no sign of any staff, and the large coffee urn she found was empty. This was highly unusual, and she wondered why Veronica didn't appear to take offense over the lack of service for her guest. What was going on? Although, Addie wouldn't put it past Veronica to have instructed her staff to not show any more hospitality to them since they were trapped here and not invited to be on board for such a long stretch.

Addie slipped through the rear door into the foyer for the stairs, elevator, and outside deck entrance. Surely one of the deckhands would be out here, wiping down the deck chairs and washing the deck, as that was a regular morning routine, or at least, it had been. But as she blinked into the bright sunlight and scanned toward the bow and then the stern, she didn't see one deckhand.

As she rounded the dining room area at the stern of the

yacht, she heard a woman's hushed laughter coming from the canopied double-wide cabana on the deck stern. She strained to hear if it was a couple of delinquent staff members shirking their duties and tiptoed closer but stopped just before she reached the curtained enclosure when Annabel's laugh rose to a hearty pitch.

"Stop it, Jean Pierre." She giggled so hard she choked. "You know I have to get back. Preston will be out of the shower by now and he'll wonder where I am."

Silence, then the unmistakable murmurings of two people locked in a passionate kiss.

"Just a few more minutes." Jean Pierre's voice sounded cracked and breathy. "Don't leave me now. Tonight is too long for me to wait to meet here again."

"Stop, get off me. I have to go. You know as well as I do that if Preston ever found out about us, he'd divorce me and fire you, and then where would we both be? I certainly don't plan on being poor, do you? Stop it." She laughed and then moaned. "Really, I have to go. I'll meet you again tonight just like most every other night. Have I ever let you down?"

"No, but I can't wait, come here . . ."

She giggled, and then the murmurs continued. "I have to go now. I'll see you later after he falls asleep as usual. Until then . . ."

Addie stepped back and glanced around for a place to hide. Out of the corner of her eye, she caught sight of Preston peering around the curtain of the cabana on the far side of the stern.

When Annabel emerged from the enclosure, she fluffed her hair, straightened her day dress, and marched past Addie taking cover behind a lifeboat. Jean Pierre appeared moments later. He tugged at his trousers, tucked in his shirt, and headed around the stern toward the other entrance into the inside deck. Addie caught a glimpse of Preston. His gaze followed the chef's every move, and his fists bunched up in balls at his side.

It seemed Simon was right about what he suspected, and it looked like Preston may have just earned a place on her suspect board.

Chapter 27

The lovers' tryst that Addie had just overheard and the fact that Preston appeared to either have known about Annabel and Jean Pierre previously or had just learned about it would be a motive to kill two reporters. If the information about the affair between Veronica's lover and chef and her daughter-in-law were made public, it would cast a very dark shadow over the family. This truly was a dirty little secret so dark that one of those involved wouldn't want it exposed. The question was which one. It could be Veronica out of jealousy. It could be Jean Pierre afraid of losing his job or access to the books. It could be Annabel so that her husband wouldn't find out. Or it could be Preston out of rage that his wife would put him in the position of losing everything he along with his mother had worked so hard to attain.

Still lost in her thoughts, she hurried back through the

lounge toward the passageway to her stateroom. She needed to take another look at the crime board and see exactly what clues she and her friends had uncovered and how they could possibly all link together. She needed a more solid idea of who the killer on board might be.

She slowed her pace when she caught sight of Marc speaking on his phone outside the closed library door. When he saw her, he clicked off his call and shoved his phone into his police-issue jacket pocket. She glanced through the wall of windows into the library and stopped.

"What's going on in there?" she asked him with a gesture of her head. "Why are all the staff in the library?"

Marc glanced into the room and then back at Addie. "Ryley and Captain Nevins are interrogating them all again."

"The captain? That's a bit unusual, isn't it?"

"I think so, but Ryley feels he has insight into them and might be able to help her figure out who's lying about what went on those two nights. She also believes someone must have seen something that they don't remember which could have some bearing on the case."

"Really? Is that what you think, too?"

"I think the books play a big part in this given the evidence found. I guess it's also a way for her to discover if one of them might be behind the counterfeiting of the books."

"I agree but allowing them to all mingle together before their interview doesn't seem like protocol."

"I agree, but she hopes it might make them looser-lipped and someone might slip up. Jerry and Officer Jefferies are keeping their ears open for any revealing conversations that might happen between them."

"Hmm." She glanced at the twenty-four or so staff seated

around the room in conversation groups and then at Marc. "Are you okay?"

"I will be. I'm just on my way to a meeting with the mayor. That's who I was on the phone with."

"Did he call, or did you?"

"I did. I think there are a few things about the management of this case that need to be cleared up. I somehow have the feeling that things might have been . . . well, misrepresented, and I want to set things straight. So, if you'll excuse me." He nodded and headed down the passageway.

"Marc?"

"Yes?" He glanced back.

"When you return, there are a few things we've discovered, and I think we'd better talk."

He nodded. "See you soon and wish me luck. I hope the mayor can see past his close association with Ryley to understand what I'm about to tell him."

"Which is?"

"You don't put the fox in charge of the henhouse." He spun on his heel and disappeared through the passage doorway.

"Thatta boy, Marc." Addie smiled to herself. "Go find yourself a killer, whoever it might be."

After all, Ryley was still a possible suspect, and until her name was completely cleared, Marc was right. She should not be taking lead on the investigation. Addie shuddered at the thought of Marc having to arrest Ryley and felt equally as guilty when a grin came to her lips. She and Ryley had their own issues, but she wasn't certain that Ryley, given her background, could be a killer. Then she recalled the altercations Lacey and Ryley had the evening of the wedding. Perhaps Lacey, but why Todd? Or could there possibly be two killers on board?

It was possible that the two murders weren't related, except by the book, which could be pure coincidence. Maybe she had been looking at this all wrong. She dashed down the passageway to her room, bolted through the door, grabbed the board, and began reading what was already written beside Ryley's name, noting Ryley's four-hour time lapse and altercations with one of the victims. She quickly added, *Ryley taking over case* and *Cozying up to Simon—person in charge of testing evidence.* She stabbed the board with the pen to punctuate with an exclamation mark.

She read her last notes and plopped down on the bed. It was possible that Ryley's behavior was all in her mind and this was nothing more than a weekend of confinement and overthinking that made her see monsters everywhere. She knew from past experience that the jealousy monster was the worst and made one think what they saw was more than it actually was.

However, Marc also had Ryley on his radar as a suspect, and that must mean something. She tried to push all personal feelings aside and look at it logically. Perhaps his hunch was being clouded by his ego and the fact that she had taken over what he viewed as *his* case. Maybe she and Marc were just both feeding each other's insecurities at the time and seeing a monster dressed as a detective where there wasn't one.

But what about the books? How did they fit into it? The books could be a completely separate case, one only disclosed by pure accident because of the torn page and Lacey's blood on it. Was she trying too hard to make it all fit together into a nice little package? Addie flung herself back on the bed, feeling more confused than ever, and hoped that Felix could find some answers soon. There had to be a lead, at least to the book mystery, hidden in those files.

A knock on the door jolted her from her thoughts. "Who is it?" she called, propping herself up onto her elbow.

"It's me, Felix."

"Be right there." She hoisted herself up off the bed. "I was just thinking about you," she said as she opened the door. "Have you discovered anything else in those files?" She couldn't help but notice the dark circles etched around his eyes and wondered if he were feeling more stress about the books than he let on.

"I've been going through them with a fine-tooth comb all night, and I have noticed a bit of a pattern."

"Really?"

"Yes, it's too soon to get excited but . . ." He glanced both ways up and down the passage. "I thought since Nevins is in the library with the other staff, perhaps you'd like to join me on the bridge to engage in a little good old-fashioned detective work?"

"Why, what are you thinking?"

He glanced around again. "It got me thinking when you said that counterfeiter, Björn Svensson, was last seen in Cuba. I want to check something."

"Lead the way," Addie said, following him into the hall, locking her room door behind her.

"I just feel so responsible for all this."

"Why would you be responsible?"

He glanced sideways at her. "Because it happened under my watch, and I won't be able to sleep until I figure out how those books were exchanged. I know for a fact that none of the brokers or dealers I put Oliver in contact with would have swindled him like that. Which can only mean that someone on board this yacht had to have had an opportunity to make the exchanges."

"So right now, we're looking at which of our top suspects had opportunity."

"Yes, you know what they say in every criminal case, especially a murder case . . ."

"Yes," Addie added, "means, motive, and *opportunity*."

"Just my thinking," he said with a sly wink as he let her ascend the stairs ahead of him to the upper deck. "We have the means. I think we have the motive. Let's go see if we can find opportunity and narrow this down to a handful of suspects instead of thirty."

They reached the alcove at the top of the uppermost deck. The sign on the door read BRIDGE, AUTHORIZED PERSONNEL ONLY. To the left was a door leading out onto the sundeck and pool area. Addie glanced at Felix questioningly.

He produced a large key ring from his black trousers pocket and smiled. "One of the many perks of being the head of security. I have masters." He pushed the bridge door open and glanced around the large room framed on all sides by floor-to-ceiling windows except for the solid corner wall where electronic panels and tall filing cabinets were placed. "It's all clear."

Addie stepped inside and was taken aback by the sight of the long desk and line of computers, switches, and monitors of various sizes. "I guess a yacht like this isn't operated the same way that smaller vessels are. Where is the ship's wheel? Outside?"

Felix let out a little chuckle as he settled into a chair

behind a monitor. "Not for a long time, especially a ship this size. There's a small one on that panel, but it's all computerized now."

"Even the steering?"

"Yes, by way of that small wheel along with those buttons and levers." He laughed and pointed to a panel beside him. "There is a large wooden wheel out on the deck, but it's just for show or in case of computer malfunction. Otherwise, this is the heart of the ship's navigation."

"So, something as small as this switch actually controls the yacht's navigation?" she asked, reaching over his arm to a switch on the table panel.

"Don't touch that one."

"Why?" She stopped mid-motion. "Will it steer us into the pier?"

"Worse, it will broadcast our presence here to the entire ship. That's the overhead speaker system."

"No, we wouldn't want to do that." She withdrew her hand and stood back as he retrieved a small black notebook from inside his blazer and began tapping on the keyboard.

"What are you doing?"

"I have the pass codes to get into the system, so let's see if I can find what I'm looking for."

The screen lit up with the words *Access Granted*, and he typed in another code.

File Not Found

"That's strange." He punched in another set of numbers. *File Empty*.

Once more he tried again. *File Encrypted* flashed across the screen.

"I can't believe it." He sat back in his chair.

"What? What's wrong?" Addie said, leaning over his shoulder.

"The log files have been locked, and I don't have a code anymore for them."

"Is that unusual?"

"Yes, security is supposed to be able to access all computerized sailing records and have navigational control in case of an emergency. I'm locked out."

"Could it have been an error?"

"No, this would have had to have been done manually to bypass the system."

"Nevins?"

"Or the junior captain, Floyd Wright, or even the first officer, Calvin Carlyle. It would have to have been one of those three."

"Now what do we do?"

"We can wait until Nevins comes back and ask him to unlock the system or . . ."

"Or what?"

"Just in case he had something to do with this, I can attempt to break the pass code. I was fairly good at this cyber stuff once." He sat back, cracked his knuckles, wiggled his fingers, and entered in another code.

Login Failed

"Okay, I only have two cracks at this again before it locks down completely." He glanced at his notebook again, then up at Addie. "Perhaps you can look in that file cabinet while I try to figure out what the code is."

"Sure, what am I looking for?"

"Logbooks. It's a requirement that all vessels carry not only a computer file of their sailing history but also a hard copy. The computer data is the best to use, as it can't be falsified, but at least a printed record can tell me if I'm on the right track with my theory."

"Are they in file folders or what?"

"They should be in large black binders marked on the spine by year. I'm particularly interested in the last three years."

"Got it, now I know what I'm looking for." Addie skirted around a table of control panels and jiggled the handle of the tall file cabinet in the corner, but it didn't open. "You wouldn't happen to have a key for this, would you?"

"There must be one in the desk." Felix pulled on the top drawer beside him, but it didn't budge. He pulled out his master key ring, sorted through until he found a small silver key, and slid the drawer open. "Gotta love these," he said with a laugh as he set the keys down and dug around in the drawer. "Here." He handed her a small set of silver and gold keys. "One of those should work."

Addie tried the assortment of keys, and just when she was ready to give up, the last one clicked, and the file door opened in her hand. The entire cupboard was filled with tall, wide, black leather binders, with the years prominently marked across a white label on the spine. Her fingers trailed over each book as she read the year. "You said you were particularly interested in the last three years?"

"Yes, bring them here. I need to check the nautical data."

"Got them." She grinned and met his gaze. "They all seem to be here just as they should be." Addie pulled each binder from the shelf one at a time and set them on a console behind her. When she had then laid out in a row,

Felix shuffled over to her side, took off his glasses, and began flipping through the pages.

"I'm glad you know what you're doing because it all looks like chicken scratches to me," she said chuckling.

"See these numbers? They are latitude and longitude, and these are nautical speed, weather conditions, and ports of call. This column is the number of passengers on board, and this is the number of staff, which would be outlined in more detail in the junior captain's and the first mate's logbooks. I don't think we need them right now."

"But wouldn't it show which staff members were on board during the times you're questioning and help us narrow down the suspect list?"

"Yes, but it also shows complaints, issues, and anything to do with personnel. Right now, I'm more interested in discovering if there were any voyages to Cuba." His eyes scanned down the pages as he thumbed past one then another. He stiffened and flipped back a page and then turned it over again. "That's strange. There's a page missing here."

"What? Let me see," said Addie, leaning over his shoulder to check the dates on the top corner of each page. "You're right, and look." She pointed. "This shows a frayed edge in the crease."

"The page has been torn out!" Felix flipped through each of the three binders and slammed them closed. "Every date in question and then some have been removed."

"Wouldn't the captain notice they were missing?"

"Not necessarily. They would only be checked under an investigation by the Coast Guard or in case of complete navigational system failure. These missing pages, like the fakes in the library, may have gone unnoticed for years."

"Now what do we do?"

Felix glanced over at the computer and then back at the logbook. "Someone has gone to a lot of trouble to hide the dockings this yacht has made over the past three years. Before I get locked out of the system, I think I can e-mail that encrypted file to my computer and clear any trace of having done that."

"But you still can't open it?"

"No." He gave her a sly smile. "But I have lots of friends who can."

As Felix planted himself back in front of the computer, she gazed around the control room. "What's that gray metal box on the wall by the outside deck door?"

He glanced up to where she had indicated. "That's where the first-aid supplies and extra flare guns are stored."

"Flare guns?"

"Yes, why?"

"Didn't Marc tell you what I found?"

He shook his head and went back to the computer.

"Do you have a key for it?"

"I think it's on the ring here on the desk beside me."

Addie picked up the master key ring and sorted through the collection until she found the one that opened the cabinet. On first glance it appeared to only contain extra first-aid supplies. However, as she started to close the door, she realized there was another door on the inside of the cabinet door and swung it open.

"How many spare flare guns are generally kept in storage?"

"Umm, usually a replacement for each deck box in case of misfire or damage. Why?"

"So that makes twelve, right? One box on the stern and one on the bow of each deck?"

"Right," he said, coming to her side. "Is there a problem with them?"

"How many orange flare guns do you count here?"

"It looks like eleven, meaning one has been replaced for some reason in one of the deck boxes. Which, I don't understand because they've never been used as far as I know."

"What's the difference in their colors?"

"What do you mean?"

"Well, say the difference between an orange gun and a yellow one?"

"No difference. It just means they were purchased from a different distributor."

"When?"

"I don't know. I'd have to see if I can find a purchase receipt. Is that important?"

"It could be," she said, looking at the lineup of guns on the rack and the one empty space.

"By the look of these, they're fairly new. I know that according to regulation, they are all replaced in the outside boxes every few years in case of corrosion. That information would be in the maintenance logs."

"We need to look at those logbooks and see if there's a purchase receipt for the new flare guns recently."

"What does the color of the guns have to do with anything?"

She glanced up at him. "The one in the emergency box on deck four, the same deck the library is on, is orange like these newer-looking ones. All the others, above and below that deck, are yellow."

He scratched his head. "But they are all replaced at the

same time, not one at a time. Therefore one changed out doesn't make sense."

"Unless it was fired recently."

"Ah-huh, and probably was the murder weapon used on that fellow on the beach."

"Exactly!"

Chapter 28

Addie and Felix made their way down the main staircase in silence. All of this was pointing to the fact that someone, obviously a crew member, had a reason to hide the yacht's sailing records. This could only mean one thing. The yacht had docked in a port of call they didn't want made known. The receipt, from a marine supply company in Connecticut, for a dozen flares guns, which Felix found in the purchase records, pointed to the reason why Marc couldn't find a distributor close to the Greyborne Harbor area for a recent flare gun purchase.

"I'm heading down to engineering. They also, by marine law, have to keep log records. Engine usage, power, fuel consumption would all be outlined in more detail than the main logs. Plus, I'll check the flare gun replacement rotation dates."

"Good, and perhaps it's time to compare the dates to the junior captain and first officer's logbooks, too. Someone on board during those times obviously didn't want a few trips to be on record."

"You're right. I'll look into that, too." He glanced at his wristwatch. "Why don't we meet after lunch in my cabin so I can e-mail the encrypted file to a friend, and then I can fill you in on what I find out in the logbooks."

"Perfect. What cabin is yours?"

"Crew quarters, C-F. See you then." He continued out the end passageway door to the outside staircase access down to the engineering deck. Addie spotted two steaming pots of coffee across the lounge on the coffee bar. Feeling the need to top off her caffeine intake for the morning, she headed directly toward them.

"Addie!"

She spun around. "Marc, how did your meeting go?" she asked as he lighted the top step into the lounge, and she couldn't help but notice the sparkle back in his eyes.

"I'm just on my way to the library."

"And . . ." She studied his face for the telltale tic he had when he was hiding something, but his deadpan expression gave nothing away. "I only ask because I've come across some very interesting information." She dropped her gaze. "I wasn't sure if I should let you"—she swallowed hard—"or Ryley know about it."

"Let me put it this way. If you come across any information that might be helpful in this investigation, please bring it directly to *me*."

"Fantastic!" Her cheeks burned at her outburst. "I mean, I really didn't relish the thought of going to Detective Brookes. She would have just dismissed me anyway."

"And what makes you think I won't?"

"Because . . ." She caught the teasing glint in his eyes and let out a short laugh. "As a matter of fact . . ."

"So, you have something?"

"Lots."

"I should have known." His eyes fixed on hers. "I knew you wouldn't be able to stay out of this."

"How can I? I'm kind of a captive audience and have nothing better to do. You can't even tell me this time to go back to doing what I do best and that's running my bookstore."

"You're right." He let out a chuckle that filled the entrance. "Tell you what, let me go speak with Ryley and get this straightened out, and then I'll come back to the library, say"—he glanced at his watch—"about thirty minutes?"

"Great. I was just going to grab a coffee and take it outside. The sunshine is calling me, and I think I'm starting to get a bit of cabin fever."

"Enjoy," he said, and marched off toward the library.

Addie sniffed the aroma of fresh hot coffee she had craved since rising this morning to Simon's kisses. Now her day could finally begin, and she contentedly made her way out onto the sundeck to catch a few rays before she popped into the library to update Marc. The deck chairs were near capacity since the promenade deck above was still closed to guests, so she meandered her way toward the stern, stopping to briefly chat with Serena's parents and nodding a greeting to the other passengers she passed. When she reached the stern, she spied one available deck chair, scooted over to it, and dropped down on it to claim it, sloshing coffee over her hand in the process.

"Smart, Addie, really smart. You waited all morning for

hot, fresh coffee, and then you waste some." It dawned on her that since the coffee carafes had been refilled, Ryley and the captain must have finished the questioning. She glanced around the deck, hoping to see Jerry or Curtis to ask them, but there was no sign of blue uniforms anywhere. Oh well, she could ask Marc when she saw him. She closed her eyes and turned her face up to the bright, late morning sun. If she could purr, she would have.

This was pure bliss. She sipped her coffee and gazed through clear deck panels out over the water far out into the harbor. A smile of contentment spread across her face. The surface glistened like glass shining brilliantly under the sun, and she shielded her eyes, cursing the fact that she didn't have her sunglasses with her. She did manage to make out an array of pleasure craft and fishing boats bobbing up and down on the horizon, and it reminded her why she loved living in this harbor town, where she was never far away from sights like this. Her gaze scanned along the jagged coast, which wrapped its arms around the harbor, and came to rest on the tall red-and-white lighthouse perched on the rocky clifftop above the bay, creating a stunning effect as the shimmering waves thrashed against the rocks below it.

She laid her head back again and drew in a deep sigh. Yes, it was too bad this wasn't a vacation. She couldn't remember the last time she actually had one of those, but if this was a glimmer of what one would be like, then she was going to take a few minutes to enjoy it. No wonder Paige didn't mind having to stay put on the yacht. The poor girl had her hands full with being a single parent and working full-time. This was no doubt a good break for her. She was lucky her sister had offered to keep Emma at the Cape with her cousins another week.

Addie wasn't certain if she'd dozed off or not, but she jerked at the raised voice coming from the cabana to her right.

"I can't believe you're still carrying on with him," Wesley's voice hissed through the closed curtain.

"But Daddy, I love him."

"Love," he scoffed. "You aren't in a position to love anyone except your husband, a husband that it took me years to arrange a marriage to. If you recall, her *Ladyship* thought you a little too trite and common for her precious son."

"Yes, I know, I know, and I'm grateful, but Preston is so . . . boring."

"Look, missy, boring or not, he's the ticket to your secure financial future, and if you blow it with him, you'll end up penniless. Much like I will if Veronica ever discovers you're fooling around with her boy toy. Do I make myself clear? What was that? I can't hear you."

"Yes, Daddy."

"Do you really think I have worked so hard all these years to keep her name unsoiled so that we could enjoy this lifestyle only to let you have it all taken away from us with a snap of her fingers?"

"No, Daddy."

"Not to mention that Veronica has a way with dealing with *people* who stand in her way of getting what she wants."

"But Preston has an insurance policy for our future, so don't worry. Even if she finds out about Jean Pierre and me, we'll all be fine financially."

"Not if you're dead and I'm kicked out on my penniless butt. I demand you end this nonsense now, or you know she could well end you."

The curtain flew back, and Wesley stomped off across the stern to the far interior deck entrance.

"Daddy?" Addie wheezed. *Wesley is Annabel's father?*

Now bits of the weird conversation she'd overheard between him and Donna made some sense, but how did Donna play into it all? Why was she so concerned about Annabel's happiness? Addie's mind raced, recalling clues on her crime board, but it was no use. Every time she thought she had something figured out something else came to light, and the web got even more tangled. Given what she'd just heard, it was obvious to Addie that Wesley did know about Veronica and the chef's affair—not to mention his knowledge of his daughter's trifling with the same man. Oh my, this was indeed a sordid web of lies and deceit, and the whole thing was starting to look like one of those British upstairs-downstairs types of television shows.

However, the statement Wesley had made about how Veronica had a way of with dealing with *people* who stood in her way was what made Addie wonder how many secrets the lawyer was keeping for Veronica. Even so, it was Wesley's last comments to his daughter that made Addie fear for Annabel's life, too. She needed to tell Marc now.

To heck with waiting the thirty minutes—she sure didn't want a third murder to happen in the middle of all this, not at least if she could stop it.

Chapter 29

Addie tapped on the glass door to the library. Elli's police officer boyfriend, Curtis, looked up from the notes he'd been reading, waved, and opened the door.

"Hey, Addie, how's it going?"

"Okay, I guess. I'll be happy to get home. How's Elli managing with running Serena's tea shop on her own through this? I had hoped I could send Paige over occasionally to help her out, but . . ."

"Don't worry. She's commandeered her grandmother Vera into working with her. I must say, I don't think I've ever seen the woman so happy. I think she's one of those not cut out for retirement."

"That's great. Serena will be relieved."

"She is. She calls Elli at least twice a day to check on things."

"That sounds like Serena. I knew she wouldn't be able to keep her hands off and enjoy her vacation."

"It sounds like she's enjoying their trip though. She keeps telling Elli about all these new ideas she has that she's picking up from the little tea shops over there. She told Elli they're having a blast exploring, when they're not cruising the waterways, and taking in the scenery of the old castles and little villages."

Addie glanced over to the closed office door and then back at Curtis. "Did Elli mention anything about what's going on here?"

"Not as far as I know. Marc gave her the lecture on ruining the honeymoon, and I don't think she wants any responsibility if Serena were to find out now."

"Let's just hope everyone is that tight-lipped and fingers crossed that Serena will forgive us when she gets back. I know she's going to be upset with us for not telling her what happened."

"I know, but what can she do from over three thousand miles away? It would only ruin their holiday. All this will still be here for her to face when they get home."

"You're a wise young man," Addie said with a laugh.

"What can I do for you? This room is still in lockdown, you know."

"I know, but I was wondering if Marc's free for a few minutes."

"He's in a meeting with Detective Brookes right now, but I can tell him that you're looking for him when he comes out."

Addie scanned the bookshelves and noticed a number of wide empty spaces. "If it's okay with you, could I just wait in here? There are a couple of things I want to check out."

"I don't know." He glanced from her to the office. "One of them might have my head for it."

"I was called in earlier to consult on the books, and I promise I won't touch anything," she said, hoping her puppy dog eyes would do the trick. "Please?"

"Okay, I guess it's all right then," he said, and stepped aside, allowing her entry.

She skirted past him into the otherwise empty room. "Where is everyone else? I thought Jerry and his crime team would still be working in here."

"No, the chief sent Jerry on an errand, and the rest of the crew is up on the promenade deck."

"Are there new developments?"

"I'm not at liberty to say." He tucked his thumbs into his police utility belt.

Addie couldn't help but think how young he looked, more like a teen dressed up for a costume party than a police academy new recruit. "Of course not." She smiled and strode over to the bookcase.

"Are you looking for anything in particular?"

"No, I was just curious to see what other books Felix removed as suspicious based on what he discovered in the files."

"So, you really are involved in all this?"

"Yes." She glanced over at him and smiled and then returned to scanning the shelves.

He slid up beside her and whispered, "Then, maybe it's okay if I tell you where Jerry went."

Addie set an eager gaze on his soft brown eyes.

"He's gone to find Mrs. Ludlow. I think the chief is about to make an arrest."

Addie staggered a step backward. "Seriously?"

"Yes, the chief has come across some information that he wants her to answer to, and if she can't . . . well then." He lifted his shoulders in a shrug.

Jerry pressed the sliding door button and gestured with his hand for Veronica to step inside. A very agitated-appearing Veronica turned up her nose and marched past him. With a glaring glance, she scanned the room, not even acknowledging Addie's or Curtis's presence.

"Where is this chief of police who has ordered you to take me away from my guests?"

Jerry knocked on the office door. It opened a crack and then swung wide open. Ryley bolted past him, smacked the door button, and darted out into the passageway. She dug her phone out of her blazer pocket and paced in the passage while she made her call.

Addie glanced from the flurry of the detective's abrupt departure to Marc in the office door. His facial expression showed no tells as he greeted Veronica and ushered her into the office, closing the door behind her.

Jerry glanced over at Addie, shrugged, and started out the door.

"Wait," Addie said in a hushed tone, and dashed over to him. "What's going on?" She dropped her voice to a barely audible whisper. "Did Marc figure out that Veronica's previous husbands died under suspicious circumstances? Does that make her the number one suspect in killing two reporters?"

Jerry pulled up to his full height and stared down at her. "Do you really think I can answer that for you? Come on, Addie, you know better."

"I know, but there's also a list of other suspects. That's why I'm here waiting to talk to Marc."

He fiddled with his belt buckle. "And just who do you have on that list?"

She leaned in closer to him. "Well, Preston for one. He knows Annabel is having an affair with Jean Pierre, the chef, who is also having an affair with Veronica and Maggie, his sous-chef."

Jerry's brows rose to his receding hairline.

"Any one of them could also be the murderer. This isn't the kind of dark secret none of them would want to come to light."

"I see." He rose up onto his toes and gazed past her to the closed door. "Is anyone else on that list?"

"Yes, but I don't have a name yet. It seems it might have something to do with the fake first editions though."

"How so?"

"Because Felix and I went to the bridge to check out the logbooks and there are some pages missing. I think someone is trying to hide some of the ports of call made over the last three years."

"Why?"

"Because the counterfeits we discovered were of an extremely high quality, and there is only one bookbinder I'm aware of who has those skills and he was last seen hiding out in Cuba."

"And the chief doesn't know any of this?"

She shook her head. "I've only just found out all this."

"Hmm." Jerry rubbed his thumb over his chin and knocked on the office door.

Marc flung the door open. The set of his jaw told Addie he was not pleased about being interrupted during an interrogation.

"Sorry, Chief. But could we have a word?"

Marc glanced over his shoulder. "I'll be with you in a moment, Mrs. Ludlow." He stepped out into the library and closed the door.

Jerry gestured with his head toward the reading alcove by the sliding doors out to the deck. Marc followed him, and the two disappeared around the corner of a bookcase.

Addie edged closer to the end of the bookcase, straining to hear what they were discussing but could only make out muffled words. A moment later the passageway door slid open. Officer Jefferies entered, stopped, and marched over to where Jerry and Marc were talking. There were more muffled words, and then Jefferies left the way he had come in. Addie heard the outside deck door swoosh open and then close, and Marc appeared around the end of the bookcase.

"Jerry just told me the information you shared with him. Thank you for bringing it to our attention. I have him collecting Preston right now, and he'll interview him again up in the deck five dining room. Jefferies just went to get Jean Pierre, and I'll speak to him in the lounge up there."

"Thanks for taking my information seriously," she said with a wobbly smile. "I wasn't sure with everything going on." She glanced out into the hallway just as Ryley shoved her phone back into her pocket and slapped the door button.

"I have to go to a meeting," Ryley called out. "I'll be back later." She spun around, not waiting for an answer.

Addie glanced at Marc and noted the telltale tic in his jaw.

"I'd better get back to my interview." He nodded at Addie and disappeared back inside the office.

Addie dropped down onto the overstuffed sofa. The leather surrounded her like a warm glove, and her hand stroked the supple covering. Never in her life had she touched leather so velvety soft. Dollar signs clicked through her mind like ticker tape. "Must be nice," she muttered, and laid back and closed her eyes, embracing the comfort.

When the passageway door behind her swooshed open, she half expected it was one of Marc's officers. She chose to ignore the minor intrusion into her momentary cozy state of mind. There was no doubt about it, she hadn't felt this relaxed in days, no, weeks, given the pre-wedding festivities and drama.

"Addie? Are you sleeping?"

"Simon." She shot straight up. "No, just resting my eyes."

"I have your bag." He tapped the extension handle to the wheeled suitcase at his side.

"I didn't expect you back this soon. Are you done in the lab? Did you get a match for those fibers?"

"Hold on there. Don't I even get a hello kiss?" He leaned over the back of the sofa, and his lips grazed hers.

"Mmm, of course you do. As a matter of fact"—she clasped his face in her hands and pulled him closer, causing the brown envelope under his arm to flutter to the floor—"I would like one more."

"Just one?" he murmured as his lips nuzzled hers.

"I think you dropped you something," she said, her lips still caressing his cheek.

"It can wait." He stumbled and barely caught himself from going over the back of the sofa onto her lap and tossed his head back in a raucous laugh. "Not the best position, I guess." He straightened his jacket and drew in a deep breath. "I saw Paige and Catherine sitting with Donna in the dining room." He held out his hand to help her to her feet. "Should we join them? I'm starving."

When Addie didn't respond to the offer of his hand, he frowned. "Aren't you hungry? It's been a while since breakfast."

"Actually, I think I'm going to wait in here for a bit."

He glanced at the office door. "Why? Who's in there?" He reached down and picked up the envelope before joining her on the sofa.

"Marc is interviewing Veronica," she whispered. "There is a rumor that he might be making an arrest."

"Veronica?"

"Yes, it seems she's at the top of his list because of the questionable circumstances surrounding her three previous husbands' deaths."

"Okay." He took her hand in his and laced his fingers through hers, resting their hands on his thigh. "We'll wait to see what happens."

"What's in that?" She gestured to the large manila envelope.

"It's my final autopsy report for Marc."

"I thought he already had it."

"No, he had the preliminaries." He tapped the envelope. "But this is the final result, and since I was bringing your bag, I thought I might as well drop it off in person. Besides"—he glanced sideways at her—"lunch smelled amazing."

She chuckled. "If you're hungry, go ahead and eat, but I know if I'm not here when they come out, it will be like pulling teeth to find out what happened."

"I can wait." He brought her hand to his lips and softly kissed it.

She grinned, leaned her head on his shoulder, and scanned the bookshelf in front of her. She sat up and looked at Simon. "Did the books on either side of *The Mysterious Affair at Styles* have Lacey's fingerprints on them?"

"No, Todd's were on a lot of them, but not hers. Why?"

Addie glanced back at the space where she had found the book and at the books standing on either side. "That proves that Lacey opening that book wasn't happenstance. She hadn't been searching through the shelf, looking for a book with a torn page. She knew which one it was. But how, and why that particular book?"

The passageway door swooshed open, and Jerry darted in and knocked on the door. Marc opened it, and Jerry gestured with his head for Marc to come out.

Marc stepped out and closed the door. "I'm in the middle of getting a confession." He stepped away from the door, glanced at Addie and Simon, and nodded.

"From Veronica?"

"Yes."

"That's what I came to tell you. I just got a full confession from Preston."

"What?" snapped Marc. He fixed his gaze on Jerry's. "How can that be? Moments ago she told me she had killed both victims."

"Did they work together?" asked Simon, rising to his feet.

"Not according to Preston," said Jerry. "He said he acted alone."

"Where is he now?"

"Upstairs. I have Curtis watching him while he writes out his statement."

"I've just left Veronica writing out hers." Marc scrubbed his hand through his thick, dark hair. "I'm going to need to see that as soon as Preston's done. Something isn't right with this."

"It sounds like," said Addie, joining them, "they each feel the other *might* be guilty and are taking the blame to cover for the other. After all, they are mother and son."

"This just couldn't be an easy case, could it?" Marc all but spat out. "First, I have over fifty suspects, and now we have people confessing left and right. Bring me his statement as soon as it's done." In an odd show of emotion, he punctuated that with a slam of his hand on the nearby bookshelf.

Addie jumped.

He glanced at her. "And why are you still here?"

"We were waiting for me to give you this," Simon said, holding out the envelope.

"What is it?" Marc turned it over in his hand.

"It's my final autopsy report." Simon grabbed Addie's hand. "But we'll get out of your way now." He tugged Addie toward the door.

"Wait," said Marc, his voice softening. "Is there anything different in here from the prelims you sent over?"

"A few things I've managed to come to a final conclusion on."

"Such as?"

"Well," Simon said, dropping Addie's hand. "I couldn't identify with absolute certainty the fibers I found on Lacey's clothes because the saltwater she'd been submerged in washed away some of the pigment and degraded the specimens, but they are definitely carpet fibers. As to the type of carpet . . ." He shrugged.

Addie glanced to the discolored area on the floor.

"Anything else?"

"Yes," said Simon. "Lacey's killer was probably male, based on the force of the blow. Given the angle of the contusion on the back of the head, he is at least between six feet and six foot three and right-handed."

Marc glanced back at the office door and then at Simon. "You figure it was a man?"

"Or . . . a very muscular woman. The fatal wound shattered the base of her skull."

"How tall would you say Preston is? Just a guess."

Simon glanced at Addie then back at Marc. "Ballpark figure? I'd say five-eleven."

"Then he might be the one she's covering for?"

"But Marc," Addie chirped in, "he's a beanpole. I don't think he's ever worked out a day in his life, do you?"

Marc heaved out a deep sigh. "Veronica is fit."

"Yes," added Addie, "and she's fairly tall but not close to six foot, more like five-ten."

"You're right." Marc tapped the envelope in his hands. "That means we have two people who don't fit the probable size or build of Lacey's murderer confessing to both murders. Why?"

"It seems to me they are afraid the other one is guilty just as Addie said earlier," said Simon.

Marc smacked the envelope with his finger. "Or

they're covering for someone else, perhaps someone they had do the dirty work for them so they could keep their own hands clean."

"Then why confess at all?" asked Addie.

"Good question." Marc placed his hand on the doorknob. "I'm interested to see the details in their statements."

Chapter 30

A ddie had not been invited to sit at the table in the library alcove, but at least she hadn't been ordered to leave. She made her way to the far end of the bookcase and strained to listen to the hushed conversation Marc, Jerry, and Simon were having as they reviewed both Preston's and Veronica's confession statements. Their words were often muffled by the noise of the A/C kicking in, but she managed to pick up a few details that told her exactly what she had felt in her gut from the beginning. There was no way either of the confessors could have committed the murder. Neither were the right height or build, and neither of them had known all the undisclosed evidence found at the crime scenes.

"So, in conclusion," Marc's voice rose, "we're back to square one, right?"

"It looks like it," added Simon. "Neither of them knew

the victim had been wrapped in a rug to move the body out onto the deck, and neither of them could name an object that was used as a murder weapon."

"Yeah," muttered Jerry. "Preston actually said he pushed her forward, and she hit her head on the bookshelf, which knocked her out, and then he carried her to the deck railing and tossed her over."

"She had no frontal contusions."

"That's what I mean. Gentlemen," Marc's voice dropped, "we're back to two family members attempting to confess to a murder which they clearly did not commit. The question is why?"

"They are definitely guilty of something though," added Simon, "and each thinks the other *could* have committed it."

"But most likely," said Jerry, "they are covering for someone else."

"At least," said Marc. "This final autopsy report helps narrow down the list of suspects. I think that this afternoon we'll be able to release some of the guests based on this."

"What do you want me to do with Preston?" asked Jerry.

"The same thing I'm going to do with Veronica. Give them access to the yacht but don't allow them to speak to each other. Watch them like a hawk and note their movements and who they do speak with. Then we'll see what happens this afternoon when I call everyone into the lounge and let them know we have come across some new information and are releasing some of them based on that."

"Do you think that's wise?" Simon's voice sounded

strained. "I mean it could put everyone left on board at risk. The killer might panic."

"Panic . . . or show their hand?"

"True," agreed Simon. "But if you allow everyone to leave who doesn't fit the characteristics of the murderer, won't that send out a signal to the murderer, who might then become desperate and do something rash?"

"What are you suggesting?"

"Perhaps allow some of the more obvious guests to leave like your parents. They were fond of Lacey if I'm not mistaken."

"*Were* is the key word there." Marc coughed. "Not for a while now, though."

"Okay," said Simon, "but your father is tall. However, he's also left-handed. Your mother isn't the right height, and neither are their friends the Andersons. Addie, Catherine, and Paige are obvious choices to allow to leave, and so is the first Mrs. Ludlow—"

"Not her. She might be one that is covering up a secret she doesn't want revealed and may have put someone up to do the killings for her."

"Scratch her then. What about the Ludlows' friends from New York?" asked Simon. "It's clear to me that the gentleman is not in good health, and his wife is too small and frail to have committed either murder. I can't imagine either of them chasing Todd Brown down the beach to catch him and shoot him let alone lifting Lacey's body over the deck railing."

"All right, they can all go, but the rest stay," said Marc. "They are either family or have a strong connection to the Ludlow family and might be covering something up." The sound of a chair scraping on the teak flooring made

Addie cringe. "But none of the staff," he added. "They haven't anyplace else to be, and someone might be thinking that by killing two reporters, they were going above and beyond in protecting their employers and securing their jobs. If we keep the police presence strong, I don't think the killer will strike again. Besides, the evidence points to the fact that whoever did this was trying to keep a secret from becoming revealed. Nothing points to them as being a homicidal maniac."

"Lunch should be wrapping up now, Chief," said Jerry. "Do you want me to go in and make an announcement that you would like to meet back in the lounge on this deck at three?"

"Yes, let's see what falls from the tree when we give it a shake."

With the voices drawing closer, Addie scooted back to the sofa and dropped into it as the men came around the corner. Marc paused and stared at her, his sheepish look telling her he had forgotten she was still in the library. "I trust you overheard the plan?"

She felt heat creeping up her neck to her cheeks and nodded.

"I would like you to stay on board if you don't have a problem with that?"

Not what she was expecting to hear. What happened to her keeping her nose out of an investigation? She glanced up at him questioningly.

"We might need your expertise on the books because I think you're right. They have something to do with the murders."

Addie's brow rose.

"Simon told me how you pointed out there weren't any fingerprints on the books on either side of the one we discovered Lacey's blood on. Jerry confirmed that he found none of her prints on any of the other books, which means—"

"She knew which book to look for." Addie snapped her fingers. "What if Todd had gotten a message to her and told her he was going to leave a note in that book for her, something that she could use in their story?"

"It's a possibility, but I also believe that your discovery of the counterfeit first editions might be the clue to what they were working on. We just need to figure out who it was and how they pulled it off," he added.

"Felix and I are working on a theory regarding just that," Addie said, "and we'll bring you any concrete information our hunch turns up."

Marc nodded and glanced at Simon. "Can we talk for a minute?"

"Sure." Simon looked apologetically at Addie and followed Marc into the office.

"Where have you been?" asked Paige as Addie took a seat after grabbing a coffee from the side table, and joined her, Catherine, and Donna in the dining room. "You've missed the best lunch ever," Paige added, handing Addie the small porcelain creamer container on the table.

"Thank you." Addie gratefully took it and poured a small amount into her cup. "It smells delicious, too, but I got tied up with something." She glanced to the nearby depleted lunch buffet table. "Maybe there's still hope of getting something," she said, stirring her coffee. "I'll be right back."

Addie made her way down the table and placed a small ladle of the last dregs of the soup from an urn into a bowl and balanced it on her plate. To her disappointment, all the buffet pans had been scraped clean, so she settled on adding a couple of sandwich wedges to her plate and returned to the table.

Catherine eyed her plate and scowled. "Is that all you're going to eat?"

"There's not much left, but this is fine," she said, and slurped up a spoonful of her lukewarm soup. "It's my own fault for losing track of the time." She glanced at Donna seated precariously on the edge of her chair as though she were about to bolt. "It's nice to finally get to spend some time with you, you know, now that the madness of the wedding is over."

"Yes," Catherine chirped in, "Donna here has been a wonderful lunch companion. We spotted her sitting alone and asked her to join us." Catherine smiled at the doe-eyed woman and leaned her elbow on the table, cupping her chin in her hand. "As a matter of fact, she was just telling us how she's worked for Veronica for over thirty years."

"Really," said Addie, "then you must know her and the family fairly well."

Donna nodded but remained mute as she wiped her mouth with a napkin and avoided making eye contact with Addie but instead focused her gaze to the table on her left.

Addie glanced over at Annabel, who was rising from her seat with Veronica and Oliver. The conversation she'd overheard between Wesley and Donna when she was trying to find her not-so-lost earring rushed back to her.

"I heard you met Veronica when you were working as her second husband's caregiver, is that right?" Addie sipped her coffee and fixed her gaze on the woman across the table.

"Yes, Mr. Buckley was such a sweet, kind man. I was in his service for a few years before he married her Lady-ship."

"And when he passed, you stayed on as her assistant?"

"Not exactly." Donna shifted uneasily in her chair. "You see, Miss Veronica had only just given birth to Mas-ter Preston when her husband passed away. She was so distraught by it all that she asked if I would remain on as the baby's nanny."

"I see." Addie set her cup on the saucer, causing more of a rattle than intended. "And Wesley? Was he employed by Veronica then, too?"

A flush came over Donna's cheeks, and her gaze dropped. "Yes, he's been her personal lawyer since be-fore she married the older Mr. Buckley."

"So, you've known Wesley for thirty years also?"

Donna nodded and pushed her coffee cup away from her. It was clear to Addie that this conversation was mak-ing her uncomfortable, but it was all ancient history. Or was it?

"Did you know Wesley's wife also?"

Donna's flush turned crimson. "We . . . met a few times. Why?"

"Just that Annabel is what, about . . . twenty-eight? So it must have been a really exciting time in their lives when she was born."

"She's twenty-seven, and yes, I was there when they adopted her."

"Oh, I didn't realize she was adopted."

"Yes. It was common knowledge that Mr. Wesley's . . .

wife couldn't conceive and then Annabel came along . . . she was such a blessing in their lives." Donna's eyes misted over, and she glanced at Annabel standing with her hand on the back of her chair sharing a laugh with one of the servers.

Addie couldn't help but notice the love in Donna's eyes as she watched the young woman and it gave Addie another idea. "So." Addie edged closer in her chair and dropped her voice. "Did you also work as Annabel's nanny? You know, look after both her and Preston?"

"No, Annabel had her own nanny."

So much for that theory. "When did you go from being a nanny to a personal assistant, if you don't mind my asking?"

Donna fidgeted with the napkin on the table and seemed to be formulating her thoughts. "I . . . um, took some time off when Master Preston was around three. My sister was ill, and I had to go and care for her," she added quickly. "When I returned to Miss Veronica's estate, she had sent Preston off to boarding school and asked me to remain on as her companion and personal assistant." She pushed her chair back. "I really must be going. I haven't seen her Ladyship for some time now, and she'll be fit to be tied if I don't manage her daily correspondence. If you'll excuse me." She smiled shyly and headed toward the main staircase.

Catherine and Paige leaned across the table and stared at Addie. "What was all that about?" Catherine's gaze held a reflection of disbelief. "You were all over the place with your questions and grilled that poor woman as though she were a suspect."

Addie's gaze darted from watching Donna disappear

down the stairs to Catherine's and Paige's wide eyes. "And she may well be."

"Based on what? Because she has worked for that witch," Paige's voice dropped, "for so long?"

Addie leaned toward them. "I told you about the strange conversation I overheard between her and Wesley when I was looking for my earring. Well, just seeing her now and comparing her appearance to Annabel's, I think I know another secret that someone wants to keep quiet enough to kill for."

"What?" whispered Paige, glancing over at Veronica's table.

"At first, I thought her concern for Annabel's happiness was because she had been her nanny, too, but then when she said Annabel was adopted, I now think Annabel is Wesley and Donna's daughter. Why else would Donna have been so worried about Annabel?"

"Really?" said Catherine. "Now that you mention it, the first time I saw Annabel. I instantly assumed that Donna was her mother and was surprised to hear that she wasn't."

"You mean"—Paige leaned into Addie—"that you think Donna and Wesley had an affair after they met, Annabel was the result, and Donna gave custody over to Wesley and his wife?"

"It makes sense to me. If they had a child together from an affair, wouldn't they want to keep the baby close, especially if Wesley, who is also the lawyer, was the baby's father? It would make sense that he would make arrangements to adopt it with his wife, who was probably oblivious to the child's lineage, but that way, Donna could still be part of her baby's life. Think about it, it makes perfect sense. After all, she just told us she took some time off to look after her sister." Addie waggled her fingers in air quotes. "Why else would she be so invested in Annabel's future and happiness? I tell you, the look in Donna's eyes when she watched Annabel a few minutes ago was love, motherly love."

"Or, maybe it's because she's known Annabel her whole life and feels protective toward the girl," said Paige. "Besides, what makes you think that Wesley is the actual birth father, it could have been anyone that Donna had a baby with."

"You're right, but from what I overheard when I was looking for my earring, those two have a personal history together aside from knowing each other for thirty years. I have a gut feeling that Annabel is their link. Look, there's Wesley out on the deck. I'll be right back."

Catherine grabbed her arm and pulled her down to whisper in her ear. "Addie, you can't just walk up to him and ask him if he had an affair with Donna and then adopted their baby with his wife."

"You're right. I'll figure something out though."

Chapter 31

Addie, still spying on Wesley through the lounge window as she made her way to the door, paused when Donna joined him at the railing. Addie excused her way out of the lounge onto the deck, stopped briefly to make small talk, and then ambled over to a deck chair not far behind the couple. She grabbed a beach towel from the stack on a nearby linen trolley and slipped into the chair, covering as much of herself as she could without looking too conspicuous.

"I think Serena's friend, that Addie Greyborne, knows about us and Annabel," said Donna, her voice wobbling as though she were on the verge of tears.

"Don't be ridiculous. Not even Veronica knows she's *our* daughter."

"Not yet but imagine how she would react if she discovered you set up her son with our little girl. Didn't you tell her the child's mother was an heiress's illegitimate baby and the family had arranged for the adoption at the time?"

"Something like that."

"Then I'm fairly certain that if she discovered her real lineage, she would have the marriage annulled, and both you and I would be out of jobs. Do you want that?"

"No, but don't worry about it. I'm certain our secret is safe now. Not even Annabel knows we're her real parents, and she never will, so keep your mouth shut."

With that he swiveled around and started toward the stern. Donna chased after him and tugged on his blazer sleeve. "It's not me I'm worried about. Too many people are starting to put two and two together."

He shook her hand loose and barged through the rear door of the dining room.

Addie pulled the towel up over her face and pushed back in her deck chair to remain as small as she could when Donna swung around and headed back in her direction. Then the coolness of shade fell across her. *Crap!* She pulled down the edge of the towel and peeked up.

"Jerry?" She glanced to his left and right and spied no sign of Donna, who must have been too upset by Wesley's words that she hadn't noticed the white lump on the deck chair.

"What, may I ask, are you doing?" He glanced down at her, a quizzical glint in his eyes.

"I . . . was enjoying the sun, but it got too hot so . . . Anyway, what are you doing out here? Aren't you supposed to be guarding Preston?"

"I was. I followed him up the back stairs but lost him. Have you seen him?"

"No, but I'll text you if I do."

"Great, thanks." He tipped his cap and headed off toward the bow.

Addie checked the time on her phone and jumped up. She'd told Paige and Catherine to meet her in her stateroom right about now so they could review any new information they all had. She couldn't wait to tell them that she had confirmed her suspicions about Annabel and Donna and how that gave another possible motive for Lacey's and Todd's murders.

As she made her way to the rear staircase, she mentally checked off all the murder motives they had discovered, and she cringed. It seemed everyone on this yacht had a possible motive for murder, but none of the evidence pointed to only one of them. This was a tough one, and she hoped Marc was having better luck than she at unraveling it all and putting the pieces together. She pulled the door open and started down the steps. As she rounded the landing to the deck below, she froze mid-step at the echo of Annabel's voice up the stairwell.

"Did you find that woman reporter's notebook or cell phone yet?"

"I thought you were searching for it," Preston hissed in a harsh whisper.

"You were supposed to check her cabin as soon as the police tape came off it."

"I have been a little busy this morning, if you recall," snarled Preston, his voice filled with disdain.

"That's your own fault for being such a momma's boy!"

"My fault?" he retorted. "If you recall, it's my mother we depend on for our livelihood."

"I know. That's why we have to find the reporter's notebook and phone as soon as we can. The police said nothing about them being on her body, so they have to still be somewhere on board. Where did you last see that reporter the night Zach got married?"

"I told you already."

"I know you did, but think. We spotted her not far from where we were talking about our nest egg, and then I saw her slip into this stairwell, writing something in her notepad."

"But it's clearly not here, is it? And speaking of our nest egg"—his voice deepened to a low growl—"you're putting all that in jeopardy by carrying on with Mother's little boy toy."

"What are you talking about?"

"I saw you and Jean Pierre carrying on in the cabana."

"What? Stop it, Preston, you're hurting my arm."

Addie flinched and edged down a step but stopped.

"How do you think Mother will react when she discovers you're playing with the same toys?"

"Preston, stop it, that hurts."

"As much as losing everything we've been working toward?"

"Okay, I get it. I'll end it."

"You'd better, or you won't see a penny from me or Mother's estate, got it?"

"Yes."

The door below into the passageway slammed, and Addie heard Annabel crying. Her heart ached for the young woman and she wanted to rush to the girl and soothe her for her husband's callous behavior, but her gut told her to stay out of it. Annabel had been playing a dangerous game given Veronica's history. She slumped back against the wall, slid to the floor, and waited until she heard the passageway door click closed.

Something poked her in the back, and she turned to see a protruding screw from the air vent. She noted it was the only screw holding the vent plate in place. The bottom screw had been completely removed. When she twisted it out with her thumbnail, the vent cover fell off and clattered to the floor.

"Whoa, what do we have here?" Her hand shook as she pulled out a black notebook and cell phone that had been wedged between two pieces of sheet metal at the corner of the vent shaft. Her heart pounded erratically in her chest as she flipped the book open. She couldn't catch her breath as she scanned down the page. "Bingo!" Addie cried, and jumped to her feet. She raced down the stairs, barged out onto the passageway, dashed toward the library, slapped the door button, and stumbled face-first into Simon's chest.

"Hold on there." He grasped her shoulder, bringing her to a hard stop. "What's the rush?"

"Where's Marc?"

"In the office, why?"

"You aren't going to believe what I found." She pulled the notepad and phone out of her skirt pocket.

"Okay," said Simon, glancing down at them.

"Okay is right. These belonged to Lacey." She smugly grinned and waved them in front of his face. "And what's in here is pure gold!"

She darted past him and hammered on the office door. Marc flung it open, his face radiating displeasure at the interruption.

"What's with all the commotion?"

"Look." She held up her finds.

"Whose are those?"

"Lacey's!"

"No way."

"Yes way, and you aren't going to believe what's in the notebook." She glanced past his arm and noticed Ryley seated in a chair by the desk. "I think you're going to both want to see this."

He ushered her in and pulled up a chair beside Ryley's. "Let's have a look." He took the notebook from her out-stretched hand, sank into the plush leather chair behind the desk, and flipped through the coiled pages of the book.

"Wow," he said, glancing from Ryley to Addie. "It's filled with details of Veronica's previous husbands, her suspected numerous affairs, including the current one with that chef, and mentions probable cover-ups by her lawyer, Wesley. There is also a notation that simply says 'books' and nothing after that."

"Perhaps," said Ryley, "her cell phone has more information in it. May I?" She turned to Addie, her hand out. "After all, I did work in cybersecurity for a time when I was with the FBI."

Addie glanced at Marc, and with a go-ahead nod, she turned the phone over to Ryley.

"Not good." She eyed the screen. "It's password pro-tected. Any chance either of you might know what her most commonly used four-digit password might be?"

"Try April nineteenth. That's her birthday," said Marc.

"Nope. Two chances left until I'm locked out."

Marc's brows furrowed as he stared off into space, lost in thought. "I have no idea then. That's the most common password people use."

"Did she ever have any pets?" Addie asked.

"It has to be numbers, not a name," said Ryley.

Addie sat back in her chair and stared at Marc's blank face. "Try Marc's birth date!"

"What? Mine?"

"Yes," said Addie, "we still have two tries left. It's worth a shot, isn't it?"

Ryley tapped in Marc's date of birth. "Bingo! I'm in."

"Really?" Shock etched across Marc's face as he glanced at Addie. "How did you know?"

"Just a hunch," she said with a soft chuckle.

Ryley scrolled down the text screen with her thumb. "It looks like she and Todd were good friends, but I don't see any love-type messages. They seem to have started discussing the Ludlows back a few months ago." She paused and read more texts. "There's one here where Todd is telling Lacey he has a meeting with a private investigator, who according to his contact, was hired by Melinda Ludlow to investigate Veronica's previous husband's deaths." She continued to read and scroll. "Everything on here points to all the main characters we have already suspected, but I don't see anything that leads us to who could have killed Todd and Lacey." She handed the phone across the desk to Marc. "Here, you take a look. Maybe I missed something."

"Was Todd planning on meeting her the day of the wedding?" Addie sat forward, trying to see the screen across the desk. "What do the last few texts say?"

Marc scrolled through the text messages and paused to read. "Todd's last message to Lacey says, 'I think I know who is responsible for what we discussed when I called you last night. I'm not sure I can get away with crashing this party again. I seemed to have raised suspicion tonight. I'll leave the name in a slip of paper in *The Mys-*

terious Affair at Styles in the library. Take a look and let me know if you agree, then call me. I'll be at the hotel in GH. Talk soon.'"

"It appears," said Marc, setting the phone on the desk, "that one of the mysteries has been solved."

"Yes," said Addie, "but it only tells us why she sought out that particular book."

"Along with her last notation in her notebook," Ryley added. "We also know it had something to do with the books for certain."

"And," said Addie, "the murders aren't related to the hundred other motives I've stumbled across."

Ryley glanced sideways at her. "Have you been conducting a little sleuthing on the side?" Her lips barely moved as she forced out her words.

Addie didn't know how to respond. Of course she had. Had Ryley learned nothing about Addie and her inability to follow police orders since they had met last year? Then Addie realized something else that Lacey's notation about the books meant.

It meant Ryley was no longer a viable suspect, either. Unless, of course, the detective had really gone off the rails and was dabbling in counterfeit books on the side, but that didn't seem too likely.

All this new information kind of tossed Addie's theory about Ryley's wanting to take over the case to steer the evidence away from her as a suspect and shine it on someone else right out the door. Saving face after a shouting match with a rival for Marc's attention might be a motive for some people to commit murder, but none of this new evidence fit with that theory of Addie's anymore.

Then Addie noticed a badge and a gun sitting on the desk in front of Marc, and she glanced down at Ryley's badge-free exposed belt. Her questioning gaze darted from one deadpan face to the other. Marc's jaw tightened, but he didn't offer an explanation, and an uncomfortable silence engulfed the room. Addie sat back. It was clear to her now why there was so much tension in the office when she busted in. Either Ryley had been in the processes of resigning her position, or . . . was being relieved of her duties.

Chapter 32

Addie settled into the chair facing Catherine and Paige, who were seated on the same sofa in the Edwardian lounge where they'd had coffee earlier in the day. Serena's parents soon joined them. Janis sank into the sofa beside Paige while Wade dropped into the other wing-back chair beside Addie's. The group discussion centered on the various theories as to why the meeting had been called, and Addie, not wanting to give anything away, busied herself with observing the other guests and staff as they assembled in the large room.

Her gaze traveled from one group to the other, and she couldn't help but notice that there appeared to be a hier-archy in play as people took their seats. The staff had been relegated to the far end of the room by the closed double-wide French doors leading into the dining room. The owners and their closest friends sat up front, facing the master staircase, where it was presumed Marc would make his appearance. Addie, her friends, and a few non-descript remaining passengers appeared to fall on the other side of the central snobbish group and were seated near the end promenade deck doors, which suited her fine because she had a full range of view over the entire room.

Addie paused when she eyed Captain Nevins waving off his junior captain and first officer when they pointed out an empty chair beside them in the back corner. In-stead, he opted for a chair near where Veronica, Oliver, Preston, and Annabel were positioned. By the jerk of his head it was clear he didn't think himself as being in the same class as his subordinates. She glanced back at Ju-nior Captain Wright, and it was obvious by the glower in his eyes that he was not impressed at being dismissed so openly by Nevins. He thudded down hard in his chair, whispered something to First Officer Carlyle, and then they both fixed icy glares on the back of Nevins's gray head as they whispered back and forth between them-selves.

Addie recalled Felix telling her that the people most likely to have access to the logbooks and the opportunity to remove the pages with the data he was questioning would have been these three senior officers. A wave of panic surged through her when she realized Felix wasn't in the room. He also hadn't been in his cabin when she went to meet him after lunch as arranged. Her gaze darted between the three men as she tried to get a read on them. One of them could have stumbled across Felix while he was going through the maintenance logbooks and si-lenced him or—she mentally crossed her fingers—his ab-sence was due to the fact that he was still poring over the books. Hopefully, he would appear soon with some news either about the missing pages or that his friend had cracked the encrypted file and opened it.

A soft tap on the back of her hand pulled her from her thoughts.

"I said, don't you agree, Addie?" Wade leaned across the arm of his chair toward her, and by the probing look in his eyes, he expected her to answer.

"I'm sorry . . ." She glanced at the blank faces staring back at her. "I was thinking about something else. What did you ask me?" She smiled sheepishly at Serena's dad.

"I said, we can only hope that Marc wanted us all to meet here so he could announce that some of us can leave as we're no longer suspects, right?"

"How can he possibly think that any of us would have killed Lacey?" Janis added.

Addie set her gaze on Catherine, who nodded in agreement.

"Because," Wade added, "once the yacht is towed out into the bay tomorrow, the only access to the mainland is by motorboat, and then we will"—his voice dropped to a whisper—"be truly trapped on board with a killer."

Addie had already considered that when Marc requested she stay on board after he released some of the passengers. For her it also meant that Simon's drop-by visits would stop, and they were one of the only things that had kept her sane through all this. But there was still a killer or killers in this group, and she never did like to leave a puzzle unfinished. Even though that might mean a day or two—hopefully only that long—that she and Simon would be completely separated because she was floating around out in the middle of the bay.

"Speaking of the meeting," said Paige squirming in

her seat on the sofa. "Wasn't it supposed to start fifteen minutes ago?"

"Yes," they all murmured, and shifted uncomfortably in their seats.

Paige was right. Where was Marc? As a matter of fact, there was no police presence in the room. Then Addie was struck by a thought. Perhaps Felix had found evidence and had taken it directly to Marc, and they were reviewing it before they came in to address the restless group. Whatever the reason, she hoped Marc hurried because by the look on Veronica's face, she was no longer amused by this gathering. She waved over staff members, snapping out orders to them and reprimanding them for not providing better service to her and her guests seated around the antique card table.

Addie noted Preston wasn't dealing well with this mandated confinement either and kept rising to his feet only to be ordered back down by Oliver. Addie winced when each incident was met with an expression of pure contempt for his stepfather as Preston dropped back onto his chair. She knew the two were not close, but today the hatred bristling off Preston toward the man was like nothing he had exhibited before.

Addie sat forward on her seat and studied Annabel, who, on the other hand, had turned her chair so she had a direct line of sight to Jean Pierre, who was seated by the dining room doors. They both appeared to revel in the opportunity to cast clandestine glances across the room. To Addie, Annabel appeared to be enjoying the thrill of flirting with her lover right under her mother-in-law's nose. At one point, Veronica swiveled in her chair to see who her daughter-in-law was engaging in nonverbal communication with, and Addie couldn't help but wince when Jean Pierre began chatting with the dishwasher seated beside him, avoiding Veronica's probing eyes. This was a game to both him and Annabel, and one that very well could have ended with the murders of two reporters whom they couldn't fool anymore.

Marc entered the room and took his place in the lounge doorway. Jerry and Officer Jefferies flanked him. Ryley stood on the sidelines, and Addie strained to catch a glimpse of her belt, where she usually wore her badge, but it was no use. The detective had buttoned her blazer, no doubt to hide the coffee stains from this morning's incident. But Addie couldn't help but notice that Ryley was not front and center with the police chief, which had become normal in their investigations.

"If I could have your attention please," Marc called, raising his voice to be heard over the murmured din in the room.

All eyes turned to him and a hush fell over the room.

"First, I would like to thank our host and hostess, Mr. and Mrs. Ludlow, for their exceptional extended hospitality these past few days, and I apologize to everyone for the inconvenience this investigation might have caused."

Mixed whispers of approval and discontent spread through the room, and Marc raised his hands in an attempt to regain control. The room quieted, and he proceeded.

"Although inconvenient, I agree, the complete lockdown was essential to the investigation of not one, but two murders that appear to be related to this vessel in some way."

This was met with mumbles of shock and disbelief

from the group as many appeared not to know about Todd's death the day before the wedding. Those were the faces Addie narrowed her gaze on.

There were poker-faced expressions from most of the main suspects on Addie's crime board. Veronica and Preston, of course, since they had confessed. Also, Captain Nevins, who had assisted Ryley with the staff interrogations and whom Marc had called in the first day to see if he could identify the body as a staff member.

The New York City friends of Veronica and Oliver appeared to be genuinely shocked to hear about a second murder, which didn't surprise Addie. They were business associates of the Ludlows', and the news of two murders related to the family or the business wouldn't have been something Veronica or Oliver wouldn't have been eager to share. Besides, Addie had already excluded them from her list based on the height and weight Lacey's murderer must have been.

However, it was the glance that she caught passed between Annabel and Jean Pierre that made her sit upright in her chair. Was that a warning glance to keep their mouths shut?

Addie was vaguely aware that Marc's voice continued to drone on in the background, but the fleeting glance between the two confirmed lovers made Addie move both of them higher on her list of suspects, especially when Annabel went back to sipping her cocktail and chatting freely with her table companions as though none of what Marc said was of any concern. Addie recalled the conversation she had overheard between Annabel and Wesley about the nest egg being secured.

Addie mentally went through her list of suspects and

glanced over at Wesley, whom she had discarded based on the fact that he was left-handed. She did note in her scan of the room that First Officer Carlyle appeared to be more uncomfortable with the announcement than Junior Captain Wright, and it made her mind click through some of the clues—the main one being the missing logbooks that they had access to. Additionally, both men were the right height and appeared to be muscular, so either of them could have wielded an ornament against the back of Lacey's head. There was also the fact that both officers would have known about the flare guns in the emergency boxes. Based on appearance, they would also have had the ability to run Todd down on the beach and use it on him to silence him.

"Well, that's the best news I've had all week," said Wade, rising to his feet. "Come, dear, let's pack up and get home."

Addie's cheeks grew hot when she realized that Marc must have said something important to the group, and she had been too preoccupied to hear it. She glanced questioningly at Paige as her friend hoisted herself off the deep sofa.

Paige stared back, a look of disbelief in her eyes. "It means we are free to go."

Addie glanced at the other passengers making their way out of the lounge. "Everyone?"

"Weren't you listening?" said Catherine as she retrieved her handbag from the floor beside the sofa. "Yes, except for the family and staff, everyone else can leave now."

"Okay"—Addie nodded—"that makes sense." Or at least she hoped it did because there weren't any passengers on her list of suspects.

Veronica stood and clinked a spoon against her wine-glass. "If I could have your attention, please," she shouted over the din of conversation. "Since Chef has gone to a lot of trouble to cook another one of his spectacular dinners for us, I would request that all those who will be disembarking remain until after dinner. You may as well enjoy one more divine meal before you head out. I really do hate to have to feed the leftovers to the seagulls, such horrid little pests."

Oliver stood as Veronica sank back into her chair and swigged the last of her wine.

"Yes, please, ladies and gentlemen, accept our hospitality for one more evening, and after dinner, our staff will be happy to assist with your luggage as you disembark."

"We would like to get home, so what time are you planning to serve this last supper, so to speak," Wade called out from beside Addie.

"We will check with the galley staff. However, I think I can be safe in saying that dinner will be served at seven," Oliver replied.

There were grumblings from behind Addie, and the look on Wade's face told her he wanted nothing more than to get off this boat and now would not be soon enough for him.

"Come on, Wade, we might as well eat before we go home. I can't even remember what's in the freezer that I could make for our dinner, and besides"—Janis glanced teasingly at Catherine and Paige—"I've been spoiled this week and don't even recall how to cook, and I don't want to tonight."

"Well, I for one am in favor of staying for dinner," added Paige. "With Emma away, this is the closest I've been to a vacation in years. I'm going to milk it for all it's worth."

"I agree," echoed Catherine. "We might as well go pack and then meet here at seven." She looked hopefully at Wade, whose brows were still knitted together in a deep scowl.

"I suppose." He heaved out a deep breath. "One more meal on this floating monstrosity wouldn't hurt."

"Thank you," whispered Janis, and she tucked her arm into his and headed off toward the main staircase.

Paige turned to Addie still seated in her chair. "What are you going to do now, go pack or more snooping?"

"Um, Marc asked me this afternoon to stay on to assist with the investigation of the books, so . . ."

"That settles that. If you're staying, then so am I," said Paige as she sat back down into her seat. "We still have a crime board filled with names, and every one of them will be staying on board."

Catherine glanced from Paige to Addie and sank into the sofa. "I never did like to leave a job half done, so count me in, too."

Addie couldn't stifle the grin that came to her face. "Thank you." She leaned forward and lowered her voice. "Have either of you seen Felix this afternoon?"

"The last time I saw him," said Catherine, "he was on his way down to engineering."

"He told you that?" asked Addie, surprised.

"He said he'd meet me here and perhaps after the meeting we could have a cocktail . . . before dinner." Her cheeks filled with a peach blush. "I, of course, told him no, but he blew that off and said he'd see me soon."

"Why, Miss Lewis," Addie said with a teasing chuckle. "I do think you have yourself another suitor."

"Pffft." She waved her hand. "What could he possibly see in an older woman like me?"

Paige stared at her in disbelief. "Obviously, you haven't looked in the mirror lately, have you?"

"She's right, you know," said Addie with a sly smile that quickly faded. "But I am getting worried. He was supposed to meet me this afternoon, and he didn't show up and—"

"That's Henry Adams, the chief engineer over there," Paige said with a head gesture, "talking to Oliver and the captain. You can ask him if he's seen Felix."

Addie turned to see a burly man with a neatly trimmed black beard talking to Oliver and the senior officers by the dining room doors. Captain Nevins glanced over at Addie with something Oliver said to them. His eyes darkened, and she didn't miss the tension in his jaw until his gaze darted to Catherine. His gaze then softened and lingered on Catherine's face. He smiled and nodded at her.

"I don't think Felix is the only one who has designs on you," said Paige under her breath, attempting to stifle a giggle.

"Don't be silly," hissed Catherine.

"I think she's right," added Addie. "I noticed at the reception that the captain was taken with you."

"In case you're both forgetting, I have a man friend, and one I am very fond of, by the way."

"Yes, but he's never here. He always seems to have an excuse for canceling your plans, like this time when he didn't attend Serena's wedding." Paige stared pointedly at her. "What was his excuse this time, work again?"

"Yes, as a matter of fact. They're in the middle of a big case, and he . . ."

"Of course, he always is. So, what can it hurt to see

what other options are open to you, especially when two
very charming men have made it clear they are more than
interested?"

Addie, whose attention was only half focused on her
friends' quipping back and forth, was more interested in
what was being said on the other side of the room. Henry
Adams nodded at something Oliver said to the group and
then ambled toward the main staircase.

"I've got to catch him before he goes back down to engineering," Addie said, rising to her feet. She glanced at
Nevins and the junior captain, who were now both gazing
at their table. She couldn't read the look in their eyes, but
something about it made the hairs on her arms bristle.
"How would you two like to create a little diversion
while I go ask the engineer if he's seen Felix?"

"What did you have in mind?" asked Catherine, still
seated on the sofa beside Paige.

"A little harmless flirting, especially since the captain
seems to be sending you come hither signals right now,"
Addie said, retrieving her purse from the floor.

"What?" Paige cried. "Won't that look suspicious if I
tag along as the third wheel?"

"By the look in the junior captain's eyes, and the
glances he keeps giving you, I'm pretty sure that your
presence would be welcomed."

"You are aware that Logan and I are in a serious relationship, aren't you?"

"Yes, just flirt and distract the captain and his junior. I
have a bad feeling that one or both of them might be behind Felix's absence."

"Oh dear, I certainly hope not." Catherine patted her

chest as though she were having palpitations and glanced over to the men. "We certainly don't need to be investigating a third murder, do we?"

"I hope we're not. Please"—Addie glanced at Paige—"think of it as undercover work of a couple of femme fatales."

"Like in spy movies?" said Paige.

"Exactly."

"We could do that, couldn't we, Catherine?"

"I suppose."

"You said you don't like to leave anything unfinished," said Paige, "and I have a gut feeling this is far from over."

"Okay." Catherine rose to her feet and smoothed out the front of her peach floral day dress. "Come on, Paige, let's turn on the charm."

"Thank you," Addie whispered, and she dashed after Adams just before he disappeared down the stairs. She reached for the sleeve of the engineer's dark-blue windbreaker and gave a tug. "Excuse me, Master Engineer Adams?"

"Yes?" He turned and set his startled dark-brown eyes on hers.

"I'm Addie Greyborne and a friend of the chief of security, Felix Vanguard."

"Oh yes." He paused on the step. "He mentioned your name this afternoon. He said he had a few things to take care of and then he had to go to meet you, something about how excited you'd be with his news."

"Did he mention what those few things were?"

"Can't say as he did, but when he left engineering, he was headed to the bridge."

"Are you sure?"

"Yes, that was a while ago though, so I doubt he'd still be there."

"Thanks." She clutched at the squeezing sensation in her chest. What if her worst fears were real and Felix had been caught in the act of exposing someone for the book fraud? She fled up the stairs, her heart hammering in her chest.

Chapter 33

Addie arrived breathless at the top of the stairs. Her mind spun with the worst possible outcome, as her heart ground out an erratic beat. Her lungs screamed for air. She closed her eyes, mentally crossed her fingers, and stepped tentatively toward the glass door leading into the bridge. She peered past the EMPLOYEES ONLY sign, and a wave of relief washed through her. There Felix was, bent over a pile of papers spread out on the console beside the filing cabinet. Hand shaking, she knocked on the glass. He jerked and spun around. A wide grin came to his lips as he strolled over and unlocked the door.

He must have noticed her panicked state, because his grin faded. "Why so glum?"

"I've been worried sick about you since you didn't meet me after lunch and then didn't show up at the meeting. I wasn't sure what to expect when I came up here looking for you."

"I do apologize." He bowed his head, but when he glanced back up at her, his eyes held a mischievous sparkle. "I guess I should have sent you a text, but everything's been happening so fast. I had to take advantage of most of the staff being at that meeting."

"What have you been up to?"

"While Nevins, Wright, and Carlisle were preoccupied in the lounge, I conducted a quick search of their cabins for the missing logbook pages."

"And . . ."

"And sadly nothing. Although, there is a locked drawer in the captain's cabin desk that none of my keys open."

"They must be in there."

"I thought about that, and the lock appears to have been tampered with at some point, like someone forced it open. By the rough shavings still inside the locking mechanism, I'd say rather recently, too. But I didn't have time to play around with it. I'll investigate that further, depending on what else I find in the senior officers' logs. But I had to hurry and get up here before the meeting was over, and by your presence, I'm guessing it is." He glanced nervously at the door.

"Yes, but I have Paige and Catherine running interference, so we have a few more minutes anyway."

"Fantastic, because you aren't going to believe what I've found." His eyes reflected the glee of a child on Christmas morning. "Just look at this." He scurried back to the console and grabbed a notepad from the top of the pile of reports and logbooks. "See this? When I cross-referenced the dates I questioned with the maintenance logs and the engi-

neer's logbooks, I discovered something very out of the
ordinary and that someone has gone to a great deal of
trouble to hide it."

Addie scanned over the notes he had scrawled in his
book. With each line, excitement swelled in her. "If I'm
reading this correctly, it appears that during the winter
months, which coincides with the dates you noted earlier,
Captain Nevins takes the yacht to George Town on the
Cayman Islands to dry-dock for the annual maintenance
and repairs."

"Yes, and that's when he and the majority of the yacht
staff take their annual vacation leave. The maintenance
and repairs are carried out by a highly reputable shipyard
that Oliver has dealt with for a number of years, so everyone, including Master Engineer Adams, has over a month
off while the family entertains over Christmas in Connecticut. Veronica has specified she wants all the repairs
to be completed by the New Year in case Preston or she
and Oliver decide to take a winter vacation in the islands."

He tugged out a nautical chart from the pile and laid it
over the notebook. "Look how close the Cayman Islands
are to Jardines de la Reina, this Cuban archipelago chain
of tiny islands."

"They're right off the coast of Cuba."

"Yes, and isn't that where you said Björn Svensson,
the bookbinder, lived?"

"My contact only said Cuba, but yes. I suppose he
could be on an island."

"Even if he's not, it's still in Cuban waters and would
be a short fishing boat trip to there, right?"

"I guess." She shrugged. "I really don't know much

about any of this, but could a boat not registered in Cuba enter those waterways and not be detected, especially one the size of a superyacht?"

"A small fishing boat wouldn't attract much attention, and my thought is that one from the Cuban-controlled islands met up with another one from the Caymans right about here." He pointed to spot in the middle of the open waterway between the two islands.

"Okay." She tried to wrap her head around what he was saying.

He pulled the nautical map away and set it on the console behind him. "When I went through the engineering logs, I discovered a discrepancy in the nautical miles and fuel consumption in the other records we've come across. It appears that *The Lady V* made unscheduled dockings on the island of Little Cayman after it was supposedly taken to dry-dock in George Town. Which, based on the engineering logs, didn't actually happen until a week later than logged, and Little Cayman is closer to the Jardines de la Reina archipelago chain. A small fishing boat leaving from there and entering Cuban waters would most likely go completely undetected by authorities."

"You mean that when *The Lady V* was recorded as being in dry dock, it wasn't actually there until a week later?"

"Exactly!"

"Which means that the captain or one of the senior officers would have had to have navigated that trip?"

He pointed to a notation in his notes. "And I discovered in the first mate's logs, where all passengers and crew on board on any given day are recorded, that those moorings appear to coincide with times Preston had flown down to the Caribbean to check on the work being done on the yacht."

"Preston, of course." She snapped her fingers. "The books are the nest egg he mentioned."

"Now we only have to figure out which of the senior crew would have made those unscheduled and unlogged cruises to Little Cayman, and then I think we know who else is behind the book forgeries."

"And most likely the murders, since it was clear by Preston's confession that he didn't commit either of them."

"I have a hunch," Felix said, "that if I keep digging through these logs of the junior captain's and first mate's, I'll find something. Perhaps who was still on board and who had the ability to navigate the yacht because I doubt that's a skill Preston possesses."

"I agree. He doesn't seem to have many skills except the ability to spend money. If anything, he might have hired an outside captain?"

"Perhaps. However, my money is on one of the staff being involved because someone on board went to a lot of work to hide the records."

"You're right"—Addie nodded—"and since all this nautical stuff is new to me, maybe you should go tell Marc what you've found. You can explain it better than I can. I'll stay here and keep looking for indisputable proof. There has to be something hidden up here—a note-book, a ledger, something that will point the finger at who exactly is behind the counterfeit books. Because at this stage of the investigation, Marc is going to want to see absolute proof and not just a few more links to a theory."

"I think it's more than a theory at this stage, but you're right. We need to find evidence that can't be contested in court." Felix glanced at the nautical maps and logbooks on the console. "I'll show him these first, though, so he understands how big this counterfeit scam is and why it's a good motive for two murders having been committed. Do you know where he is right now?"

"As far as I know, after the meeting, he went back to the library office, but he could be anywhere by now."

"Okay, don't unlock this door for anyone," he said, gathering up the papers from the console and tucking them under his arm. "If they have a key, hide and make sure you leave out the end sundeck door as fast as you can, and just in case you need to make a hasty exit, I'd better leave it unlocked." He strode over to the end door, fit the key in the door lock, flipped the thumb bolt, and returned to the console. "We don't want to show our hand before we have another name to go along with Preston's. The sooner we can find all the players in this forgery ring, the better. Oh, and you'll need these." He dropped his master key ring in her hand and headed out to find Marc.

Addie sat down hard in the captain's chair at the console and surveyed the bridge. If the missing pages weren't in any of the senior officers' cabins, they had to be here somewhere. Her mind clicked through all the places they had searched previously but couldn't spot anywhere that might second as a hiding place. Her gut feeling told her there had to be some evidence hidden on the bridge somewhere.

She examined the navigational console closer. The steering mechanisms, the control panels, radar and sonar screens, and numerous other screens and dials that she had no idea what they were or did. Her gaze traveled down to the locked drawer under the top of the console, and on a hunch, she gave it a tug, but it was locked. It really didn't matter though because it was one place Felix had already searched on their previous visit.

Frustrated, she leaned her elbow on the top and cupped her chin in her hand, being cognizant of not hitting the overhead speaker switch. She scooted her chair closer to the console with her feet to release the strain on her back. A stabbing pain exploded across her kneecap. She flinched, and her hand shot down to rub it. Her knuckles scraped across something protruding from under the drawer, and she pulled it back. Curiosity took over, and her fingers searched for what her eyes couldn't see. She found the source. There was a bulky object sticking down from the underside of the drawer.

She slid off her chair, got on her hands and knees, and crawled into the kneehole. She glanced back over her shoulder, hoping her friends were successful in their distraction assignment, flipped onto her back, and gasped. There was something taped under the drawer. Her fingers quivered as she released the tape bindings and unwrapped the plastic covering. Her heart swelled in her chest. It was a notebook.

It was a ledger of book transactions that had been brokered between Preston and the old bookbinder. The date of delivery of the original book and the date of return of a fabricated copy were clearly recorded. Exactly the proof they had been looking for, but whose handwriting was this?

She froze at the jingle of keys rattling in the door lock behind her. She had Felix's keys, so it wasn't him. Panic surged through her. She sat upright and slammed her head on the top of the drawer. Rubbing the top of her head with one hand, she scooted out from under the console. Still clutching the book in her fingers, she stood upright and spun toward the door and pasted a smile on her face. At least she hoped it was some semblance of a smile and not the mortification of her being caught with her hand in the cookie jar. Heat crept up her neck.

"Miss Greyborne?" asked Captain Nevins, shock written across his face. "What are you doing in here?"

"Umm . . . I was—"

"Better question, how did you get in here?"

"Oh"—she waved her hand toward the end door—"it was unlocked, and I came in looking for you or one of the other officers to ask about the procedure tomorrow when we are towed out into the bay."

"Really?" His gaze dropped to her hand, which she pressed down on the console for support as she sprawled awkwardly against it. Her other hand still clutched the book behind her back. His brown eyes darkened, and he strode across the bridge to the door in question and pushed on the handle. It swung open. "That's odd. This door is always locked unless an officer is on the bridge."

"When I saw that no one was in here, I thought it must have been an error and . . . and I was just about to leave a note for someone to contact me to answer my questions and then leave . . ."

A skeptical glint sparked his eyes. "And were you going to lock it behind you with those keys you have on the console?" His back stiffened and his voice warbled as he fixed his gaze on hers.

Her gaze dropped to where he had glanced when he

first came in. *Crap!* She palmed Felix's key ring and
shoved it into the pocket of her skirt.

He opened the emergency storage cabinet by the door,
flipped open the compartment, and retrieved an orange
flare gun from the rack.

"Do you have to replace one of the guns on the deck
box?" she asked, fighting to keep her voice even.

"Yes, that's exactly what I'm going to do with this."
He waved the gun in front of him. "When I checked the
deck boxes this morning, I noticed one appeared to have
corroded, so . . ." He slid open a drawer in the cabinet,
pulled a cylinder out, and clicked it into the flare gun bar-
rel. He waved the gun in her direction. Given the cold-
ness in his eyes as he turned the gun over in his hand, she
knew then who Todd's murderer was.

"You should be careful. I hear those can do a lot of
damage. And you'd hate for it to go off in here and damage the instruments."

His gaze flashed from suspicious to malicious, and she
slid farther down the console away from him in hopes she
might be out of the line of fire.

"Yes, we wouldn't want that, would we?" He bran-
dished the flare gun in one hand and held out his other as
he stepped around the far end of the control console, edging his way toward her. His gaze darted to her hand behind her back, then his darkened eyes fixed on hers. "I
think you have something that belongs to me, if I'm not
mistaken. Give it to me." He took another step toward
her. "Now!"

She slid back. Thrusting the notebook in an upward
motion behind her, she prayed it hit its target. "This is
your book? I should have known. Of course, it all makes

sense now." Her voice wavered as she fought to find the courage to face his threatening glare. "You're the one involved along with Preston in the book forgery scheme, aren't you?"

He lunged toward her, a venomous glare flashing in his eyes. She darted to her left and slithered around the end of the console out of his line of fire.

"You have no idea what you're doing." He smashed his fist on the top of the console and stalked closer to her, forcing her to back up into the file cabinet. "I knew you'd be trouble when it turned out you were some kind of book expert." He let out a short harsh laugh. "Who'd have thought that someone like you or those two damn nosy reporters would be at the wedding?"

Addie glanced at the end door, then over her shoulder at the main door, and then back at him. With each step he took toward her, his body seemed to quake in rage, and her access to the only two escape routes dwindled.

"So, what happened? Why kill them?" She pressed her back against the cabinet, trying to wedge the notebook into the latch opening. If she could make it click open behind her, perhaps she could use the door as a shield.

"On the evening of the rehearsal dinner, Preston and I were having a *private* discussion about our little business arrangement. He was expressing his concern over his mother's affair with the chef and that if Oliver discovered it—well, let's just say, there would have been a good chance he and his precious wife would be out on their butts. You see, any sign of a scandal meant he would lose his inheritance."

"Especially if further investigations into Veronica's background were also to come to light."

"Exactly," he snarled, taking a step closer to her.

"What about you? Were you afraid that if Preston were gone, you'd lose your job? Is that a reason you went along with the counterfeit scheme?"

He tossed his head back. A sardonic laugh filled the bridge. "Hardly, my intentions were purely monetary and my survival depended on me making a lot of money."

"How so?"

"Let's just say that the casinos in the Caribbean are very attractive to a man like me, and shall we say . . . over the years, I owed a lot of very scary people a large amount of money."

"That doesn't make you a killer, just a gambler, right?"

"Murder wasn't my objective in any of this, but that night when Preston and I were talking about our next trip I happened to glance over at the lifeboat and saw that fellow skulking around in the dark. I couldn't take the chance he overheard us, so I chased after him. I just wanted to talk to him, but he bolted down the rear door to the stairs, and I lost him on one of the decks below."

"But then you found him, didn't you?"

"Yes," he hissed, "in the library. When I caught him, he waved his phone in the air and said he had photos of the documents he had found in the desk in *my* quarters. He bragged that they'd make great headlines along with the other evidence he had of the book fraud being committed right under Oliver Ludlow's nose."

"He found the missing log pages?"

"I didn't know then if he had that notebook that you're not very good at concealing from me, but I couldn't take the chance of him exposing our business venture. So, I made a grab for his phone and the book he was holding.

The page tore, but that reporter guy slipped away from me and darted out the library deck door. I ran after him and grabbed the first thing I could find."

"A flare gun like the one you plan on silencing me with?" Her gaze fell on the gun he wielded in his hand.

"I finally caught up to him on the beach. He laughed and told me it was too late, that he had just sent a message to his partner." He waved the gun erratically in her face. "I didn't believe him because he'd been running since I caught him in the library. But to be sure he couldn't send a message to anyone, I—"

"Shot him with the flare gun."

"Don't you see? I had to. He would have ruined everything."

"What did you do with his phone after you shot him?"

"I threw it in the harbor along with the flare gun, of course."

"Then you had the little problem of a missing gun and had to replace it, right?"

"Yeah, but I didn't count on someone like you figuring out that the colors were different and were replaced at different times." His jaw tightened, and he lunged for her.

She slithered out of his reach and darted to the deck door, stumbled, and staggered into the far end of the console. "What about Serena's friend Lacey? Why did you kill her?"

"I heard that obnoxious woman bragging about working as a big-time reporter in New York and put two and two together. So, I kept a close eye on her to make sure that reporter fellow hadn't actually sent her a message. But later after everyone had called it a night, I spotted her in the library. She was bent over the table and going through the same book that Todd guy had. I couldn't take the chance that he had told her about the counterfeit books, could I?"

Addie shook her head and edged around the console as he stalked toward her.

"I grabbed the Shakespeare bust off the table and . . ."

"And you hit her?"

"I had no choice."

"What did you do with the body?" Addie glanced out the window by the deck door, and a wave of relief surged through her. She stood upright and thrust her chin out. "I'm guessing she was bleeding pretty heavily after that."

"Oh yes, I had to wrap her in the carpet and drag her out onto the deck to the railing. I knew she had been drinking all night, and I needed to make it look like she was drunk, hit her head on the rail, and then fell in and drowned."

"What did you do with the carpet and statue?" Her gaze flitted to the movement on the deck outside. "The carpet would have floated, so I don't imagine you threw that in the bay, too."

"No, it's tucked safely away where no one will think of searching. The bust sank nicely, so there were no worries there."

Nevins raised his hand. The shaking had stopped, and he narrowed his dark gaze on hers. "This has all been fun, my dear, but it's time to get this over with." He aimed and gripped his other hand on his gun wrist.

"If you're thinking of doing what I think you are"—she gestured to the window behind him, where the bridge was surrounded by police officers, their guns drawn and pointing at him—"you should know that the police have been listening to every word you've said and are just waiting for the chance to shoot you."

He glanced over his shoulder and then at the control panel, where the intercom switch was turned on. His face turned ashen, and all sense of triumph slid from his eyes.

Chapter 34

Addie made one more round of her stateroom, checking the bathroom, drawers, and wardrobe for anything she might have missed packing. She paused. Her makeshift crime board still leaned up against the mirror of the dresser. She turned it over and reread the notes she, Paige, Catherine, and Simon had made over the course of the extended weekend.

How could she have missed it? The captain wasn't even on her radar. She had either overlooked an important clue or the fact that Marc and Ryley had recruited Nevins to assist with the staff interviews had eliminated him as a suspect in her mind.

She read over what they had written. She could see why she could have missed it. There were a lot of different people and motives. Any one of which could have led to the murders of two reporters, but still . . . ? Maybe it was time to do what Marc was always telling her to do. Leave the investigating up to the police—even though they had missed that one, too—and stick to selling her books.

She folded the cardboard wedding announcement in half to make it fit into the top of her suitcase. She folded it again, crammed it in, and slammed the top of her case down hard before it popped open. Addie took one more glance around the spacious room, and a tinge of sadness tugged at her when she gazed over at the second bed that had remained empty over the last few days. It would have been wonderful to have had Simon as her roommate, but—perhaps another time.

Addie wheeled the suitcase behind her, and with her other hand, she clutched around the handle of her overnight bag, her arm draped with her bridesmaid dress. She managed to swerve her suitcase, herself, and her load through the door at the end of the stateroom passageway before it closed back on her. She stumbled out into the passage by the library.

"I'd offer to help," said Marc, wedged between the hallway and the partially closed library door, "but as you can see . . ."

She took one look at the large file box in his hands, dropped the handle to her suitcase, and pulled the door farther open for him. "What's going on in there?" she whispered, glancing into the library.

"Oliver and Veronica," he muttered under his breath, "are discussing the future of their marriage, I believe. At least that's what I gathered by the bits of conversation I overhead when I was packing this in the office."

"I imagine they are." She glanced at the apprehensive look on Veronica's face as she listened to what Oliver was saying to her from the opposite ends of the sofa. "A lot of information about her affair with Jean Pierre and then about Preston and Annabel came out in the investigation."

"It certainly did, especially when we arrested both her son and daughter-in-law for conspiracy and theft, along with another string of charges."

She stood back, dodging the file box as he staggered into the passageway, allowing the door to slide closed behind him.

"It's only too bad we couldn't get any evidence proving her previous husbands had been murdered. But those cases were investigated, and no evidence of foul play was discovered at the time."

"Still, it doesn't mean the authorities didn't miss something." Her mind recalled the captain. "That does happen sometimes even when the best investigators are on a case."

"True, we are only human, but we're also conditioned to follow the evidence. If it doesn't point to anything or anyone in particular . . ." He shrugged and balanced the box on his hip.

"I hope"—she glanced back at Oliver—"that he takes the possibility of her guilt of involvement seriously enough to fear for his own future and does something about it."

"I heard the word 'divorce' when I was coming out and then him telling her that she had until noon when the yacht would be towed out to deeper water to leave by, and that he'd have her belongings sent to her."

"That's a relief and you have to admit that Serena and Zach might be relieved, too, when they return and discover that Veronica won't play a part in their future, and they won't have to constantly worry about Oliver's future." Addie glanced at the closed office door. "Should I wait to hold the door open for Ryley? She'll probably have a box, too, right?"

"No, she's gone and this is my last load."

She glanced at him questioningly. "Do the two of you have big plans tonight to go through all these?" She gestured with her head as she grabbed the handle of her suitcase and followed him down the passageway.

"Ryley is home, packing."

"I didn't know you were planning a trip right now. Does that mean the case is wrapped up completely?"

"We're not, and it's going well with only a few things left to tie up. But we did find those missing logbook pages in Nevins's cabin, and the carpet from the library stuffed in the garbage compactor. Between those and the evidence in here"—he motioned with his head as he started down the stairs—"of the book forgeries, plus your fast thinking of turning on the overhead PA system with that notebook you had in your hand, I think we have a pretty solid case for a double homicide, plus a whole string of other charges not only against Preston and his wife, but the captain, too."

"That's great! Well, you know what I mean." She thumped down the stairs behind him but then paused. "Wait a minute."

"Let me get this down to the lower deck." He stopped but didn't look back at her. "And then I'll come back and help you with your bags."

"I don't need help," she said, trouncing down the next step to stand beside him. "What do you mean Ryley is packing but you're not going on a trip?"

His gaze dropped to the stair below him. She thumped down to the step below him forcing him to look at her. "What do you mean, she's packing?" she repeated.

"She's moving out," he said, his gaze not meeting hers.

"I'm so sorry to hear that. Are you okay?"

He shrugged. "It's been coming for a while now, so it's no shocker, I guess, but . . ."

"But what? It still hurts? I know that feeling," she said, fidgeting with her suitcase handle.

"No, it's the fact that she put her career over everything else and finally got what she wanted all along." He dodged around her and started back down the stairs.

"Which is what?" Addie asked, following on his heels as he quickened his pace down the steps to the deck below.

"She apparently is now the new police chief of the Salem Police Department."

"What? How did that come to be?"

"As I'm sure you were aware, she resigned when she didn't get her way to take over this case."

"I thought as much, but then she appeared to have calmed down, and I thought everything was back to normal."

"No, it could never be normal after that, and as you saw at the wedding reception, she and the mayor's wife have become close friends. Zoe persuaded her husband to do something to stop Ryley from leaving. That's when he came up with this plan. It seems his second cousin or something is the mayor of Salem, and they happened to have an opening coming up with their chief's retirement."

Addie chuckled and shook her head. "Ryley gets the

command position she tried to steal from you yet stays close enough to continue her friendship with Zoe."

He nodded.

"Marc, I'm really sorry. You must be devastated by all this."

"Not really." He stopped at the landing of the main deck, and his eyes met hers. "As I mentioned to you before, things haven't been good between her and me for the past few months, and recently I came to understand something you told me a long time ago."

"Me? What did I say that would break the two of you up?"

"You didn't." He shook his head. "It was when you told me you weren't ready for our relationship because you weren't over David or his death, but I didn't listen, and I pushed and ended up pushing you away."

"That was a long time ago. What does that have to do with you and Ryley?"

His jaw tightened, but his eyes softened as he studied her face. "Because I wasn't ready for Ryley. I, too, wasn't over someone in my past."

"Lacey? I knew it."

"No, not Lacey." His gaze broke with hers, and he strode down the steps to the gangway entrance, stopped, and glanced back at her. "I think I even called her Addie once." He shrugged. "And you know better than anyone what happens when someone whispers the wrong name in the heat of the moment." He spun around and marched down the pier toward the parking lot.

Chapter 35

Addie leaned over the British country cottage garden image on the new backdrop she had created for her window display and balanced a copy of Agatha Christie's last book in the Hercule Poirot series, *Curtain: Poirot's Last Case*, alongside a copy of *The Mysterious Affair at Styles* in which the great Belgian detective made his debut. She stood up and grinned. The Golden Age of Detectives had to be her favorite murder mystery period. She glanced over the collection of books her distributor had shipped—by Dorothy L. Sayers, Dashiell Hammett, and Ngaio Marsh—placed alongside her beloved Agathas. If this window display didn't whet the appetite of the cruise ship passengers, then nothing would.

"It's still June," said Paige, sliding up beside her. "I'm surprised you've changed the wedding theme display already."

."I know, I am a bit, too, but ever since word got around town of a double murder on a luxury yacht right here in Greyborne Harbor, we haven't been able to keep up with the demand for murder mysteries. It seems all the locals can't wait to share the story with the tourists."

"Tell me about it," Paige said with a soft laugh. "I get stopped on the street and asked if it's true."

Addie smiled her final approval of her new display. "If they want them, then here they are. Personally, I've had enough of weddings to last me a long while anyway."

"Don't say that. I've noticed a certain doctor's been popping in more than usual this last couple of weeks."

"I think that's only to keep an eye on me."

"Why would he do that?"

"Since Marc and Ryley broke up, Simon's been . . . well . . . a little out of sorts. I think he feels threatened, and he's afraid things might go back to the way they were." Even though she hadn't seen Marc since that day they disembarked, her mind traveled back to his last words to her. "Of course, I've tried to reassure Simon that there's nothing to worry about on my end, but I'm afraid he still feels a little wobbly about it all."

"Speak of the devil." Paige nudged Addie in the side. "To me," she whispered, "I think he's just a man in love, and the whole wedding thing has got him thinking." She gave Addie a teasing wink and busied herself, straightening books on the far wall.

The overhead bells jingled out Simon's arrival, and his lips brushed her cheek before they reached hers. "Mmm, I've been waiting for that all morning."

"I thought you were working today." She clasped his collar and pulled him close for another kiss.

"I am, or will be, soon. Just thought I'd pop in for

this"—his lips grazed her cheek—"before I head over to the hospital, and . . ."

"And what?" She nibbled his bottom lip.

"And . . . I got a call from Serena asking me to be here."

Addie pushed him away and gazed up questioningly at him. "Why would she do that?"

"I was hoping you could tell me."

Addie shook her head. "I hope everything's okay. I saw her last night. She seemed to be doing better than she had earlier this week. I heard through Zach that Marc finally got through to her, and she's forgiven us all for not telling them about what happened until they got back last weekend."

"She didn't say anything to you then about calling me?"

"No, nothing. I wonder what's wrong." Addie's gaze dropped, then she looked back into Simon's sea-blue eyes and smiled. "Maybe she just needs your calm in the middle of her emotional storm. It has been a lot for her to take in lately with the wedding, the honeymoon, and then coming back to . . ." She waved her hand over the murder mystery collection of books.

"I guess we'll find out in a second. Here she comes."

"Simon!" Serena shrieked as the door chimes tinkled in the background. "I'm so happy to see you." She flung herself into his arms and gave him a tight hug.

He glanced over her head at Addie, a mystified look in his eyes. He unwrapped Serena's arms from around him and took her hands in his. "Is everything okay, Serena?"

"Yes, of course. I just haven't seen you since we got back, and I was . . ." She glanced out the window.

"And you were what? Having a hard time dealing with all the news?" he said, his voice soft and soothing.

"No." She stared up at him. "I'm okay now. It was a shock, but I've done my grieving and . . ." She glanced back out onto the street.

Addie followed her gaze. "Who are you looking for?"

"What time is it?"

Simon glanced at his watch. "A few minutes past twelve, why?"

"No reason."

Addie eyed her skeptically. "Then why are you grinning like a Cheshire cat?"

Serena's face lit up, and she spun away from the window as Gloria entered the bookstore. "Ta-da!"

"Hi, Gloria and Pippi," Addie said, ruffling the little Yorkipoo's head. "How's my favorite little girl today?" She laughed when the little dog's pink tongue lapped at her cheek.

"Did Serena tell you the news?" breathless Gloria panted as she shifted the little dog in her arm.

Simon and Addie stared blankly at the women.

"Good, I hoped she could keep a secret."

"What are the two of you cooking up?" Addie glanced from one not-so-innocent-looking face to the other.

"I'm getting married!" Gloria squealed, and thrust her left hand in Addie's face. "See? Isn't it gorgeous? Cliff finally proposed after all these years."

"Congratulations!" cried Addie, staring at the huge diamond glistening in the sunlight streaming in through the window. "I'm so happy for you." She wrapped her arms around the short, stout woman.

"Yes, that's great news." Simon leaned down and kissed her round cheek. "Cliff is a lucky man." He gave Addie a side glance. A soft smile touched the corners of his lips.

"I say he got a touch of wedding fever because he proposed right there under the moonlight on the dock when we were leaving the wedding reception."

"That long ago, and you're just announcing it now?" Addie glanced from a grinning Serena to a glowing Gloria.

"We had so much to figure out before we announced it, like where we were going to hold the ceremony and then live afterward."

"I assume you'll be married in Greyborne Harbor, right?" Addie grinned and scratched the little dog behind the ear as Gloria nestled Pippi into her chest. "And then the living arrangements would have been a tough one since you both own your own homes. What did you come up with?"

Gloria glanced mischievously at Serena and the back at Addie. "Well, the wedding will actually be next month at a small family ceremony at Cliff's daughter's ranch in Arizona."

"Not here with all your friends?"

She shook her head. "It's for the best. After all, we aren't in our twenties anymore and want to keep it low-key."

"But this is your first marriage, and even if it was your second like Cliff's, it's something your friends will want to celebrate with you," said Addie, hoping her disappointment wasn't too evident.

"Yes, but we're trying to save money for our future, so getting married on the ranch works out the best for us."

"I, for one, am disappointed," said Simon. "Would it help if I were to walk you down the aisle?"

"That is a lovely gesture." Her eyes reddened as she smiled up at him. "One I hadn't considered, but no." She shook her head. "You see, my cousin, who is getting on in years and doesn't travel well anymore, and two of Cliff's four children and their families live nearby. I think what we have planned now is for the best in the long run." Her face beamed, taking on the same Cheshire cat appearance as Serena's. "Besides, we've decided to take up his daughter and her husband's offer of us moving into the guesthouse on their ranch after . . ."

"After the wedding? You're leaving Greyborne Harbor?" Addie fought the sting of looming tears as she looked at the little ball of fur snuggled into Gloria's arm. "I guess I won't be having my weekly visits with my little friend anymore, then."

Gloria pulled herself staunch. "The problem is we're not moving into the guesthouse until next year, as we're taking a yearlong world tour first. Cliff has never traveled outside the United States, and he's a bit jealous of the trips I've made over the years with the perks of my job as a travel agent, so I'm going to introduce him to some of my favorite places."

Addie smiled at Pippi. "I know for a fact that this little one travels well, and she'll be happy to be included."

"That's the thing." Gloria brought the little dog to her face and nestled her chin into the fluffy fur, as tears welled up in her eyes. "We can't take her with us, and I don't think it fair to my baby to pawn her off on various family members until we get back. It will only confuse the poor little thing." She thrust Pippi into Addie's arms. "I want you to take her . . . for good."

Addie clasped the wriggling ball of fur in her hands, and Pippi lapped excitedly at her palm. "What? You can't be serious?"

"I am," said Gloria, wiping away a stream of tears from her cheek. "I need to know she's gone to a good forever home to someone who will love her as much as I do," she choked out between sobs. "I have to go." She swiveled toward the door. "I'll drop off her things later." She waved her hand, burst into full sobs, and fled out the door, the chimes jingling out a merry tune not fitting the tears the woman shed.

Addie nestled the ball of fur to her neck and kissed the little dog's head. She had no words for the two grinning faces staring at her.

"This is amazing," whispered Simon. He scratched Pippi's head, and she licked his hand with doggy glee.

"That's not all," said Serena, grinning like a cat that shared its latest hunt with her.

"What do you mean?" Addie was still trying to grasp the meaning behind Gloria's words, *I want you to take her for good,* and squelch the flood of emotions that raced through her right now. "I'm not sure I can take any more news now. Unless . . ." Addie's eye widened, and she glanced down to Serena's tummy. "You're not preg—"

"No! At least, I don't think so." Serena ran her hand over her belly, and then shook her head. "Zach and I bought a house!"

"What, really?"

"Yes, we've spent the morning at Gloria's, and I'm happy to announce we've just drawn up the papers and been to the bank and are now the proud owners of her fabulous little Craftsman bungalow."

Addie couldn't wipe the smile off her face, and then it faded when Serena's words sunk in. "That means you'll be moving out of the garage suite."

"Yes, which is why I asked Simon to be here. Wouldn't it be perfect for you?"

Simon's face reddened.

"You're at Addie's all the time anyway, and you don't like that little apartment you live in. The garage suite would be perfect for you." She beamed and glanced from one stunned face to the next. "I thought you'd jump at the chance." Her smile faded. "I guess I was wrong."

"Not wrong, Serena," Addie said, shifting Pippi into the crook of her arm. "It's just something that Simon and I have never considered. I guess I thought you and Zach would be there forever, and I didn't think that one day . . . never mind. I'm so thrilled for you. Gloria's house will be the perfect place to start your new lives together." She squeezed Serena's hand.

"Yes, it will, and as for the other arrangement you mentioned"—Simon stared down at Addie, and a soft smile tugged at the corners of his lips—"it's something we can talk about after this little one gets settled in her new home." He kissed the top of Addie's head and whispered, "You never know what the future will hold, do you?"

"No," Addie whispered, and nestled her chin against Pippi's head and gazed into Simon's eyes. "The future is both a gift and a mystery, and you never know what it will bring." The surge of emotion that bubbled through her was something she hadn't felt before. Her life was complete in this moment with the love she had for the little fur ball that had stolen her heart a long time ago and the man who still filled it every day.